The haters have had their turn.
It's up to the lovers now.

A BERKLEY SHOWCASE ORIGINAL BY

GORDON EKLUND

THE GARDEN OF WINTER

GORDON EKLUND

BERKLEY BOOKS, NEW YORK

THE GARDEN OF WINTER

A Berkley Book / published by arrangement with
the author

PRINTING HISTORY
Berkley edition / September 1980

ISBN: 0-425-04568-4

A BERKLEY BOOK® TM 757,375

PRINTED IN THE UNITED STATES OF AMERICA

PART 1:

The Teacher

History (which can be defined as pieces of time seen whole) derives its form from the pattern of the four successive seasons. Winter gives way to spring, to summer, to autumn, then stands resurrected. The cyclic flow of human events exists as surely as the turning of the earth. And yet this is not mere duplication—an exact and banal repetition of things past. Think clearly: the winter of your birth differed dramatically from the winter of mine. One experienced more snowfall, the other less rain. So, too, with history. The duty of any gentle man plainly demands that he adapt himself not only to the pattern of the changing seasons but also to the transformed aspect of each particular season. The man who lives one winter exactly as the one before is a fool as surely as the one who attempts to resist the cycle, who plants corn in autumn to be harvested in spring. A gentle man must identify each moment in its infinitesimal, individual splendor; each consequential instant exists, must pass, will never be repeated.

William Stoner, The Book of Stones, *circa 2045*

1

*If nobody's willing to lay money on the exact
date when the Great Dark Age first descended
upon our little round planet, we do know with
some certainty when it reached its logical end: that
was the moment when the clattering, banging,
belching internal combustion engine first
reappeared upon the land. Rattle on all you want
about a renaissance of learning or a reassertion of
science and I'll say hooey. It was the internal
combustion engine that brought pre-Stoner
civilization crashing down in the first place, and
here it was back again, chugging, gasping,
popping, and heaving the same as always. Take
2258, for instance.*

> Daniel T. Janson,
> A History of Human Events
> Subsequent to Stoner's
> Time, 2378

Beyond the snug sanctuary of this dust-choked basement, the
snows of late December toppled in steady procession, while in
here, underground, wrapped in the folds of a deerskin jacket,
hands firmly encased inside thick wool mittens, Christopher Janson was beginning to sweat as he stood watching the flickering
shadows cast against the farthest concrete wall by the lantern held
above his head.

From without, a muted voice reached him: "Christopher! Ned!
Are you here?"

Ned Janson turned from the workbench where he crouched,
a wooden-handled screwdriver clutched in one hand. "That's
Mother."

"I know," said Christopher.

"So what do you think? Should we tell her or not?"

Christopher shrugged. The black smoke from the oil lantern
made his eyes water. The old basement was a cramped, airless
place; the broken shards of the ceiling boards loomed less than
a meter above his head. A third boy, Bill Walker, sat directly
across the bench from Ned. Bill's eyes shone as big as twin moons
in a nighttime sky.

"You're not done yet," Christopher told Ned.

"One more minute. Two at the most."

"Then I'll go." Christopher edged away. "It must be cold out there."

"It's fine in here," Bill said, wiping his lips and grinning ingenuously. His shoes were worn moccasins. His shirt was tattered and his trousers frayed. He wore a round cloth cap on the wiry bush of his hair, but it was small and failed to cover more than the tips of his ears.

Christopher went over to the broken window through which the three boys had gained access to the basement. Standing on tiptoes, he poked his head outside, blinking to see past the falling snowflakes. "Mother!" he called. "Here we are!" A frail, stooped figure weaved through the white mist. "Over here! In the old house!"

Sinking into the snow with each step, Sarah Janson followed the sound of her son's voice. Dropping to her knees beside the window, she thrust out a gloved hand and caught Christoper firmly by the nape of the neck. "So there you are. I could have looked all day and never found you down here."

Christopher laughed. "We snuck in."

"Ned, too?"

"And Bill."

"Why? Isn't our house good enough for you? I'm not sure this place is safe."

Christopher winked and dropped his voice to a conspiring whisper. "It's a secret project."

"Oh, my." Releasing her grip on his neck, Sarah dropped her head and kissed her son suddenly upon the forehead. "A secret from me, too?"

"Not necessarily. Actually, it's Ned's project."

"Then do you think—" she leaned back, measuring the open space of the window with an exact eye "—this old lady can squeeze through?"

Christopher glanced back at Ned, who raised a hand, indicating he was ready. "Give it a try," he said, stepping out of the way. A moment later, Sarah's booted feet came through the window and touched ground. The rest of her soon followed. She was only thirty-five years old, with the delicate pure features of a porcelain statuette. Standing inside the window, she slapped her gloves together, sending puffs of snow scurrying into the dirty air. "You shouldn't have come out in this weather," Christopher told her.

"No, I like the cold." She moved toward the workbench and Ned. "So what's this secret project you've got going?"

"We started work last Wednesday," Christopher explained.

"And now we're nearly done." Ned hunched his shoulders so as to block the workbench from Sarah's view. His elbows churned like pistons as he continued to work. "Another thirty seconds," he said.

Respecting Ned's privacy, Sarah faced Christopher. "And I also have a surprise for the both of you." She sniffed the air tentatively. "What's that burning?"

"It's just the lantern," Christopher said, raising his hand and showing her.

"No, you're burning something else, too."

"Not yet we aren't," said Ned. He leaned back like a fat man finishing a fine meal and dropped the screwdriver.

"What I came to say is that your teacher has arrived," Sarah said. "He's just now reached the house. I want you to come and meet him at once."

"Don't you want to see this first?" Ned wasn't about to let anything supersede his project as the center of attention. He slid quickly to the left, exposing his work to full view. "And it's not just a toy. Watch this." He reached down and pressed a tiny lever. Sparks flew as an engine chugged to life. "See what I mean?"

Sarah's face registered genuine awe. "How did you ever built that?"

Ned beamed proudly. "I made every part myself, though Bill and Christopher both helped some. What do you think, Mother? It works perfectly, doesn't it?"

"I think . . ." Capless, she reached up an pushed several errant strands of black hair out of her eyes. "I think it's a car, isn't it?"

"An automobile," Christopher said. "Just a model, of course. The real ones were much, much larger."

"They carried people," Sarah said.

"We looked at pictures," Ned said. "This is just like the real ones, except for being smaller."

"And it runs, too?"

"Sure." Lifting the model car—four tiny wooden wheels attached to a wire frame dominated by the miniature engine in the front—Ned placed it on one end of the bench. When he let go, the car jerked forward. Ned observed its halting progress like a mother watching her child's first, hesitant steps. He caught it before it reached the other end of the bench and shut off the engine.

"So that's what I smelled. Gasoline."

"Not really," Ned said. "It's just lamp oil. It smells differently because there's no wick to burn. Want me to do it again?"

Sarah hesitated. "I'm sorry. Mr. Lacy is waiting and we should be polite."

The four of them left by way of the window. As they crossed the stretch of white terrain that separated the old abandoned house from the big white house where the Janson family resided, Christopher and Ned walked side-by-side with their mother. The snow, driven by flurries of wind, swept down upon them in successive waves of whiteness. Bill Walker followed several paces behind.

"We're not sure Father should be told about the car," Christopher said. Ned had brought the model with him tucked inside a jacket pocket.

Sarah seemed surprised. "He'll be as proud of Ned as I am."

"Are you sure? Precept is Precept. Stoner never drove a car."

"This is just a model."

"But you won't tell Father?"

"If you don't want me to."

"Then I guess I don't. It's just . . . well, there's no reason to upset him."

"No." Sarah squeezed her son's arm. "It'll be our secret. The three of us."

In the den, the teacher waited, occupying Father's favorite chair, with its thick cushioned seat, frayed armrests, and the broken spring in the back. Charlotte Janson, the boys' only sister, knelt on the carpet at his feet, her eyes wide in wonderment as she observed the strange cloud of gray smoke that flowed from the teacher's lips and nose. Nor was this smoke the most peculiar aspect of the man. He also wore a beard, a great mass of shaggy gray-and-black hair that grew like wild grass along the ridges of his chin and cheeks. The teacher was a huge man, almost fat, with yellowed skin, tiny black eyes, and dirty broken fingernails.

He stood as soon as Sarah Janson entered the room. "Your daughter and I have had a most interesting talk," he said, bowing his head in proper deference.

Charlotte looked embarrassed. She was staring at the teacher's right hand, where something was burning. It was a thin stick wrapped in brown paper. The odor was pungent and overwhelming.

Sarah occupied the chair immediately beside the teacher. Once she was seated, he sat down as well. "Christopher and Ned," Sarah said, "I want you to meet Jeffrey Lacy, your new teacher."

Both boys bowed their heads and tried to recite the proper greeting. "We are most honored to make the acquaintance of so learned a gentle man." Ned, perhaps distracted by Lacy's imposing presence, lagged a beat behind. The result made Charlotte titter.

"And I'm glad to know you boys, too," Lacy said quickly, before Ned could feel embarrassed. "Let me see if I can guess which is which." He rose to his feet and lumbered across the room. "The tall one here must be Christopher. Is this your bright one, Sarah?" Lacy reached out and ran his fingers quickly through Christopher's hair. "He's got the head bumps of a genius."

"Christopher does well at scholastic matters," Sarah said. (Lacy had called her by her first name—the children failed to suppress their surprise.) "Ned is extremely adept at mechanical things."

"I suspected as much." Lacy stepped over in front of Ned. When he spoke his voice huffed, as though the effort of speech was enough to tire him. "Let's see what his bumps have to say." Lacy fingered Ned's scalp carefully. He grunted, dropping his hands. "Not a damn thing about mechanics." He shook his shoulders wearily. "So much for that system."

Sarah was smiling. "Don't tell me you've taken to following head bumps, Jeffrey."

"It's just curiosity." Lacy went back to the chair and sat down heavily. He crossed his legs at the ankles and puffed at the tip of his fire stick. "Hell, Sarah, anything is worth trying. If it works, fine, and if it doesn't, who cares. Separating the profound from the absurd has never been easy." He leaned forward suddenly, almost lunging, and put his elbows on his knees. "What about you, Christopher? What do you think about head bumps?"

"I don't . . . I mean . . ." Christopher tried to answer too quickly and his words caught on his tongue. "Isn't that something the peasants follow, sir?"

"So? Are you telling me to disregard anything a peasant believes?"

"Well, no. Not exactly, sir. It's just—"

"Lacy."

"Sir?"

"My name is Lacy. Sir was Galahad's first name." He glanced at Sarah, grinning. "I don't resemble him in the least."

"I can confirm that," said Sarah, smiling openly now.

"As a matter of fact," Lacy went on, "I have worn a variety of names over the years, but Jeffrey Lacy was the one I was born with, and I find I keep coming back to it as the years pass. Hell, I'm not young anymore. I'm apt to die damn soon. When I'm gone, I think I'd like to find Jeffrey Lacy enscribed on my gravestone. It shouldn't matter a damn, but it does."

"I'd like to change my name," Charlotte said, from her place on the floor.

Lacy looked at her for the first time since the boys and their mother had entered the room. "Then you ought to do it."

"But what name should I choose?" she asked.

"Don't you have a preference?"

"I think . . ." Charlotte glanced at her mother, as if seeking permission to speak further. She was small, fragile, and dark-haired, like a will-o'-the-wisp. "Joan," she said. "Because of Joan of Arc. I read a book about her once. She was very . . . brave."

"A dope," said Lacy.

"Oh." Charlotte was not able to conceal her hurt. "I just thought . . ."

Lacy tilted toward her. "You mean you don't agree?"

"Well, I . . . no. No, I don't agree."

"Well, good for you." Lacy leaned back, smiled, and clapped his big gnarled hands. "You see, I happen to presently believe that all martyrs are dopes, that no good is ever served by dropping dead, but I've felt differently in the past—when I was twenty-eight and living in Capital, I went by the name of Sebastian Lincoln—and suspect, assuming I live a few more years, I'll feel that way again some day."

"Well, I do like Joan of Arc," Charlotte said, her voice ringing with conviction.

"And so do I," said Ned.

Lacy chuckled and looked at Sarah. "What do you know? I'm supposed to be the teacher and they're already ganging up to tell me I'm full of shit."

"I think the children like you, Jeffrey."

"They do. Except for Christopher over there. He doesn't like my looks, my language, or my cigars. He's wondering what in hell ever got into you, hiring a vulgar smelly old man like me."

Christopher didn't flinch. Lacy had described his thoughts accurately.

Mother stood up. "I'll get my husband now."

Christopher felt a flash of anxiety. The very thought was disturbing: a meeting between Father and this man Lacy. They didn't seem to exist in the same world.

After Sarah had gone, Charlotte said, "He's not going to like you, Mr. Lacy."

"Does he like Joan of Arc?"

"I really don't think so."

Lacy nodded his head sagely. "Then that gives us one thing in common right off the bat."

Christopher was appalled. He couldn't say why but he wished he could tell Lacy what to do: put your feet on the floor and throw away your fire stick and don't say *hell* or *damn* or especially *shit* and cut the hair off your face and don't speak to children as if they were the same as you. He remembered once when he was a little boy and he had gone walking with a pet dog, when ahead on the trail he had spotted another dog approaching. It was the same here. Lacy was one dog and Father the other. Conflict was inevitable; the tide could not be turned.

Christopher went over and sat down against the wall. He gestured at Ned to get out of the way too.

Lacy was smoking again.

Christopher thought that perhaps Lacy failed to understand the exact circumstances he faced. "My father is a very devout Stonerist."

"As am I," said Lacy. His mouth formed an oval; he blew smoke rings.

"He's the chief county bureaucrat."

"I held a ministerial position in Capital."

"Everyone in County Kaine regards my father with the highest esteem."

"I have no reason to doubt their perceptions."

"But with my father you can't—"

Christopher fell silent. Firm, deliberate footsteps sounded in the hallway. It was Father. He was coming now.

A bare instant before the door opened, Lacy bent down and stubbed out his fire stick against the bottom of his shoe. He put his feet on the floor, wiped his lips with the back of a hand, and sat stiffly in the chair.

The door opened and Sir Malcolm Janson stepped through.

The moment he did, Lacy sprang to his feet. He crossed the room with amazing speed, stopped in front of Sir Malcolm, and bowed his head. "Sir," he said, "I am most honored to make the acquaintance of so learned a gentle man." There wasn't a trace of coarseness in his voice or bearing; he could have been a courtier bearing tidings from Capital.

Malcolm, a lean man, sixty years old, with snow white hair, bowed in return. "And I, sir, am honored equally by your presence in my home."

Sarah, who had waited by the door, came into the room and took possession of her chair. Malcolm sat down beside her, while Lacy remained on his feet, hands clasped upon his belly.

For a long moment, the men regarded each other silently.

Malcolm said, "I assume your journey to County Kaine was a not unpleasant one."

"This is an excellent part of the world," said Lacy. His tone was polite but not obsequious. "Stoner's home was in County Kaine—or so the legends claim. I consider it a privilege to be allowed to visit here."

"You've been living in the East?"

"For nearly twenty years. I went originally in hopes of discovering certain old documents, but it's a terrible land, where Stoner's name is seldom mentioned or even known. All of the once great cities—destroyed in the collapse. Only rubble remains to show their passing."

"I am familiar with some of your past writings," Malcolm said, after another long moment's pause.

"Then it is they which are honored by your interest."

"I found them—your papers—often penetrating."

"The work of a young mind, I'm afraid, but I thank you for the kind word."

"Though I did not always concur with your point of view."

"No man is ever right all the time. The mark of a gentle man, as Stoner observed, is to be right once."

"Ah, yes, indeed." Malcolm let a faint smile cross his features. He turned to Sarah. "Perhaps Ned and Charlotte should be excused."

"Of course," she said, gesturing at the two children.

Ned and Charlotte stood, bowed, and departed. As he passed Christopher, Ned glanced at his older brother with open envy.

Christopher was afraid to move. Had his father somehow overlooked him or did this really mean what he hoped it meant?

Sarah caught his eye and smiled reassuringly. Then he knew he was right. A feeling of pride swelled inside him.

Malcolm never looked at his son. "I have only one minor factor I'd like to discuss further, Mr. Lacy. You have met my children. I'd appreciate hearing your impressions of them."

"I have the same general impression of all three."

"And that is?"

"While enormously bright, they are distinctly uneducated."

Malcolm's face showed no reaction; he and Lacy might have been discussing someone else's children. "In what manner do you regard them as uneducated?"

"In any manner you choose to name."

"Were they rude to you?"

"Only as I expressly requested. Etiquette is not education. I was speaking of raw knowledge. Wisdom must be learned, not taught."

"My wife and I have taught the children to read and write—even Charlotte. Christopher and Ned know mathematics and some history."

"My intention is not to criticize what you have accomplished."

"But you feel more could be done."

"By you, no. You are a busy man, sir, with many responsibilities."

"By you, then."

"I am a teacher by trade."

Malcolm nodded slowly, then came to his feet. He bowed, then Lacy. Sarah quickly left the room. Without another word, Malcolm followed her out.

As soon as the door closed behind his father, Christopher released the breath he had been storing in his lungs.

Lacy dropped into the chair Malcolm had vacated. "So what do you think, Christopher? Did I get the job or didn't I?"

"I don't know, Mr. Lacy. It's difficult to say. My father has always been proud of us children."

"In other words, I shouldn't have said you were uneducated."

"I don't think he liked hearing that very much."

"But it's true."

Christopher hesitated, trying to decide. "I suppose in a way it is."

"Then what kind of man is Sir Malcolm?" Lacy lit another of his fire sticks—cigars, he called them. "Is he the sort who can bear hearing the truth?"

"I think he is. I guess he is."

"You should know, Christopher. He is your father."

"Sure, but he's still . . . he's a very difficult person to know."

Lacy shrugged his shoulders. "Aren't we all? Still, I'm not worried, even if you are. I know I have the job."

"But Father never said anything."

"Sure, he did. You just have to know what to listen for."

Christopher shook his head. The whole adult world sometimes seemed so complex, so fraught with ambiguity, that pure confusion overwhelmed him. What was Lacy talking about?

"Remember how he sent Ned and Charlotte away and let you stay," Lacy said.

Christopher nodded. It was not an event he was apt ever to forget.

"He'd never done that before, had he?"

"No."

"Then you should have figured it out right then. Why would he let you stay unless he considered you worthy as an adult, and how could he feel that way unless he believed you were ready to learn?"

"But he hadn't even talked to you."

"No matter. He'd read my papers. He made that clear enough

at the very beginning. I don't think he likes me. I'm positive he doesn't approve of me. But Sir Malcolm is a very intelligent man and he knows I'm one too. When it comes to facts, I've got few equals and no superiors. I teach people how to think, not what to think. Malcolm will tolerate me. He knows it's best for his children, especially you."

"Me?" said Christopher surprised at first. "Oh, you mean because I'm the oldest."

"I don't mean anything of the kind. I mean, because, when Malcolm dies, you're going to be the one to take over this county and run it. You're the one who's got the most to learn."

"But I'm not even—"

Lacy held up a hand. "You can't tell me anything I don't already know," he said smugly. "I read your head bumps, didn't I?"

Christopher shook his head, unable to decide whether Lacy was serious or not.

"By the way," said Lacy, "how familiar are you with the local geography?"

"What do you mean?" said Christopher, startled by the abrupt change of subject.

"Geography. Local landmarks. That sort of thing. Specifically, I'm interested in any caves."

Christopher thought for a moment. "There's only the diamond mine."

"What's that?"

"It's a cave, I guess. I mean, it used to be a mine. Not diamonds, I suppose, but we kids used to play there when we were young."

"Is it far?"

"A few miles."

Lacy stood up. "Then you'll have to tell me how to get there." He moved swiftly past Christopher and out the door. Before Christopher had more than an inkling of what had occurred, he was suddenly alone in the den. The diamond mine, he thought to himself. Why would Lacy be interested in visiting that old wet place?

Late that same night Christopher Janson moved on bare feet through the dark tunnel of the upstairs hallway. When he reached the central staircase and saw a light shining from below, he stopped. From down in the living room a familiar voice reached him: it was Mother. Christopher had not anticipated finding her awake this late. He listened for a moment to discover whether a second voice joined hers, but apparently Sarah was alone. She often read to herself late at night—usually poetry—and he assumed she was doing that now.

Christopher went on, padding into the deeper darkness of the other wing. The first door he passed showed a line of white light burning underneath: Lacy's room. The next door was dark but propped open a bare crack.

Christopher edged the door ajar and slid through. "Ned?" he whispered. "Are you awake?"

"Yes."

"Then stay quiet. I want to talk." Reaching back, he shut the door, taking care not to let the hinges squeak. Ned's room was a mess—toys, tools, puzzles, and games strewn everywhere. Christopher picked a path to the bed and dropped to his knees. "Mother's still awake."

"I know. I could hear her."

"I thought you'd be asleep, too."

"No, I was thinking."

"Look, I came here for a reason. That car. Do you know where it is? I want to see it."

"Sure. It's here." Ned thrust out a hand. Christopher felt the touch of something hard and cold. "I was just looking at it myself."

Christopher raised the car in his hand and looked at the sleek, knobby, jagged form. He wished he could start it running.

"Do you see something?" Ned asked.

"No, not really." Christopher lowered his hand. He just wanted to hold the car, feel its touch against his flesh. There was really no reason. Tomorrow they would return to the basement; tomorrow they would run it again. "I was just thinking. This car is as real as any other. If we had the parts, the resources, we could build one as big as any in the pictures we saw."

"Sure, but we don't."

"Well, what if we did? That's what I was thinking. What would happen then?"

"For one thing, Father would kill us. Cars are forbidden by precept. They were used to fight wars."

"That was a long time ago."

"Tell that to Father."

"There hasn't been a war in two hundred years. Who would we fight?"

"I don't know."

Christopher let the car slide off his hand onto the floor. He stood up. "That's why I think it's crazy. Stoner's dead. So's the world he lived in. Why should we—you and me—why should we be bossed around by what he believed?"

"Because he was right."

"Always?"

"I don't know, Christopher. Why are you asking me all this? I'm no expert. Ask Father—or Lacy. Ask him all about it."

"Maybe I will." Christopher turned on a heel. In the excitement of the moment, he had forgotten to whisper, but the hallway was as dark and vacant as before. The light under Lacy's door had gone out. In the living room, Mother continued to read.

Reciting from the pages of a paperbound book, Sarah Janson uttered each word distinctly, though she barely heard a sound she made. Sarah wasn't reading aloud from any desire to understand these old poems better—she already knew each one of them, Keats and Shelley, Swinburne and Browning, Thomas and Poe, as well (or better) than her own three children—but rather for the sheer noise alone—the swiftly repeating rhymes like ocean waves (Vachel Lindsay now) which helped free her mind for more essential thoughts. If anything, she was thinking of how Malcolm had proved so much less resistant than she had expected. He disapproved of Lacy of course, but she had known he must. But he had not refused her entreaties, either. She wondered what had done it, what had turned the trick. What Lacy had said about the children. That had stung poor Malcolm—her, too, truth be told. Uneducated. Well, weren't they? Why else had she invited Lacy to County Kaine?

Earlier this evening, seated in the opposite chair, Malcolm had asked, "Was this man always like this, Sarah? You knew him in Capital. He has a vast reputation in certain circles."

"Jeffrey was always rather eccentric, but he's a devout Stonerist, I'm sure."

"Yes, but is his Stoner the same as mine? That's what I wonder."

"Don't you like him?"

"I don't approve of him."

"Then I should send him away."

"I—no." His shoulders sagged. It was so unlike Malcolm to let his outer self reflect his inner emotions. "If you want him, retain him, but I . . . I'd prefer seeing as little of the man as possible."

"I'll give him grandfather's room upstairs by the children."

"Fine."

"And he can take his meals with the children too."

"That might be best."

"I'll speak to him."

"No. That would be . . . impolite. There's no need. A man of his stature . . . no."

"As you wish, Malcolm."

"I . . ." He fell silent.

"Yes, Malcolm."

"I . . . oh, nothing, nothing at all. I suppose it's for the best. I suppose it has to be done."

It was then—for the first and only time—that she wondered. Does he know? Has he guessed? Did he once hear?

But no, she firmly decided. It wasn't suspicion. Malcolm could never possibly suspect her of deliberate duplicity; such a concept lay wholly outside the range of his private experience. Malcolm was simply sad, disappointed. At one time he had believed that his children had no need of any education beyond that which was contained within the few hundred pages of *The Book of Stones,* but first Sarah had attacked that belief and now Lacy. Perhaps it wasn't fair. It might even be cruel. Malcolm was not deliberately unrealistic. Christopher was headed straight for the bureaucracy, and Ned, too, if he could pass his examinations, and the only requirement for such service was a thorough knowledge of Stonerist doctrine. And Charlotte was a girl—a woman—and not even one book was required to master that trade. It was just that Sarah had not agreed. For the first and only time in their marriage, she had acted without consulting her husband and answered Lacy's original letter affirmatively. The children, especially Christopher, were getting old: the time for mannered discussion had passed. What she sought for them was knowledge. She wanted them to

know botany and biology, astronomy and painting, poetry and
music, history and literature. She wanted them to realize that more
than one opinion existed within the fabric of the cosmos, and that
there was more to a learned life than bowing, nodding, smiling,
obeying one's father, loving one's child, respecting one's wife or
husband. Sarah wanted her children to know more than she did.
To be blunt (which Sarah never was, except with herself) she
wanted them to know more than their father. And that was cruel.
Malcolm, sensing the truth, was wounded by it.

She regretted that. But now Lacy was here and the children
would have a chance to learn from a brilliant and adroit master.
That was more important than any one person's feelings. Malcolm's. Or her own.

In truth (she thought as she recited) Charlotte worried her as
much or more than the boys. It wasn't only her peculiar nature—
she was as strange as Christopher and Ned were normal—but the
bleakness of her future. In a few years Charlotte would have to
marry, and when that happened, her life would end. What a terrible, deadening world Stoner created for us women, thought
Sarah, exulting in her private heresy. It was as if the Great Man
had expended such energy erecting a perfect society for men that
he'd had no pep left to deal with women. She loathed Stoner,
hated his book, despised this world he had made. That was her
secret. She had never told Malcolm—not even Lacy. Nor would
she. But there were tricks, ways of surviving. Charlotte must learn
them too. Lacy could teach. That was why she wanted him here
desperately now and it was why she had wounded Malcolm deeply
in order to ensure that it happened.

So Sarah Janson was satisfied. Not happy—that could never
be—but pleased. As her lips moved, uttering rhymes aloud, she
continued to think these secluded thoughts.

As she touched the door with her bent knuckles, Charlotte
Janson peered at her feet, where the toes touched the pool of light
that spilled forth from under the door.

Dimly, she heard steps moving in response to her knock. For
a moment, stiffening, she battled the impulse to flee.

The door opened. Charlotte lifted her eyes and stared at the
face in front of her. "I—I wanted to talk."

Jeffrey Lacy shook his head. "Isn't it late?"

"I—yes, I know it is, but...but I've got...there isn't time..." Her words tumbled like dominoes falling in a row; she couldn't control them.

Lacy laid a hand on her bare arm. "Come in," he said, holding the door.

The room—barely disturbed since Grandfather's death many years ago—already bore the stamp of Jeffrey Lacy. Books and papers cluttered the corners, and the old bed had been lowered and the canopy removed.

"So what is it?" He went to the bed and lay down. She was pleased to discover that he was not smoking.

"Well, it's silly."

He didn't contradict. (Mother would have.) "What isn't? You tell me your silly thing and I'll tell you one of mine."

She giggled, putting her fist close to her lips. She hated her skin. It was pale—and splotchy. Underneath, where no one could see, there were brown moles like blots of caked mud.

"I hear voices," she said.

"That's not silly. Whose?"

She had never thought about that before. "No one in particular, I guess. Just voices."

"Are they gods, devils, demons, or spirits?"

"They might be."

"Don't you have an opinion?"

"I...aren't you surprised?"

"Not especially. People have been hearing voices like yours for quite a few thousand years."

"Then you've heard them, too?"

Lacy shook his head slowly. "Unfortunately, no. But I've listened—I've tried. Your voices—what do they tell you?"

Charlotte had to think. "Well, many different things."

"Are they oracular?"

"I'm afraid I don't—"

"Do they tell you about the future?"

"No, not that. They talk. It's like a friend—personal things."

"Have you ever told anyone else about this? Your mother?"

"Not her, no."

"Anyone?"

She hesitated. When she first came here, she hadn't intended to get into this. "Well, one person. A monk at St. Sebastian's. His father used to work in our stables. He's very intelligent—and devout. Brother Julian."

"Then you must trust him."

"I do. Very much."

"Then I feel privileged that you've extended me the same trust."

"It's just ... well, sometimes it's easier to talk to a stranger than someone you've known all your life."

"I know." He stood, wobbling toward her, and caught her hand. "You better go now."

She turned toward the door, then stopped. "There is one other thing. I'd like ..."

"Yes, Charlotte?"

"I'd like to be able to come here again. To talk to you. To explain. Brother Julian—I hardly ever get a chance to see him. You'd be somebody in the same house. Somebody to trust."

"I'd like that very much, Charlotte," he said, guiding her the rest of the way to the door.

"And you won't tell anyone? Not even Mother? You'll promise me that."

He patted her shoulder. "I promise."

She smiled. On the way back to her room, she passed Ned's and heard him and Christopher whispering together.

Turning on his stomach, Bill Walker shoved his face into the tight angle where the dirt floor touched the adobe wall and pulled the blanket up over his head until it covered his ears.

It wasn't enough. He still heard clearly. Mother, asleep on the floor at the opposite end of the hut, spoke in a flat, dull monotone:

"Machines breathing fire ... lips spewing flame ... the chapel burns ... the dark man laughs in glee ... the monk is alive with the inferno inside ... metal insects slither forward, stinking of death ..."

Bill knew he shouldn't be lying here. He should be springing up and dashing out and rousing the elders so that they, too, could hear the future.

Bill didn't care. He hated the damned elders and he hated the damned future. He wanted to lie as he was, pretending sleep, pretending not to hear, straining with all his might not even to listen.

Sometimes, when she dreamed, Mother shouted. When that happened, the sentries often heard and brought the elders. A few months ago Elder Anders had taken a stick and struck Bill on the shoulders until his skin shredded and the blood ran. "Don't ever let that happen again," the elder said. "When your mother dreams, call us. Her talent is a gift from the gods."

Bill shoved his face even closer to the floor. He pressed his fingers in his ears. Still, he heard her. She wasn't shouting (fortunately) but it was a small hut:

". . . the dark man rides a mount of black steel . . . the master's son must fight . . . swords clash at vast distances . . . death like rain falls upon the land . . ."

In the morning when she woke, Mother would recall nothing. The dreams came only at night. Sometimes months passed and nothing happened. At other times the nights when she dreamed outnumbered those when she didn't.

Bill hated her. He wanted his mother to be a gentle lady (like the master's wife—like Sarah Janson), with smooth skin and a way of moving as graceful as the wind. Bill's mother was skinny. Her hands were like sores, her touch like dust, her voice like an old man's cough. And her dreams. He hated their torment more than anything else.

Christopher said not to believe. He said the oracles were peasant foolishness—a superstition. He said the future was like a face behind a veil—no one could see it.

But Bill believed. He knew his mother's dreams were true. He knew the gods spoke through her lips. He hated her more for that. He hated her for his own fear—and awe.

She spoke: ". . . the chapel burns . . . the monk is afire . . . death rains . . . a black steel hand strangles . . ."

He wouldn't listen. Once Christopher had promised that when they were both grown up Bill could come and live in the big white house. Bill had told his mother. She laughed at him. "Sure, they'll say that now, letting their children play with one such as you, but wait, just you wait, that time'll come when they'll kick you aside and laugh and taunt and call you ignorant peasant. I know—I can see—I've smelled the stink of tomorrow's damnation. Does your father speak with Sir Malcolm? Does he share the food placed on the master's table? He does not. And do you know why? Because to them, to those gentle people, we are less than their dogs or their horses or their cattle."

Bill shut his ears. He wouldn't listen. But he heard. And ever after that, even until now, his friendship with Christopher had not been the same. For now he was afraid. When would Christopher finally speak, withdrawing his promise and proving Bill's mother a prophet again? It hadn't happened yet. Christopher had never spoken of his pledge after that first day. But Bill remembered. Even today in the basement with that funny machine Ned had built that blew smoke and stank like a wet lantern: he was afraid then that Christopher might speak.

"The old man dies unmourned . . . the woman is unloved . . . death rains upon the . . ."

He wouldn't listen—he wouldn't.

PART 2:

The Heretic

Tradition as a means for effecting social fusion may be seen as existing in two ideal forms, one temporal and the other spatial, with the former, where customs are simply passed between generations from father to son to grandson, easily the less complex. This temporal form of tradition has most likely existed since the beginning of human society and may be largely instinctive in nature.

But what of the spatial form of tradition? How is it defined and where and when do we find it?

To discuss these questions, the use of the term class is unavoidable. During the Terrible Years, when tradition in all forms became a subject of ridicule, the goal of a classless society was often advocated. Unfortunately, what our ancestors failed to realize is that any such society is, by definition, ultimately decadent, possessing within itself the seeds of its own collapse, for a classless society must lack the spatial form of tradition and thus perish.

Class should never be confused with caste; the two are, in fact, polar forms, quite unalike. In the properly classified society, an informal group of citizen-philosophers (gentle men) must stand at the

21

*top and by their very example of right living infect
and influence those beneath them. This second
class, in turn, will influence a third and so on,
until the entire social fabric is permeated with
propriety and fused into a single harmonious
whole.*

*How should this upper class be chosen? Not, to
be sure, through hereditary means, for therein lies
the real danger of caste. The question ought to be:
what is required of a truly upper class? The reply:
full knowledge of proper tradition.*

*To determine this, no more complex means is
required than some simple system of honest
evaluation: an examination. Any such test, once
established and made open to all men regardless of
station, shall become the pulsing artery of a
properly modulated society. Leaders will be
discovered, chosen, and sent out to lead—through
example—all others.*

> William Stoner, The Book
> of Stones, *circa* 2045.

*During the Great Dark Age, the common
assumption was that things ought never to be
allowed to change. This was crazy, but what had
happened was that even the keener minds of the
time had confused simple transition with general
chaos. What resulted was a lot of men darting
about the landscape, pointing long fingers: this or
that was a violation of precept and thus horrible.
What nobody ever figured out was that, when you
cap a bottle and shake it, pressing the cap down
tighter all the time, then sooner or later the whole
bottle will blow sky high and, when it does,
chances are, you're going to go straight up with it.*

*Which is pretty much what happened back
then.*

> Daniel T. Janson, A
> History of Human Events
> Subsequent to Stoner's
> Time, 2378.

The rhythmic patter of horses' hooves beating against the dirt
road; the gentle tickling of dry dust caught in the nostrils; the

bouncing and rattling of the old wooden coach; the heat of the noonday sun against a bare arm: these sensations and others swirled around young Christopher Janson, but they failed to reach him consciously. Instead, his attention was fixed to a spot on the landscape where, beyond an acre of ripening corn, a pillar of black smoke rose into the sky higher than his eye could follow.

"That must be it," Sir Malcolm Janson said, leaning past his son and shading his eyes against the fierce glare. "That's Blake's steel mill. The man doesn't even attempt to conceal its existence."

"Do you think he should?"

Malcolm dropped wearily back in the padded seat. "Let's simply say that I would feel more comfortable if he did."

"Because it's a violation of precept?"

"Because..." Malcolm grew suddenly cautious. "Precept is a matter of interpretation, after all."

Christopher didn't believe that, and he knew that his father—in all honesty—did not, either. What could possibly be more at odds with Stoner's philosophy than a steel mill? The two of them had left County Kaine the previous morning. The coach, driven by a pair of loyal house peasants who took turns handling the reins, had barely paused in that time. They had crossed two separate ranges of low rolling hills—one in the night and the other just past dawn—and once, when a river blocked the road, swerved and crossed an ancient concrete bridge that still contained the grooved rails of the old locomotives. A number of tall rocky cliffs served as a border between the adjacent counties. There was no sign to mark the actual dividing line, but this was County Tumas, not County Kaine. It was Sheridan Blake's county, and Christopher had noted even in the first few miles a different scent to the air.

As they passed the column of smoke that marked the site of Blake's mill, the horses seemed to quicken their pace, as if sensing the approach of a final destination. Turning in his seat, Christopher looked back once more, but he still could not see the factory itself—only the smoke it cast. He had met Sheridan Blake on several previous occasions when Blake had visited the big white house. He was a stout, florid man, with graying hair and a loud voice.

Christopher faced his father. "Are you saying that Mr. Blake has a different interpretation of Stoner than you?"

"I'm saying that the viewpoints of any gentle man are valid." Malcolm was remaining cautious. It was an old habit in the bureaucracy and one Malcolm plainly found difficult to shed even with his own son.

"Have you read the book he wrote?"

Malcolm nodded slowly. "Have you?"

"No. I tried, but it was hard to fathom. Jeffrey Lacy read it, though."

"And what did he think?"

Christopher hesitated, well aware of his father's opinion of Lacy. "He said it was utter heresy."

Malcolm laughed without amusement. "Then, for once, Mr. Lacy and I appear to agree."

"What do you intend to do about it?"

"Do?"

"Well, yes. If Blake's steel mill is a violation of precept, shouldn't someone stop him?"

"How?"

Christopher started to answer, then closed his mouth. He realized that he couldn't honestly answer that.

Malcolm smiled drily. "Perhaps you can see the dilemma involved, Christopher. The trouble with Stoner's precepts is that they are not laws. They are not enforceable."

"But—"

Malcolm held up a hand. "Hush. Not now. This land belongs to Mr. Blake, and I do not wish to speak critically of him."

Christopher sighed, returning his attention to the coach window, knowing that when his father felt something was improper it was impossible to convince him to change his mind.

A sudden sharp noise like the crack of a whip caught his attention. The coach jerked violently, as the horses, frightened by the noise, surged forward. Christopher tumbled off the seat and his father toppled beside him. The sharp noise came again, then a third time. Above, the driver swore furiously as he fought to control the horses.

Christopher picked himself up as the wild rocking of the coach slowly subsided. "What was that?" he said.

Malcolm Janson sat as stiff as a statue. "It was, I believe, a gunshot."

"A shot? But guns can't—"

Malcolm raised a hand, silencing his son again. "Not now," he said softly.

"But, Father, you can't—"

"Not here, I said."

Shortly afterward, rounding a bend in the road, Christopher sighted a huge stone castle looming directly ahead of them. He could barely believe his eyes at first. A set of railroad tracks ran beside the road and they looked almost new. Up ahead a whistle blew. Christopher leaned out the window and tried to see through the heavy dust. A puff of white smoke floated in the air.

The huge oak dining table made Christopher feel shrunken and insignificant in comparison, and he wondered why such a massive piece of furniture had been chosen for tonight when, after all, only the four of them were dining. Sheridan Blake and Malcolm Janson sat at opposite ends of the long table, while Blake's daughter Adrienne occupied the chair across from Christopher. Blake had done nearly all the talking thus far, and now, pointing a fork at Christopher, he was describing the miniature railroad he had recently constructed for his own amusement.

"It's only a model really, just a toy. I use steam to power the locomotive. Anything more would be beyond my present resources, I'm afraid. An intriguing idea but not a very practical one."

Christopher nodded in apparent agreement, glancing at his father's masklike features as he did. Once, years ago, Christopher and his brother Ned had constructed a model automobile but a full scale car had not then seemed practical, either.

"In fact," said Blake, "I sometimes think that all of my inventions, including that big steel mill out by the corn fields, are nothing more than mere toys."

"Very impressive toys," said Malcolm Janson.

"Perhaps." Blake laughed suddenly. "It's all a matter of interpretation, I suppose. Some men disagree with my views and that, according to Stoner, is their natural right. I understand that you have one such man in your own house. When I first unveiled my mill, Jeffrey Lacy wrote a letter of condemnation."

"Lacy is a very impetuous man," Malcolm said.

"Unlike yourself, sir," said Blake.

"Jeffrey Lacy is my teacher," Christopher said.

Blake seemed surprised. He glanced at Malcolm but continued to address Christopher. "In precept?"

"No, just in general subjects. Biology, astronomy, literature, and so on."

"This man Lacy must be very knowledgeable."

"Oh, he is," said Christopher. "In fact—"

Blake's laughter drowned his reply. "Sir Malcolm, what's wrong? Don't you trust your own boy to resist Lacy's heresy?"

"It's not that, Mr. Blake. My wife and I simply feel that philosophical training is best left in the hands of the parents. Jeffrey Lacy is a respected member of my household and free to speak his mind as he wishes."

"Which, I'm sure, he's not hesitant to do." Blake swung his attention back to Christopher. "As your father is aware, Jeffrey Lacy and I are not unacquainted. When I was a young man and he was a minister in Capital, our paths crossed on several occasions. Then years passed and I heard nothing of him. You can imagine my surprise when I learned that he was now living in your house."

"My mother knew him," Christopher said. "The same as you. In Capital."

"But what happened to him then is what I wonder. After he left the city."

"He lived in the East," Christopher said.

"Among the savages?"

"Yes. He visited the old cities. He's writing a book—about Stoner. That's why he went there."

"But Stoner, as everyone knows, lived in County Kaine."

"That's why he's come here now."

Blake shook his head with sudden sadness. "It's all a pity, really. Lacy was regarded as a great man once, a scholar second to none."

"He still is a scholar," Christopher insisted.

"Perhaps." Blake continued to shake his head. "He was driven out of Capital, you know, sent into exile by the Governor himself. Perhaps that has more to do with his travels to the East than this supposed book about Stoner."

Christopher fought to conceal his surprise, glancing at his father to discover how much of this he knew, but Sir Malcolm's restraint was total; his face revealed nothing. "Whatever his past, I consider it a rare privilege to have a man of Mr. Lacy's learning teach my children."

If anything, Christopher was doubly surprised now. He had never heard his father praise Lacy before.

Blake grinned broadly. "But what of yourself, Sir Malcolm? What is your opinion concerning my mill? Is it a violation of precept or is it not?"

"The matter is open to individual interpretation."

"And yours—your interpretation?"

Malcolm shook his head. "I have none."

Christopher sensed that more was occurring here than was outwardly apparent. Blake and Sir Malcolm seemed to be playing a game, a fencing match. There was a tension in the air that their neutral words could not fully disperse.

"Capital is aware of my mill," Blake went on. "I can show you a letter from the Governor himself expressing approval."

"Of your mill, yes." Malcolm reached out and took a sip of wine. "But what of your guns?"

Unlike Malcolm, Blake was not capable of concealing his inner feelings. His face registered surprise—and shock. "Guns?" he repeated softly.

"On the way here, my horses were startled by the report of gunshots."

"In my county?"

"On your land."

Blake had recovered much of his composure. He made an abortive attempt at laughter, but the gesture lacked any of its earlier resonance. "You are mistaken, I'm sure. What you heard was something else, another loud noise."

"Such as what?" asked Sir Malcolm.

"Why, any of a hundred things." Blake squirmed visibly. Christopher never doubted for an instant the man was lying. "A falling log, or thrown rock, a minor explosion in the mill. Yes, that's what it must have been. Something in the mill."

"Of course I've never heard gunfire before."

"Of course not."

"So it might have been as you say."

"I'm telling you, Sir Malcolm, that it was. Surely, you believe me."

"Why shouldn't I, Mr. Blake?"

Suddenly, Christopher's attention was diverted by the sound of a soft voice from across the table. It was the first time Adrienne, Blake's daughter, had spoken all evening.

He looked at her. "I'm sorry. What did you say?"

"I asked whether your house was still the same as it was the other time."

"My house? But we haven't met—have we?" She was as delicate as her father was vulgar but nearly as dark as he.

"You can't mean you don't remember." Her voice was unexpectedly husky. "You were nine and I was six. It was eleven years ago, almost exactly. I came with my father."

He shook his head. "You have a better memory than I do."

"It was hardly a day I was apt to forget."

He felt pleased by her attention without exactly knowing why. "Was it that special?"

"A girl doesn't become engaged every day."

"But you're not married."

"Of course I'm not. It's you I'm talking about, Christopher. Don't you even remember that much?"

The rooms Christopher and Sir Malcolm occupied sat opposite one another at the end of a broad stone corridor, where the slightest sound echoed a hundred times over. As Christopher waited in his room, the footsteps in the corridor, as loud as gunshots, finally came to a halt. He heard a door creak painfully open. It slammed shut.

His father had returned at last.

With a weary sigh, Christopher stood up, went out, and knocked on the opposite door.

"Christopher?" said a voice from within. It was soft, muffled, barely audible. The oak doors were as thick as a man's fist.

"Yes, sir. I'd like to talk to you, sir."

"Then come in. The door's not locked."

Christopher entered to find his father perched on a corner of the tall bed like a spindly bird waiting to be fed. "I was expecting you, son. Why don't you sit here beside me?"

The unexpected warmth of the gesture caught Christopher by surprise—and momentarily distracted him. He sat on the edge of the bed and glanced furtively at his father's thin figure. "It's something Adrienne—Mr. Blake's daughter—it's something she said at dinner tonight."

"I know."

"She said that years ago, when both of us were little, we were engaged to be married."

Malcolm nodded. "It's true."

"But couldn't you—shouldn't you have told me?"

Malcolm twisted his head. He had to tilt his neck at an awkward angle in order to gaze directly at his son. "I intended to. All during the trip over here. But you seemed so . . . intrigued. I knew it was your first time away from County Kaine and everything must have seemed so new and different. Then, again tonight, I intended to tell you. I never thought the girl would blurt it out that way. I'm sorry. I should apologize."

For a father to apologize to his son was an occurrence unprecedented in Stonerist doctrine, but Christopher barely noticed. "Then it is true."

"Yes."

"But it's a mere formality, right? It's not as if anyone can force me to marry her against my wishes. It's not as if I don't have a choice in the matter."

"That's true." Malcolm's bony fingers toyed with the edge of the yellow bedspread beneath him.

"Then that's all there is to it?"

Malcolm shook his head slowly from side to side. "I wish it was."

"But—what else can there be?"

"Me, Christopher. I want you to marry her."

"Blake's daughter?"

"Yes." Malcolm was no longer looking at Christopher. "Isn't she pretty?"

"A lot of girls are pretty. I've seen peasants who are pretty. That doesn't mean I want to marry them."

Christopher had never been angry at his father before, and the force of his present fury frightened him.

But Malcolm seemed not to mind. He stood abruptly and moved across the wide room. "You're right. I shouldn't have been ...petty. It's not her beauty that matters. It's only that... well, would you believe that all the way here I worried that she might turn out to be fat?"

"It wouldn't have made any difference, Father. I just can't understand. Why do you want me to marry her?"

"Because of Blake."

"Blake? I'd think that would make you feel just the opposite. A man like that—a part of our family."

"Blake's the rising power in this world, Christopher."

"I don't care."

"In a few years, he'll be able to crush me with one hand."

"I'm not afraid of him."

"No, but I am."

"Because of his guns?"

"Partly. And because of what he is. Blake is a tinkerer—he acts without thinking of the consequences. He's built a locomotive and a steel mill. And now guns. What comes next?"

"And how will my marrying Adrienne put a stop to that?"

"Blake loves his daughter. You could use her as a...as a sort of bargaining lever." Malcolm suddenly looked very old. His body seemed to shrink inside its suit of clothes. "The man frightens me, Christopher—he really does. If I could think of any other way, any other means of controlling his unbridled ambition, don't you think I'd prefer it?"

"And you knew all this back then, eleven years ago?"

Malcolm laughed. "No, isn't that funny? Back then it was Blake, not me, who wanted the marriage. I agreed to the engagement as a simple formality—as a polite gesture between neighboring counties—but now...now Blake doesn't want it and I do."

"I don't love her, Father."

Malcolm came close to the bed and placed a hand on his son's shoulder. "Do you know her?"

"Even if I did, what difference would that make?" Christopher looked up, meeting his father's tired eyes. "Marriage is supposed to be for life, for eternity. What if I agree to marry this girl and then I meet someone else, someone I love?"

"That is a risk every man—and woman—takes when they marry."

"You didn't take it."

"Ah, but you're wrong. I never set eyes on Sarah until the day we exchanged vows. I knew her by reputation alone. She was the daughter of a minister in Capital and I was an obscure county bureaucrat. I was ambitious, Christopher, and old—older than your mother by twenty-five years. I knew she and her family could help me achieve the position I sought in life. So I married her."

His father's honesty disturbed Christopher. It was difficult to regard his parents in these terms—as real people, with feelings and faults. "Can I ask you one thing, Father?"

"Yes, of course."

"In my place, what would you do?"

"Marry her," Malcolm said, without hesitation.

"Because of Blake?"

"Because my father asked me to."

Christopher stood up. He couldn't explain to Malcolm that, for him, that just wasn't reason enough; he couldn't hurt the old man that way. "Can I have time to think?"

"Until tomorrow."

"That's all?"

"I'd prefer not to stay here longer. Tomorrow Blake wants to show us his steel mill. I agreed—there was no proper way to refuse. After that, I'd rather go home."

"I understand."

"I wish I could give you more."

"No, I said I understood." The door seemed very far away as Christopher headed toward it. Halfway there, he stopped. "What if I can't decide? What if I just can't make up my mind?"

"Then refuse. It's better to take no action than one that is wrong."

"Stoner?"

"Malcolm Janson." He smiled thinly.

"There is one other thing. Mother. Did you tell her about this?"

"I did."

"And what did she say?"

Sir Malcolm stared at a remote corner of the room. "She said she despised me for even considering it."

"I'm sorry, Father."
"So am I, Christopher."

What shocked Christopher most deeply was the fact that he was not shocked at all.

Observed from a distance, with the pillar of smoke vaulting toward the sky, Blake's steel mill had seemed like some ominous, decadent force, but once inside the brick building, what had once appeared sinister stood revealed as merely explainable. As Blake guided him and Sir Malcolm through the interior of the mill, describing in careful detail the smelting process necessary for the production of finished steel, Christopher listened with deepening interest, intrigued by what he heard. These concepts were entirely new to him and very exciting as a result.

Malcolm, on the other hand, barely seemed to hear a word; he was like a devout Christian held prisoner by atheists. He moved with lassitude, rarely speaking, and when he did, his voice came haltingly, his body held tense.

A dozen or so peasants—big men stripped naked to the waist— labored inside the mill. The heat in here was nearly unbearable, which appeared to increase Malcolm's discomfort. Blake led them to a round vat set in a recessed part of the floor where the molten ore was kept boiling. It was here that Malcolm finally turned away. "I don't think I can bear any more," he said.

Displaying concern, Blake hurried over to him. "But you haven't seen the final product yet, Sir Malcolm. You don't want to leave now."

"Yes, I'm afraid . . . the journey wearied me. You and Christopher go on."

"No, I'll go with you, Father."

"Thank you, Christopher. I'm not sure . . ."

Christopher supported his father's weight on one arm. The old man's breath came quickly. For a moment, Christopher feared that something might seriously be wrong.

"I'll join you outside in a moment," Blake said. "I have a few details to discuss with my foreman."

As soon as they stepped out in the sun, Sir Malcolm seemed noticeably improved. He pushed Christopher gently aside and moved under his own power. He sat down on a patch of blackened earth and wiped his forehead with the back of a hand.

"Are you all right, Father?"

"Better, I think. In there . . . it was difficult to breathe."

"The heat was pretty intense."

"Yes . . . the heat."

"Here." Christopher removed his shirt—it was a hot day and he didn't really need the garment—and placed it in a bundle on the ground. "Why don't you lay your head here and try to rest?"

"Are you going back in—with him?" Malcolm made a gesture toward the open door of the mill.

"I'll stay here with you."

Malcolm seemed relieved. He stretched out, put his head on Christopher's shirt, and closed his eyes. The ground was smooth. There were only a few small pebbles to interrupt the surface of the land. At one time grass must have grown here.

"I'm surprised the filth in the air doesn't destroy his crops," Malcolm said, opening his eyes.

"Does it make a difference?" said Christopher.

"Oh, yes. I thought by now Lacy would have taught you. Think what it must have been like, son. Two hundred years ago, three. The whole world was like this. Not one steel mill, not one factory, but thousands and thousands of them. There were factories for building this and building that, every possible machine your mind can imagine. And the automobiles. The locomotives, the jet air-planes. All of these things choked the air with their stink until not only the crops but even the people could not breathe. Thank God for Stoner's wisdom. Without him, it might all happen again." He shut his eyes wearily.

Christopher waited until his father's chest rose and fell with rhythmic regularity, then moved away. Halfway to the door of the mill, he met Sheridan Blake coming in the opposite direction.

"How's the old man doing?" he asked, in apparent concern.

Christopher pointed back the way he had just come. "He's taking a nap."

Blake shook his head. "A long trip for a man at that age—it must be exhausting." He turned, surveying the mill from without; the pride on his face was easy to read. "Well, what do you think? It's quite an achievement, isn't it?"

Christopher sought the exact proper words to use. "It is impressive."

"Thank you." Blake dropped to the ground and slapped the

earth beside him. "Here, sit with me."

Christopher sat down.

"You have no idea what I had to go through to build that mill. The materials, the supplies, the resources. I had to travel nine counties away to obtain certain ores that I needed. It was just a dream at first. Nothing but a crazy vision in my head. I made it come true. That's what pleases me the most."

Christopher didn't think he could compliment Blake without sounding like a traitor to his own father's philosophy. "What made you decide to do it? I mean, why build a steel mill in particular?"

"Because it's a basis. You know, like a house. When you build a house, the first thing you do is lay the foundation. My mill is like that. With the steel I produce, a million other things are suddenly possible. Like my little railroad."

"We saw that on our way here."

"I know you did. Of course it's not full scale. It's just a toy, really. But, goddamn, I love that thing. At night I like to come out and hop aboard the engine and *putt-putt* around for hours. With steam power, all that's necessary is a healthy supply of fresh water. It's not dirty, either, like coal. Hell, you and your father ought to build one."

"A railroad?"

"Sure, why not? If you want it, do it. Even a steel mill, for all I care. If you want something, build it. That's my motto."

"Well, I would never—"

"I know." Blake held up a hand. "Your father wouldn't like it."

"He believes in Stoner."

"Don't you think I do?"

"I don't . . ." Christopher decided to be honest. After all, if he wasn't an adult, why would Blake be talking to him this way? "I don't see how you can and still do all this."

"Easy. Because belief and worship aren't the same. Stoner was right—ninety-eight percent of the time. He knew his own world and he knew the one before and he knew what had destroyed it. But Stoner's dead, Christopher. He's been dead a hell of a long time."

"That doesn't make him wrong."

"Or right, either. Look, don't worry. I understand about your father and, frankly, I like the old guy. He's a great man, a fine man, but sixty-odd years is a long time to be alive. When you get that old, there's a tendency—I've noticed it in myself—you start getting too damned involved in your own past. The memory plays nasty little tricks, making yesterday seem a lot prettier than today. The past is always springtime and the future is like the first day of February."

"There is one other factor, Mr. Blake. My family isn't rich. We don't own half the land in the county. We couldn't build a steel mill even if we wanted to."

"Hell, I'd gladly give you the money."

"You would?"

"Sure. Call it a dowry. You are marrying my only daughter."

Christopher didn't say anything. He hadn't made up his mind about Adrienne but sensed that it would not be wise to let Blake see his hesitancy.

Blake stared out in the distance. "I'll admit that I wasn't too pleased when I was first reminded of it. We do a lot of things when we're young and poor that don't make quite as much sense eleven years later. When your father told me last night that he intended to make me stick to my promise, I was damned mad."

"Because of what you said—about my family being poor."

"Sure. Eleven years ago the Jansons looked like kings to me, but I've worked damned hard since to get where I am today. I could marry Adrienne to almost anyone I pleased, except maybe the old Governor himself." Blake reached out suddenly and put an arm around Christopher's shoulders. "But I've decided not to be bitter. You're a good boy and I like you. Adrienne says she likes you, too. And County Kaine is right next to County Tumas. That can't be a bad alliance to form."

"I suppose not," said Christopher.

"And also—"

Right then Malcolm Janson cried out. It was a mournful sound. Startled, Christopher sprang to his feet and hurried to his father's side.

By the time Christopher reached him, Malcolm was awake and rubbing his eyes. He smiled weakly. "I guess I must have fallen asleep."

"You screamed, Father."

"I did? When?"

"Just a moment ago. I thought you might be ill."

"A dream." Malcolm climbed unsteadily to his feet. He shook his head and peered at the sky. "Odd," he said, with a shrug. "I can't remember anything about it."

"I'll leave you two alone now," Sheridan Blake said smoothly, backing toward the door. The room, though large, was as spare as a dungeon. Several shelves were set in the stone walls but they contained only dust. Christopher occupied one of two chairs around a square table.

"If my father wakes up," he told Blake, "please tell him where I am."

Blake shook his head. "I don't think that will present a problem. You two talk and get acquainted. I'll be back later."

Blake turned and departed, leaving the door ajar behind him. For a long moment, Christopher stared at the gap.

Then Adrienne leaned across the table and gripped his arm. "He may be trying to listen in, so speak softly."

"Who?"

"My father of course."

"But this was his idea."

She grinned. "It was mine. You don't know how glad I am that you finally came."

"I'll . . . I'll be leaving soon, you know."

"Tomorrow. But I don't care. It's only for a while."

He tried to smile reassuringly but his lips refused to make the gesture. Blake had lured him here without explanation. If he'd known Adrienne was waiting, he would have made some excuse. She was lovely, though, her cheeks powdered white, her lips painted red.

"Eleven years is an incredibly long time, even if you say you don't remember. I was always asking my mother about you. I remember, whenever Father went to visit Sir Malcolm, I'd try to sneak into the carriage and go with him. He always caught me. I don't think he knew what was on my mind, how much I remembered."

"Maybe you shouldn't have . . ." It was difficult to put his thoughts into words; he didn't want to hurt this girl. "After all, we were young, just kids. You didn't have any idea how I might turn out."

"No, but it didn't matter. Last year, when Sir Malcolm came here to talk to Father about the mill, I kept staring at him for hours and hours until finally even he noticed."

"My father? Why would you want to stare at him?"

"Because of you. To try and see you. To see how you might look."

Christopher laughed self-consciously. "I don't look very much like him."

She laughed, too, but in a completely different way. "I know. You're much prettier."

He felt warm with embarrassment. She seemed much younger than her years. It was difficult trying to talk to her, finding a safe subject. He hoped Blake was listening and might choose to intrude. "My father was quite old when I was born."

"My mother was just the opposite. She was young. Her father was a minister in Capital."

"So was my mother's father."

"Well, there are something like two hundred different ministries, you know. Some are much more important than others. My uncle is a minister now. Minister Talstead. You may have heard of him."

"Sure, " said Christopher.

"But my mother died. In a plague. I was only thirteen. I seldom saw her for years before, though. She and Father didn't get along. He preferred to keep me for himself."

"I see." She had not wholly managed to conceal her bitterness. Christopher felt as if he had been granted an unwanted peek at something very ugly.

"I really do want to marry you."

He looked at her, no longer able to resist her entreaties. "So that you can get away from here?"

"Partly. I just wish...I wish we could do it today,."

"You're not of age. We have to wait at least a year."

"Then tell me about it."

"About what?"

"Our home. Where will we live? What will it be like?"

Christopher felt himself drawn unresistingly toward her reality.

"Our family has a large house, but we won't want to live there. There's a smaller house nearby. I think we could use it. Nobody's lived there for at least a hundred years. When I was a kid, my brother and I used to sneak in there and play."

"What about them? Your family? Don't you have a sister, too?"

"She's two years younger than me. Charlotte. My brother's another year younger."

"What's his name?"

"Ned. It's Edward, but everyone calls him Ned."

"I'm glad."

"Why? What about?"

"I meant because it'll be so different for me. Here I've hardly known anyone except Father. Only the peasants ever come to call. Once a year we go to Capital to stay with my aunt."

"I've never been there."

"It's awful. I don't like it."

In the intervening silence, while Christopher shifted uncomfortably in his chair, Adrienne came to her feet and move around the table and stood behind him. Suddenly, she lowered her head and kissed his neck.

Christopher tensed.

He turned around and then her lips were on his.

He resisted. But only for a moment—only infinitesimally.

Mounted on the black steel spine of his miniature locomotive, gloved hands wrapped tightly around the pillar of the smokestack, Sheridan Blake let the wind whip through his long hair. A lantern set in the locomotive's face illuminated the darkness on both sides of the tracks, while Blake, with a foot, tooted the horn fixed to the engine's side. *Honk-honk* went the horn, blasting in the night. Blake grinned at the noise. *Toot-toot.* He laughed aloud. Poor old Janson, he thought. Well, the bastard had asked for it.

As far back as he could remember, Sheridan Blake had never disliked anyone quite so fervently as he presently disliked Sir Malcolm. Oh, he had hated a man like Talstead to be sure, but that was a long term emotion spread across many years, and what he felt for Janson was sudden, sharp, intense. Nor was that son of his, in spite of the boy's assumed naivete, much better. Both had come to County Tumas with no other purpose except to steal another man's only daughter. A crime—an unforgivable offense—and one for which Blake, in due time, intended to extract an appropriate revenge. Hell, you couldn't outwit Sheridan Blake. Not in the long run, where it mattered. For a single day—even a week or month—yes, perhaps—but for longer than that—never.

Blake knew exactly how to respond; he had firmly made up his mind. From this day forward he would erase from his mind and heart any lingering feeling toward the daughter he had long adored. The next time he saw Adrienne, he intended to nod, smile, speak politely—but no more. She would be treated as a distant casual acquaintance. His strategy was plain: a man who refused to care could not be manipulated. And that'll be me, thought Blake. I'll trounce the bastards at their own game. He hurt; he felt pain. Yet this defense was necessary. His goal in life was too important to let private emotions interfere with its pursuit.

He thought of the girl's mother. A pretty girl, sharp-eyed, given to plumpness in her later years. They had tried a similar strategy there—Talstead had—but Blake had won. His wife was dead now—killed in a plague years ago—but Blake had never cared.

Malcolm Janson was a fool. The love of a father for a daughter, the love of a husband for his wife, he refused to let such weaknesses bring him low. Blake laughed without mirth. I will spit on your grave, he thought. I cannot be tricked. I cannot be beaten. I am invincible from wounds of the heart.

Some things on earth were far more precious than individual love, no matter how fond.

They couldn't understand. Not them—not with their families—their ancestors—their silver spoons. Not the Jansons or Talsteads or any of that breed.

Blake understood. He remembered his own father: a shepherd. Big red hands. Black teeth. Foul, dirty nails. Murdered in a drunken brawl when his son was just ten. One year later the mother disappeared. Blake understood about hunger. Cold. Loneliness. He learned how it felt to choose between feeding one's stomach or one's herd and electing the latter. He learned what is was like to cry without the strength to make tears.

He taught himself to read. A stolen copy of *The Book of Stones*.

(He had no money in those years with which to purchase anything.) A hundred times or more he recited the words of the philosopher until they were committed to memory, as intimate a part of his soul as his own private thoughts.

At eighteen he journeyed to Capital. He appeared at the examination center and asked to be administered the tests. The scholars stared at him. Some laughed aloud. His clothes were torn, his face and hands soiled, his feet bare. "Go away, peasant," they said. "You cannot take a test if you cannot read."

Politely, Blake showed them his personal, tattered (and stolen) copy of *The Book of Stones*. He said, "It is written that the exams shall be open to everyone regardless of class or station."

The scholars laughed again.

And yet, in the end, they let him enter.

Why? he had always wondered. Was it mere whim? Or genuine kindness? A chance for additional laughter or true devotion to the words of Stoner?

No matter: Blake achieved the highest mark scored by any examinee in more than five years.

It took eight more years and a skillful marriage before he achieved his initial goal in life: appointment as chief bureaucrat in the county of his birth.

From the beginning, Blake determined never to forget his own origins. He would do everything in his power to ensure that no other boy would ever suffer the same agonies that had scarred the years of his youth.

He believed he had succeeded. If nothing else, he had tried.

And no one—no Janson—would ever prevent him from continuing to try.

The locomotive sped through the night. Past a shoulder, Blake observed the stone castle where a single light burned in the second story.

Sir Malcolm called him a heretic. Sir Malcolm thought he was willing to plunge the world back into the horror and turmoil of the Terrible Years.

It wasn't that at all. Blake sought only one thing: he wanted a world where no man need go hungry.

We must strive to create consciously our own vision of the future, he thought, basing our design upon the errors of the past.

Sir Malcolm had come to County Tumas in hopes of winning a significant victory.

He had won nothing.

It would take more than a daughter to bring down Sheridan Blake. I have lost a wife, he thought, and now a daughter as well, but I shall never lose my own will to succeed. If Christopher Janson must be his son-in-law, then so be it. He would find a use for the boy. And there was always County Kaine itself. The rumored library of proscribed books hidden in the monastery at St. Sebastian's, for example. That was something worth considering.

Straddling the locomotive, Blake shut his eyes and suffered a vision of the one true future. It is mine, he thought with savage clarity, mine to create.

Sir Malcolm Janson awoke in darkness, a loud rumbling sound echoing in his ears. For a long moment, listening intently, he sought to divine the nature of this intrusion, but the sound soon faded and he lost interest in the mystery.

He sat up in bed. The aging body he had come to despise protested at the sudden motion. He looked at his hands. They were trembling, drenched in sweat.

A dream, he now remembered. Just before waking, he had been having a dream.

What was it about? He tried to remember, but like many other dreams, this one, too, had faded.

It must be death, he decided. The dream, that is. Nothing else could explain this trembling, the sweat, the lifeless taste in his mouth. Death alone had the power to instill dread in a man's soul. It had happened before. For months now he had dreamed his own death, only to cry out, waking himself. And he was afraid. Not because of the dream itself. No. Rather, it was the fear that one night, weary and exhausted, he might sleep too soundly and the dream, when it came, would never end and he would be dead.

Why should he fear death? He was not a young man. His life, a long one, had been lived gently and properly. He had loved his children, respected his wife, obeyed his father, cherished his friends, followed the meaningful rituals, taught others from the wisdom of his years, and been blamelessly loved by the people he served.

42   THE GARDEN OF WINTER

Yet death frightened him. Life, no matter how good or deep or long, seemed insignificant compared to the infinite reaches of that certain end. He was not a Christian. Stoner had written, "There may or may not be a God, but in either event the doings of heaven and earth are separate."

That no longer seemed enough to satisfy.

God and heaven? Death and life? How brutal to thrust such predicaments on a man at this late hour of life, when one's clearest and keenest thoughts lay far behind. Clarity these days was as rare and brief as a lightning bolt. I should thank Sheridan Blake, he realized in a burst of insight. When I see that man, only then can I be aware of how well I have lived. Would Blake fear death? Never. Only one who has lived well can regret the coming of the end.

He heard footsteps. In the corridor. Climbing out of bed, he padded to the door and listened. Christopher. Yes. There was a knock. He opened the door.

"Father?"

The lantern light blinded him momentarily. "Yes, what is it?"

"There's something I need to tell you, sir."

"Come inside." He stepped back, letting Christopher pass.

They sat side by side on the edge of the bed.

"I've made up my mind," Christopher said.

"About the girl?"

"Yes, I've decided that..."

But Sir Malcolm was no longer listening. He knew exactly what Christopher intended to say, every word. He thought instead of death—that most supreme of cosmic mysteries. It made him feel tiny, inconsequential, shrunken and petty. He embraced that feeling now more than ever.

As soon as Christopher left and made his way upstairs, Adrienne Blake realized that she no longer possessed any alternative except to go outside and meet Dav Lindstrom.

Adrienne would have given almost anything in the world for a good excuse not to go tonight. After Christopher, the very thought of Lindstrom—with his hairy arms, beefy smell, heavy breath—revolted her.

Yet what else could she do?

Her father wasn't—as she had slyly suggested to Christopher—listening in. He wasn't anywhere nearby to send her to bed without a chance to leave. And she had promised Dav—eight days ago, what seemed an eternity now, the last time they had met, two days before she learned that Christopher was coming at last.

It was so completely different now—so changed. She would have to tell Dav the truth. It was over between them forever. Would he listen? Would he understand? She was worried, almost frightened. Dav Lindstrom was a peasant and a peasant might do anything.

Maybe she shouldn't tell him.

But, if she didn't, wouldn't that be worse? Then she would have to lay with him. Not just tonight but other nights a whole year's time, till she finally went away to marry Christopher. And she didn't think she could bear to do it even one more time. Not after Christopher. Not once.

Adrienne took a lantern, ignited the wick, and went outside. The night proved unexpectedly cool, with a strong breeze blowing, and she was glad she had chosen to wear a heavy gown.

In the distance she could see the bonfires of the peasant enclave. Dav lived there when he wasn't working in the mill. Much farther away, only a dim red streak against the black sky, she could make out the flickering glow of the mill itself.

Stepping down the cobbled path that led from the castle to the road below, Adrienne discovered what had become of her father. The steady rumbling of the locomotive reached her ears. She could hear the horn tooting senselessly. Once last year, right after he'd finished laying the tracks, she had agreed to go riding with him, but the speed had frightened her so much that she'd begun to cry and begged him to stop. After that, she'd never gone close to the locomotive. Father continued to go out almost every night.

The land sloped gently. Adrienne left the path and followed the edge of the road. The high grass, whipped by the wind, made a gentle whistling noise. Dav should be waiting near here. They always met here and then went into the grass. Maybe he hadn't come tonight. She felt a wave of hope. Maybe he was ill or injured.

"Adrienne?"

She stopped and turned the lantern. "Dav?"

"Did you expect another?" He stepped onto the road beside her. A tall man, four years older than she, with a gruff voice like a pig's grunt. "I started to think you weren't coming."

"I was delayed."

"Because of those men?"

"What men?"

"The two that came to the mill with your father today. One was as old as a mountain and the other just a boy."

She knew this was her chance, her opening. "Yes, it was because of them. You see—"

His arms went around her. She had no opportunity to resist. He shoved his lips against her mouth and tried to force his tongue inside.

She squirmed free of his grasp.

He stood with his hands on his hips, glaring at her. "What's wrong with you?" She could see him clearly in the lantern light. "You angry with me?"

"Should I be?"

"Then what is it? Since when don't you like me kissing you?"

"It's because I can't—I shouldn't."

"Who told you that?" He drew closer and put his hands on her shoulders. "What's that supposed to mean?"

For the first time she realized the depth of the revulsion she felt for him. He had first seduced her more than a year ago. A chance meeting on this same road early one evening. Her father in Capital. She recognized Dav from the mill, where he served as foreman. He kissed her and she, for whatever reason, responded. It was just boredom, she told herself, just the fact that she had no other friends, no one but her father. The first time she remembered the pain most clearly. And the blood. A big pool of it. Dark blue, not red; the sight made her feel ill. Dav said he had a potion that prevented pregnancy and she laughed, for she hadn't even thought of the possibility. When he asked, she said, yes, she'd meet with him again. She did. And again. A hundred times now that she must have lain on her back in the soft grass with her gown bunched around her waist while his hips thrust against her.

You're my lover, he liked to say when he finished. He revolted her.

She wiped her lips with the back of a hand, a half-conscious gesture. "I came to say I can't see you again. I'm sorry."

"Who do you think I am?" His grip tightened on her shoulders and he shook her.

There were tears in her eyes. Fear was like a taste on her tongue. "Don't hurt me," she pleaded.

He let her go. He stepped back. "You'd better explain so that even a peasant like Dav Lindstrom can understand."

"It's that boy—that man. He and I are to be wed." She said it quickly, hastily, wanting to get the words out before they stuck on her tongue.

He showed no emotion. She clutched the lantern in one hand and saw his dark eyes clearly.

"When's this going to happen?" he said.

"Soon."

"How soon?"

"In . . . in a year." .

He grinned. "In county?"

"What?"

"Is it going to happen here? Are you and him going to live at the castle?"

"No. He's from County Kaine. His father is—"

"I know all that." He moved forward. He was smiling broadly now and she could see his teeth. "So what's the problem?" he asked smoothly.

She tried to run. His huge arms circled her waist. His thick lips pressed against her. She tried to scream. Tried to twist away.

He slapped her.

She fell in the road.

There was a taste in her mouth. "I'm bleeding," she said, gazing up at the huge figure looming above. The lantern had squirted from her grasp. It lay in the road, casting shifting shadows.

"Come here," he said, reaching down and grabbing her. Adrienne shut her eyes as firmly as she could. She knew exactly what he intended to do, knew it was futile to resist. He carried her through the air. She smelled the grass, felt the moist blades against her face. She opened her eyes, seeing only darkness, the sliver of a moon, and waited for his body to fall upon her.

Instead, something kicked her in the side.

She moaned.

He kicked her again. An explosion went off in her head. She cried out. Surely, someone must hear. Just peasants. Her father and his locomotive.

His voice reached her. She felt his breath close to her ear. "You won't tell. Hear me? Because, if you do, I'll tell more, and that boy will never want to see your face. A hundred times you rutted with a peasant. You screamed and panted and begged for more. I know it all and I'll tell."

"Yes," she said. Her hands brushed his hair. Like wires. Not smooth and sleek, not like Christopher. He'll kill me, she thought, but deep down she knew that he would not. Her life was not in danger.

His hands squeezed her throat. "I want you to promise."

"I do."

"What?"

"I promise I won't tell."

"Say that you tripped in the night, say anything, just don't say my name."

"Yes."

He stood up. She could see him dimly, a darker shape against the night. She shut her eyes. He would fall upon her now, take her as she lay. She clenched her fists so tightly that the nails cut into her palms.

After a while, she opened her eyes.

She was alone.

He had gone away, after all.

Sarah Janson sat alone in the warmth of the big living room, head tilted back, eyes nearly shut, and recited poetry aloud. Her tongue moved slowly as she read, for the verse she had chosen to recite tonight was extremely complex: Donne, Hopkins, Yeats, and Auden. The intellectuals. Men with minds as well as hearts. Her throat felt raw. A pile of books lay stacked beside her chair. The lantern burned on the table. Outside, the wind slashed and howled. A bleak night. Her voice grew louder. The words came faster. She barely paused to take a breath.

And, as she recited, her mind never for an instant stopped whirling.

I am a woman of many parts, she thought. They are like masks, she concluded, a thicket of shifting faces. No single identity existed purely alone; there was no private self—no genuine Sarah Janson. Long ago she had first created the faces not for reasons of subterfuge or concealment but rather for strength and greater depth. She thought of her father, mother, two brothers, aunt, uncle, friends, and finally Malcolm. She thought of the children— Christopher, Charlotte, and Ned. She thought of Lacy. Each of these people, whether then or now, past or present, served as the model for yet another of her faces. Deprived of the people she knew, Sarah herself would soon cease to exist. I am they: they are me. And that is why, she realized, I am so damned afraid. For they are going. Leaving me. One by one.

Her family and friends had left long ago. Malcolm came next. She knew full well he was dying, but that mattered little, for the spiritual death always preceded the merely physical. Had he ever truly cared for her or she for him? Did it matter?

Christopher, too. Marriage meant that. Not death—only an utterly selfish person would think that way. But it was an end, a leavetaking. Charlotte and Ned would soon follow.

Then what of me? she thought. Who will I be when I'm alone at last? She recalled when her father had died unexpectedly and her mother had been transformed overnight into a cold, gray spirit, a presence merely, no longer a substantial human object. Her mother had loved her father but she did not love Malcolm. Did that matter, either? Will it be the same with me? she wondered. Can it be happening now, even as my heart continues to beat? Can I be dying already and not know it?

She went on reciting.

Jeffrey Lacy entered the room. Stooping, he placed a glass of wine on the floor beside her chair, then sat down opposite her.

He waited motionlessly until she had finished reciting the poem she had begun.

She looked at him, smiling. "You brought wine?"

"I had a feeling you might need a swig."

"My throat feels like I haven't stopped talking all night."

"You haven't."

She sipped the wine. "This is different."

"I know. I've heard you down here before. It's a new habit, isn't it? You didn't recite poetry when we were first together."

"I didn't even like poetry."

"It's an acquired taste. We educated people are taught to read quickly. A book is like a barrel of mediocre beer. The faster you gulp, the better it tastes. Poetry has to be sipped. It's like a rare wine."

She smiled back at him. "I'm not even sure I like it now."

"Wine?" His eyes twinkled.

"Poetry. I don't think I heard a word I read all night."

He shook his big head. "It's not the words that matter—it's the music."

She tossed her hair. "If you say so. But, if that's true, then why bother with the words in the first place?"

There was a pause. Sarah drained her glass. Lacy stood up and came across to her chair.

He put an arm on her shoulder. "They'll be coming home tomorrow. Is that what you've been thinking about?"

"It started with that. Other things came up."

"It's been quiet around here."

"Without Christopher, it has."

"You're worried, aren't you?"

"I don't know."

"Meet the girl," he said. "Talk to her. Get to know who she is. We both knew the family in Capital. Forget about Blake. The mother was a fine woman."

"I don't care about that. At least I don't think I do. It's just . . . well, this makes me feel so old."

He nodded. "Me, too."

"You? Why you?"

"Because I am old." He offered his hand. "Shall we go to bed?"

She looked up at him, smiling tentatively. "For the night?"

"If you want it that way."

"I do." She stood, kissing his cheek lightly. "Who are you, saying I'm old?"

As soon as he heard her breath coming with even regularity, Jeffrey Lacy drew back the bedcovers and placed his feet on the floor.

His clothes lay draped over a nearby chair. It was dark in the room—the curtains drawn against the faint luminosity of the early moon—but his fingers moved with agility as he dressed; his eyes were accustomed by now to the absence of light.

He went over and opened the door, then glanced back. In the bright light spilling from the corridor, he could see her pale face outlined clearly against the white pillow. Her jaw tilted slightly up, as if in a gesture of defiance, and the sight somehow made him want to smile. Poor thing, thought Lacy. In this world that Stoner made, there is no place for one such as you. Sarah was a woman, and yet she was more intelligent than any but one or two men he had ever met. What a waste, he thought wistfully, but was that really true—or fair? Sarah a waste? No, no, he decided. He knew her too well to believe that.

The children slept soundly in their upstairs rooms. Well, Ned, at least. (Charlotte seldom seemed to sleep.) If he hadn't been convinced of that—of their privacy—he would never have offered to sleep with her tonight. It was the first time since his arrival here. They had made love twice before, but never in that bed, her bed, never for the entire night. On previous occasions, they had been like adolescents, meeting in the high grass, the back of her curtained buggy. Tonight, he had sensed her special need.

Lacy opened the door further, stepped out, then closed it gently behind him.

Well, isn't that petty of you? he thought. Special need? Whose? he thought. Yours or hers? Sarah was a strong woman. She had lived with Malcolm without love for enough years that he was sure she could have died that way. He had written the first letter—not she. He had asked for employment—she had not offered it.

Sarah had not been his first lover. He doubted that he had been hers. That was, oh, decades ago. (Twenty years.) In Capital. He, a brilliant scholar; she, the reigning princess of the civilized world. (A delicate and sensitive beauty which had not lessened with the passing years.) She, who could have chosen any of them, had picked him. Why? It was his intelligence, of course. And his respect—the respect he held for her. After a few blissful months she had gone to marry Malcolm Janson, and he, falling into dis-favor with certain ministers, had begun his journey to the East. His exile. For a few weeks he had hated her; for several years he had despised Janson. That was all behind him now.

Plucking a lantern off the wall, he went outside and peered at the sky. A fine clear night, clouds chased away by a steady driving wind. He wished he could have stayed longer with Sarah, but caution and restlessness had eventually won out. Better to sleep in his own bed. Charlotte might come wandering. In any event, he hadn't slept a full eight hours in more years than he could remember. It's my rootless youthful nature, he thought mockingly, my bold questing self.

He smelled smoke. A dozen or more campfires burned in the peasant enclave, flames whipped high by the wind. A bizarrely primitive tableau, like something out of the East. He heard drums beating. *Boom-thump-thump, boom-thump-thump*. A familiar sound from his twenty years of exile. The peasants ruled in the East, if anyone could be said to rule at all. He was glad to be home. For twenty years, he had roamed the devastated cities, seeking information, searching for a measure of the forgotten truth. He smiled tightly. And I found it, he thought. When least expected. Where least expected. In County Kaine. In Stoner's home. All my life, he thought, I searched for William Stoner, and now I have found him. That search had ended the week after his arrival, a cold winter morning, snow ankle deep on the ground. A place known locally as the diamond mine, though the records in the East had given it another name: Gunbolt Site. He preferred the former designation. It was the place where children often played.

Boom-thump-thump, boom-thump-thump. The wind had altered direction, carrying the sound more clearly, hurling dust against his face. Bowing his head, Lacy moved toward the enclave. He had not dressed adequately. Even the dark of night ought not to be this cold during the summer time of the year.

So young Christopher was to marry. The daughter of Sheridan Blake. He sympathized with Sarah's hesitancy and pondered Malcolm's eagerness. Blake was indeed a dangerous man. A Cassius of the counties—he thought far too much. Lacy had known Blake in Capital. The son of a shepherd, it was rumored. A dark swarthy man with yellow stained teeth. Well, the world was changing. Christopher might do well. The boy often concerned Lacy. He was smart but glib. He read Stoner, memorized the required passages, but he didn't live Stoner; that was the change. The boy's world was too damned different from the book for him to accept it, as Lacy himself once had, as revealed gospel. He sometimes preferred the company of Ned, the slow, plodding, gentle brother, but it was Christopher who would surely place his mark on the world. Yet, whose mark? His own, or Blake's? That was what worried Lacy most of all.

From the enclave he heard voices rising. He slowed his step and extinguished the lantern, approaching the fires surreptitiously. He had spent too many early years in the city, missed too much. Life was more real out here somehow; Sarah had made a wise choice. Some sort of religious ritual, he decided. The peasants carried around a host of assorted beliefs. They upheld Christ, thus pleasing Brother Horace at the monastery, and yet also worshipped a hundred other gods, finding divinity in the rain, the wind, the trees and flowers. Who was to say they were wrong? Not even Stoner. The voices reached him more clearly now. He stopped to listen, crouching behind a well-placed bush. The multiplicity of apparent voices fused into one. He couldn't identify the source. A woman? An old woman? The voice, shrill, almost a whine, emanated from inside the circle of fires. He couldn't see a thing.

"Flames sweep across the land . . . machines like insects hurl the gray death . . . blood flows like river water . . . the sins of a brother plague the daughter . . ."

Ah, he thought, an oracle. Lacy knew of such people, but he had never actually witnessed a moment like this. The peasants seldom acknowledged the existence of their own superstitions. Fear of the monastery. In a Christian land, Christ must prevail in word if not deed. Brother Horace would have been appalled; Lacy was fascinated. Sometimes drugs were ingested, certain vines smoked. He sniffed at the fumes about him. Tree branches, he decided.

" . . . an end to all beginnings must commence . . . a man without legs will—"

Suddenly, a shadow rose up in front of him. Lacy fell back and nearly cried out in surprise.

"Mr. Lacy, is that you?" said the shadow.

"Bill. Bill Walker. What are you doing here?"

The boy dropped beside Lacy. "You shouldn't be here, sir."

"I was taking a walk. I heard voices. I—"

"Well, don't let them catch you. The elders. They'd be angry if they knew you were here."

"I didn't mean to spy. It's just that . . . well, I've never heard anything like this before."

"It's madness," Bill said flatly.

"You mean you don't believe?"

"No, sir, I don't."

"But the others do?"

"Some of them. Mostly the old ones. They can't read or write. They don't know any better."

They spoke in whispers. With half-an-ear, Lacy continued to listen to the old woman's prophecies. There was an odd, almost frightening sense to what she was saying. She could have been describing an ancient battle she had witnessed with her own eyes. But this was prophecy, not history. This was the future.

"Can you take me down there?" he asked.

Bill Walker shook his head quickly. "I can't. The elders . . ."

"They won't harm me."

"But why do you want to go? Do you want to laugh?"

"I want to listen."

Bill stood hesitantly. "All right. Come on."

Lacy went with him. The fires were arranged in a neat circle twenty yards in diameter. The old woman lay in the middle. She was naked, her clothes laying in shreds nearby. Lacy stopped and stared, fighting to control his initial revulsion. None of the men inside the circle took notice of him. Their faces were slack, their eyes empty. Beyond the fires, the huts of the enclave stood dark and silent. Apparently, only a few elders came to hear the oracle. Lacy sat down in the dust. Bill Walker, a troubled expression on his face, knelt beside him.

The woman was silent now. Her body lay motionless on the ground, but her eyes were open. Saliva foamed at her lips. Her abdomen and legs were covered with welts and scratches. The fresher wounds gleamed red in the harsh light.

Suddenly, she was speaking again. The voice seemed to come

from deep inside. "Fire rains upon the chapel . . . the men of God are rendered blind . . . the dark man from beyond the hills wreaks his vengeance upon the land . . ."

Lacy tilted forward. This did make sense, he decided. *The chapel?* St. Sebastian's. *The men of God?* The monks. *The dark man from beyond the hills?*

Out of the corner of an eye, Lacy glanced at Bill Walker. There was fear on his face as well.

Charlotte Janson sat on the edge of her bed and pressed the heels of her hands against her ears.

It didn't help. She still heard them. The voices came from inside, not without. There was nothing she could do to make them fall silent.

Fire rains upon the chapel. The men of God are rendered blind. The dark man from beyond the hills wreaks his vengeance upon the land.

What did it mean? Even when she refused to listen, she couldn't help hearing. Lacy admitted he didn't know. Brother Julian said he didn't know. No one knew.

Yet she heard. The voices kept coming. Nearly every night. She couldn't sleep. She couldn't think. She couldn't even dream.

Why me? she thought. Why do they speak to me? I am not Joan. I am not a saint. Why me? Why is God picking on me?

PART 3:

The Wedding

Some many years ago a most gentle scholar from a neighboring county came to visit my home and school. After he and I had shared a vial of precious red wine, the scholar bowed his head and asked timidly if he might be permitted to put one question to me. I nodded my assent and the scholar asked, "Mr. Stoner, is there a god?" Smiling, I replied that this was a question better put to a peasant than to me. The scholar, persisting, then asked, "Is death the total extinction of the spirit?" Again, I politely referred the matter to a peasant. "But can you explain the creation of the universe?" This time, my patience very near its end, I stood to fetch the peasant.

The scholar, with a sad face, begged me to remain. "Mr. Stoner," he said bluntly, "I fear your wisdom has been greatly exaggerated. You are not only unable to answer the most relevant questions known to man, but you appear to refuse to regard them seriously."

I admitted that this was indeed so. "But that," I said, "is exactly why I am a wise man."

The metaphysical polarities of theism and atheism are wholly irrelevant to the functioning of a properly modulated human society. One may

55

admire the totally theistic state of ancient Egypt,
while simultaneously acknowledging the supreme
social achievement of agnostic China. The
Christian nation of United America and the
atheistic state of Soviet Russia stand equally as
pitiful abortions within the social fabric of human
history. A good and gentle society may worship one
god, one hundred, or none at all; the same is true
of an unsuccessful nation.

The sole duty of a gentle man consists in
learning to live harmoniously with other men.
Obey the stated precepts, do not do to others what
you do not wish them to do to you, follow the
prescribed rituals. If all this is accomplished, then
the society formed by such gentle men shall be a
good one. Religious beliefs are matters for the
heart, not the mind. The social fabric must be
woven from wholly rationalistic threads, those that
can be seen, felt, or heard; questions of the spirit
remain for the individual to decide.

It is not that I cannot or will not answer such
questions as those put to me by the scholar.
Rather, in the privacy of my heart, I have
answered them to my own satisfaction. Yet my
personal answers are no more or less valid than
those held by any other, for I can prove none of
them. When I discuss society, as I often do, my
views are subject to immediate testing. My precepts
may be shown to be either right or wrong. This
can never be done with a god or devil.

William Stoner, The Book
of Stones, circa 2045.

Actually, it was two nearly simultaneous forces
that helped ring down the curtain of history on
what we now call the Great Dark Age. The first of
these, which I've previously described at length,
was the reemergence of the internal combustion
engine as a locomotive force. The second (and
who's to say which was more important?) was the
big transformation in social mores that struck
around the middle of the twenty-third Christian
century. What was one to make of it? All of a
sudden, like ants in pursuit of jelly, the women
came pouring out of the family homes they had
willingly inhabited for two centuries. It's hard to

> *say which frightened the older generation more:*
> *their first sight of a smoking automobile or their*
> *initial glimpse of a pair of moist, red, painted*
> *female lips.*
>
> Daniel T. Janson, A
> History of Human Events
> Subsequent to Stoner's
> Time, 2378.

Despite what day it was, Christopher Janson stood waiting patiently in the doorway while his brother Ned wandered aimlessly across the length and breadth of the huge, high, hopelessly cluttered room, stroking his chin and scratching his head like a depiction of Christ judging sinners on the Last Day. "Well, what about it?" Christopher finally said, when it became clear Ned might go on like this for hours. "Do you think we can use the place or not?"

Ned turned with a look of surprise on his face. "Oh, sure. Why not? It's big enough."

"And a mess," said Christopher, pointing at the piles of junk, garbage, and dust scattered around the room.

"Oh, that's nothing."

"It's plenty enough for me." A tornado might have struck the place. The door itself dangled from a single screw. The previous owner, Mr. Bixby, leaving the county, had apparently removed anything salvageable. There was a wooden workbench buried beneath cobwebs in the middle of the room, for instance, but three of its legs were missing.

"I'll clean it," said Ned. "While you're gone." He poked at one of the piles with a broken stick. Something seemed to stir inside. A rat?

"Well, we'd better get going," Christopher said.

Ned poked at the pile again. "We've got five minutes, haven't we?"

"I suppose so."

"I'd like to look around a little more."

Christopher knew it was futile to argue with his brother in one of his distracted moods. He gave the door a gentle shove. "I'll wait for you outside."

"Sure," Ned said dimly. Holding his stick, he turned to another pile. "In a second."

"Five minutes."

"Sure. Five."

Christopher went outside. He had inspected the place earlier in the day and, in spite of the mess, had already made up his mind to proceed with the deal; Ned's agreement only made things easier.

He sat in the untrimmed grass in front of the door, taking care not to snag his clothing as he moved. He was wearing a knee-length white cotton tunic, blue tights, and black leather boots. The costume was the traditional garb for the occasion, but it was also hot, uncomfortable, and itchy. He did not look forward with much anticipation to the rest of the day. He didn't mind the ceremony so much; it was the frills that went with it—like the tunic—that gave him a pain.

As he sat, his eyes happened to come to rest on something he had somehow failed to notice before. There was a paper sign, tattered and streaked by time and the weather, tacked above the door. The neatly hand-lettered sign read:

BIXB CAR IA E WO KS

Christopher smiled. For some reason, he liked that sign very much. It would have to stay—only the name would be changed:

JANSON MOTORCARS

The name—and the job to be done.

The horses he and Ned had ridden stood nearby, munching at the tall grass. Christopher wondered what the animals would think if they could comprehend the ultimate result of this visit. We intend to make you obsolete, he thought. We intend to give you a chance to spend all your days munching sweet grass. Not that it would happen that fast. Not these horses, but their sons and daughters perhaps. If he could accomplish that much, Christopher would be pleased.

He stood up and called to his brother through the door. "Hey, Ned, hurry up in there! You don't want me to be late today!"

"Just another second," came Ned's voice from within.

"Okay, but that's all!"

Christopher went over to the horses and stood holding his mount by its bridle. From out here, the old wood-and-concrete building didn't look nearly so bad. It dated back to the Terrible Years. An army had originally constructed it, he'd been told. Sir Malcolm had acted surprised when Christopher had revealed his interest in purchasing the place, but of course Sir Malcolm was unaware of the real reason he and Ned wanted the building.

"The Bixby Carriage Works?" Sir Malcolm had said. "But that place has been shut down for at least five years."

"Yes, sir, but we intend to open it again."

"And build carriages?"

"Yes, sir."

"But why? I never knew you had the slightest interest in such a trade."

"It's not really a trade, sir. More of a hobby. Ned and I just thought it might be fun to build and repair carriages."

"And you're willing to spend your own money for that purpose?"

"Well, sir, it's not exactly our money, either."

In fact, Christopher thought that most of his father's final reluctance stemmed from the source of the money Christopher intended to use to purchase the building from Bixby's relatives: he had borrowed the funds from his soon-to-be father-in-law, Sheridan Blake.

"Ned, come on!" Christopher called. "I can't wait another minute!"

Ned's face appeared in the crack of the doorway. "Not even one?"

"If I don't get there in time to marry his daughter, you can bet Blake isn't going to loan us a thing."

Ned emerged from the doorway. "Since you put it that way, I suppose we'd better hurry."

Blake's interest in the proposed motorcar factory was more than financial. The steel produced by his mill would be essential in their work.

Actually, from here, it wasn't more than twenty minutes' ride to St. Sebastian's. Christopher mounted his horse and made sure that Ned set off before following. He glanced at the pocketwatch his mother had given him only this morning. Thirty-eight minutes to go.

"How long to you expect to be gone on this trip?" Ned asked Christopher, when their horses moved side by side.

"Three weeks or so." After the marriage, he and Adrienne had agreed to spend time with Blake at the castle. Christopher felt a tightening sensation in his stomach. Now what was wrong? He glanced at the green land lying ahead, the sharp crease of the horizon, the blue sky beyond. Was he finally starting to get nervous?

"That's what I was trying to see when I stayed in there so long. In three weeks I can have that whole place cleaned up. I'll even install some of our equipment. As soon as Blake's first shipment of steel arrives, we'll be ready to start."

"No, we won't," said Christopher.

"Why? What do you mean?"

"I mean I don't want you spending all your time over here while I'm gone. This has to remain a secret—from Father if no one else. There hasn't been a functioning automobile in this county for two hundred years. We're in no hurry."

"Maybe you're not," Ned said sullenly, "but I am."

"I just don't want to see Father hurt."

After climbing a gentle incline of grass and wildflowers, Christopher turned his horse toward the white streak of the sun. Suddenly, topping another rise, he saw below the stone buildings of the monastery at St. Sebastian's. Ned saw them, too, and nudged his horse in that direction. Christopher deliberately hung back for a moment and took a deep breath. The soaring spire of the chapel glittered like a piece of the evening moon. His hands sweated on the reins. His stomach felt queasy. Well, he thought to himself, I suppose it's not every day when a man gets married.

Christopher dismounted in front of the chapel. Ned was waiting for him. From within, Christopher could hear the sharp strains of a piano. Music meant little to him, and the exact nature of this melody eluded him. A group of peasants, drawn to the spot through curiosity, stood near the door. As the brothers approached, the peasants moved politely back. Christopher suddenly noticed his old boyhood friend, Bill Walker, and raised a hand in greeting.

Bill waved back.

Ned preceded Christopher into the chapel. When it was his

turn, Christopher entered with his head held high, a man fully prepared, mentally and spiritually, for the new responsibilities of married life.

It wasn't until several hours after the completion of the ceremony that Christopher finally found an opportunity to exchange words with his bride. A sumptuous meal had been consumed in the chapel dining hall—precept required that Christopher sit with the bride's family and she with his—and the reception had followed immediately. To Christopher, Adrienne had either changed markedly during their months apart or else the mental vision he had carried with him had somehow gotten distorted in the interim. She seemed older now, which was understandable, and less beautiful, which was explicable—the memory always played that trick—but there were other, less obvious alterations as well. Seen from afar, Adrienne appeared to move with more grace, with additional confidence, with newly found certainty. She was a woman now, no longer a child, and perhaps that was the best solution he could devise for what puzzled him. He knew she had spent most of the past year in Capital with her maiden Aunt Hilary. The reception had been going on for nearly an hour before Christopher reached her through the crowd. He caught her bare arm and bowed.

She smiled. "So what did you think of them?"

The question suprised him. "Of who?"

"The family who came. Aunt Hilary refuses to travel, so she sent these people, cousins and things. Do you like them?"

"Well, they were interesting," he said.

She laughed and brushed his cheek with her lips. "Do you really mean that?"

He glanced self-consciously around to see if anyone might have noticed the intimate gesture. It was hard to keep in mind that he was married—hard to remember how to act. She smelled like fruit petals—a perfume, he guessed. She had worn none a year ago. "But I was confused. Your father did most of the talking, and I forgot who half the others were."

"Oh, I always do that." She squeezed the meaty part of his arm. "Don't worry. It's just my mother's family. They have as little to do with me as possible."

He started to ask why, then caught himself. The answer was

plain enough. Her father. "And mine?" he said hurriedly. "What did you think of my family?"

"I thought they were marvelous, of course. Shouldn't I?"

He couldn't answer that question. Or any other, for that matter. All at once, for no logical reason, he felt tongue-tied. Turning his head desperately, he spied Jeffrey Lacy trudging through the crowd, a mug of ale in one hand, a smoldering cigar in the other. Christopher waved to him.

"Have you had a chance to meet Mr. Lacy yet—my teacher?"

"No, but I've heard of him."

"From your father?"

Reaching the couple, Lacy beamed at Adrienne with a brilliance that threatened to eclipse the glory of a full moon and, in spite of his girth, executed a smooth, swift bow. "I am most honored and delighted to make the acquaintance of so beautiful a gentle woman."

Adrienne nodded in reply. "And I am most pleased to make your acquaintance as well, Mr. Lacy. You are a teacher, I understand. Please tell me. Exactly what is it that you teach?"

Lacy grinned and puffed at his cigar. "Oh, nothing at all," he said blithely.

"Nothing?" Even Adrienne seemed taken aback by this reply.

"Sure. Nothing—and everything. Even Christopher here is beginning to understand that it's not what you know that matters as much as what you can forget."

"Perhaps you could teach me, too."

"I could try."

"I'd like to know how to forget."

"That's the easy part. It's knowing what to forget and what not to forget that's hard." Lacy glanced around the room. "It's funny, but I've been trying to catch your father's eye all evening without any luck. I'd almost think he was avoiding me on purpose. Years ago he and I knew each other in Capital."

"Did you hold an official position there?" Adrienne asked.

"I was the Minister of Transportation. I did it badly and was asked to leave."

"Then you must have known some of my mother's family."

"I knew Arthur Talstead. He was one of those who asked me to leave."

She laughed. "I've only met him a few times myself. He's not very friendly."

"And I knew your mother."

"You did? Really? Was she . . ."

"A fine woman. As for the rest of the family, well, they mean little harm."

"Except for Minister Talstead."

"He's a sly one. A man of prudence. He did not approve of me."

"Why?"

Lacy winked. "Ask him, not me."

"Then his attitude is not an uncommon one?"

"Lord, no. Nearly everyone disapproves of old man Lacy. Except for Christopher here." Lacy reached out, punching Christopher softly on the arm, startling him. "And sometimes I'm not too damn sure about him."

Christopher tried to laugh. The conversation between Lacy and Adrienne disturbed him. It involved matters distant from his own knowledge—the personalities of leaders in Capital. Not for the first time, he felt almost awed by Adrienne. She had indeed grown in the last year. Too much? Well, his own time was coming.

Lacy was saying, "Your mother asked me to come over here, Christopher. She said to tell you that Sir Malcolm is preparing to depart and wishes to say good-bye."

"Oh," said Christopher. "I thought he'd left already."

"You'll find him in the kitchen. He ate there."

"Alone?"

"Brother Horace is with him."

"Then I'd better go." Leaning down, Christopher kissed Adrienne on the lips. Standing upright, he felt a flush spread across his face. The gesture had been a quick, bold move, leaving him uncertain. Neither Adrienne nor Lacy appeared to notice his discomfort.

Lacy put an arm around Adrienne's dark bare shoulders. "I'll guard her for you. That way, the only bore she need worry about is me."

Christopher nodded quick approval and slipped inconspicuously into the crowd. He no longer cared to be the center of attention but anonymity was an impossible pose to maintain. After all, it was a fact that nearly every person he had ever known in his life was presently standing somewhere in this room. It was also true that most were here more from reverence for Sir Malcolm than any devotion for him, but that hardly seemed to matter. His hand was shaken. His back was slapped. Words of advice were whispered in his ear. He passed his sister Charlotte deep in conversation with a thin-faced young monk, and something in the way the two of them stood with their heads close together, as if no one else in the room truly existed, made him pause and turn in their direction. Charlotte looked up when he touched her arm.

"I think you'd better go and stand with Mother," Christopher said.

Charlotte frowned. "Why should I?"

"Because I have to see Father." Christopher knew the identity of the monk. It was young Brother Julian, whose father had once served as a steward in the Janson family stables. He didn't know for sure what made him want to intervene. He knew people were watching Charlotte, and something told him it was his duty to make them stop.

"Then get Ned," she said.

"No." He tried to keep his voice soft and firm, gripping her arm. "I want it to be you."

There was anger in her eyes—and something deeper, too. Resentment? Bitterness? Real hatred? She spun wordlessly away from him and moved through the crowd.

Christopher turned to Brother Julian, waiting for him to say something, but the monk merely lowered his head. Christopher waited another moment, then moved back in the direction of the kitchen. Charlotte was a strange one, that was for sure. Why should she want to talk publicly with this peasant monk? It was as if she was either unaware of her position in the county or totally unconcerned. Either way, it angered him. It would have angered Sir Malcolm, too, and perhaps that was why he had acted as he had.

Christopher found his father seated at a small table in the monastery kitchen. The odor of roast meat pervaded the air, while various monks and nuns scurried about, scrubbing pots, scouring pans, loading dishes, bearing trays. Old Brother Horace, who had presided at the wedding earlier, sat across the table from Malcolm.

The two old men were like islands of silence amid the ocean of clamor surrounding them.

Christopher bowed to his father first, then to Brother Horace. "You wished to see me, sir."

"I did." Sir Malcolm's voice resembled a whisper of wind. The stroke that had felled him a year ago during the return trip from County Tumas had left the entire right side of his body paralyzed. It was only in the last month that he had regained a modicum of speech. "This must be a grand day for you, son."

"It's been very pleasant." There was an empty chair at the table, but Christopher wasn't sure whether precept allowed him to occupy it. He remained standing. That was another of Lacy's maxims: it was better to do nothing than the wrong something.

"I wish I could have been there to share the wedding feast."

"Adrienne's family was very kind."

"And Blake? He was there?"

"Even Blake was polite today."

"It must have been a strain." Malcolm tried to smile, his lower lip trembling with the effort. Brother Horace looked away, pretending not to see. "Don't let him know I'm like this. It would only make him glad. A year ago we pinned his shoulders. This would be his revenge."

"He saw you at the wedding."

"I know." Malcolm seemed to wish to express some deep inner feeling, but his tone of voice was beyond his conscious control and only the bare words remained. "I wanted to see the wedding very much. I'm dying, you know. This meant a lot to me."

"I'm glad, sir."

His left hand suddenly snaked out from his side, clasping Christopher's wrist. "I wanted you to know . . . know that I'm damnably . . . sorry."

"Sorry for what, sir?"

"And proud. Pleased. Happy that things turned out as they did. I don't expect to live much longer."

"The medical men say . . ."

"Witches. The hell with them." His voice assumed a harshness of tone Christopher had no longer known it possessed. "A man damn well knows when he's dying. Give me one month, a week, a few days. When I'm gone this county will belong to you.

I want . . . want . . ." He faltered, momentarily unable to proceed.

Christopher glanced at Brother Horace, who lowered his eyes and shook his head.

"I haven't even taken my exams yet."

"But you will. And when you do you'll pass. That's no problem. It's that I want . . . want you to make me a promise. Just one—one thing."

"Of course, Father."

"I want you to promise not to forget."

"Forget?"

"Stoner. William Stoner. Don't forget his words. He knew more . . . more than any of us can ever imagine. Believe me. My work—it's in your hands. Promise me."

"I do."

"And Blake. He's mad. Don't forget that, either."

"I know him, Father. We're related now."

"And you think that means something to him?"

"Well . . ."

"I know I told you it would. I was wrong. Don't do what I did—don't underestimate that bastard. And don't—don't . . ." He stopped, shaking his head, a mighty effort. His fingers closed tightly around Christopher's wrist. "I have nothing more to say."

Christopher nodded. "Then go home, Father. Get some rest."

"You forgive me?"

"For what?"

"For today? This marriage?"

"Of course I do. The girl—Adrienne—I like her very much."

"You could have done better."

"I don't think so, sir. I'm happy."

"Good." His voice was soft again, a weary whisper. Whatever animation it had temporarily possessed had now vanished.

Brother Horace stood and opened a side door. Two brawny peasants stepped inside and the men together managed to lift Sir Malcolm to his feet and steer him toward the door. The old man never glanced back. The door shut. A moment later Christopher heard the squeak of carriage wheels and the beat of horses' hooves.

He looked at Brother Horace. "He means it, you know. He is going to die."

"I'm afraid so."

"He just gave up. It happened a year ago. When he had the stroke—before that. It's almost like he wanted it to happen, wanted to die."

"Perhaps he no longer had any reason to live."

"Why shouldn't he? He's not that old. He's got Mother, us, his work. That's no good reason just to die."

"My religion would agree with you."

"Father isn't a Christian."

"He is, though he doesn't know it."

"That's doubletalk." Christopher had never spoken so bluntly to an elder before, but Brother Horace appeared unoffended. "I'm going for a walk."

"Do you want company?"

Christopher shook his head. "No. Thank you, but no."

"I understand."

He went out the same door through which his father had been carried. In spite of the warm day, it was cold now. The wind blew harshly. Dressed only in his wedding tunic, Christopher moved swiftly in order to avoid the chill.

The monastery grounds provided little space for walking. The buildings were placed snugly side-by-side, with only narrow concrete walks between. A sliver of moon illuminated the night. He passed darkened, shuddered windows. Once upon a time, before Stoner, the monastery at St. Sebastian's had ruled the county, but this was a secular age, and many of the buildings, once pulsing with life and activity, had not been used for a hundred years. According to Lacy, Christianity survived only because of the peasants' occasional tolerant interest. And, thought Christopher, because a man needs some place to be married. The chapel behind danced with light. Christopher fixed his eyes on the darkness ahead.

All of a sudden, he stopped. There was another source of illumination out here. A bright light. A flame—a torch.

Intrigued, Christopher turned down a path toward the light.

He saw a figure holding the torch high above its head.

When he recognized the figure, he stopped again.

It was Sheridan Blake.

Blake had noticed him too. "What brings you out in the dark, Christopher? Not bored with marriage already?"

"I might ask you the same thing, sir." Christopher approached again. Blake stood in front of one of the vacant buildings. The door was made of iron, and there was a padlock affixed to the latch.

Blake pointed at the building. "Do you know what this is, Christopher?"

Christopher shook his head. "Should I?"

"Your father does. It's an interesting place, isn't it? Did you notice the windows as you approached?"

"I don't have a torch."

"You don't need one for this. There aren't any—not a single window. Doesn't that strike you as strange?"

"Nobody's used the building in years."

"So? It was obviously that way when it was built. Take a look. See for yourself."

He waved the torch over his head. All Christopher could see was a very ordinary-looking stone building. There were no windows—that was true—but he saw nothing necessarily ominous in that. "Maybe they didn't want to see outside."

"Or have anybody see inside?" Blake suggested.

Christopher frowned. "Exactly what are you trying to say?"

"Just this." Blake tapped the side of his head. "I think I know what this building is. It's the library—that's what it's got to be—the monastery library."

"This whole building? A library?" Christopher found that hard to accept. He hadn't seen that many books in a lifetime.

"I'm surprised you don't know yourself. It's surely the most valuable piece of property in this county."

"Books?"

Blake winked. "Proscribed books," he said. "An entire building stuffed from floor to ceiling with nothing but proscribed books."

"But those books have been destroyed."

"That's what they want you to think." Blake lowered his voice carefully. "I know better. Every secret of the industrial age is locked behind that door. Want to build a fast, efficient automobile? There's a dozen books in there waiting to tell you how. Plans, blueprints, formulas. A mountain of knowledge that no one can touch."

"But the monks—"

"Exactly. It's a task they long ago took upon themselves. To protect us from ourselves, from the wisdom of our ancestors. I'd bet a leg Horace himself has never set foot in that building. Stoner knew what the monasteries were doing, but he never said a word. Who better than the monks to hold the keys? Hell, they wanted order and stability more than anyone."

Christopher shrugged and started to turn away. "Then there's nothing we can do about it."

Blake reached out and grabbed his shoulder. "I can't, but you can."

Christopher looked back. "What do you mean?"

"I mean, in time, your poor father is going to die. I saw him today at the chapel and while it hurts me to say it, that moment may not be long in coming. When he does, you'll succeed him."

"And I can get into the library then?"

"Your father does now."

"Why?"

"To read the books. Why else?"

"My father would never read a proscribed book."

"Then ask him."

"Maybe I will."

"Don't necessarily believe what he tells you."

"My father wouldn't lie."

"He would to protect you from something he felt you weren't ready to know."

"You told me."

"That's different. I'm not Sir Malcolm. I'm a realist—I live in the world as it really exists. Eventually, no matter how Sir Malcolm presently feels, you'll hold the key to that door."

"And when I do?"

Grinning broadly, Blake hooked an arm around Christopher's shoulder. "Well, then I'd certainly expect you to let your father-in-law have a peek inside."

Aware that he was already late, Christopher hastened downstairs, drawing Adrienne behind. When he reached the swinging door that led to the pantry, he turned automatically and had a hand on the edge of the door before realizing his error. Then he stopped. "Wrong way," he said to Adrienne, striving to conceal his embarrassment. "We're supposed to eat in the dining room today."

"Don't you usually eat there?"

"I used to eat with the others."

"What others?"

"The children. Ned and Charlotte."

She still seemed puzzled. "And your mother and father ate alone?"

"Until today. Now that I'm—"

"But why?"

He shook his head. It was too complex to explain. "It's just the way we've always done it. Look, we'd better hurry. My father hates it when people are late."

She shrugged, reached out, and took his hand. "This must be a very important occasion for you."

"I suppose it is."

"Like an initiation," she suggested.

Christopher drew back, grinning. "Only the peasants do that."

"My father says we do all the things the peasants do, just differently."

"Well, your father used to be a peasant."

She frowned and grew silent. Christopher realized he might have hurt her. Tightening his grip on her hand, he urged her toward the dining room. Once he had entered the room and looked at the big table, he halted in surprise, for Mother was alone at her end of the table and only two other places had been set at right angles to hers. Sir Malcolm's seat at the head of the table was vacant.

Sarah could see where he was looking. "Your father decided to take breakfast in his own room," she said, smoothly and quickly. Then she smiled at Adrienne. "Won't you please sit down, dear?"

Christopher slid into his chair, while Adrienne sat across from him. He felt stunned, as if struck by a solid blow. "Is Father ill?" he asked Sarah.

"No more than usual. I think—after yesterday—he's just tired."

"But he left early."

"He's still not a well man, Christopher."

"Then—tomorrow—will he come then?"

"Here?" She shook her head. A house peasant, a pretty young woman, her wiry black hair drawn into thin braids, appeared through the kitchen door, bearing a tray with three plates. "I can't answer for Malcolm."

"Then you think he won't?"

She was still smiling. "Why don't you ask him, Christopher?"

He thought now that he understood what she was saying, but that understanding, if valid, left him more worried than ever. If Sir Malcolm no longer intended to take breakfast in the dining room, it could mean only one thing: he had already chosen to step aside and surrender his role as head of the family. Christopher had no way yet of estimating how far this abdication might reach—not into the county, he guessed—he hadn't even passed his exams—but he nonetheless felt as if a heavy burden had been dropped unexpectedly on his shoulders. He remembered his conversation with Blake the night before. Too much was happening too quickly. He felt as if he were being propelled ahead through life at a dangerous and reckless speed.

Breakfast consisted of fried eggs, hot cereal, fresh bread, and tomato juice. Christopher ate in thoughtful silence, while Sarah and Adrienne discussed and dissected the events of the night before. It was Adrienne's opinion that the reception had been overly crowded and that certain of the less distinguished members of her mother's family might have left earlier for Capital. Sarah said that she did not agree. "The more people at a party, the more chance there is for everyone to find at least one compatible soul."

"I don't think my father ever found anyone," Adrienne said.

"I happen to know Mr. Lacy was looking for him."

"I don't think he wanted to be found."

Christopher looked up from his plate. "Has anyone seen Lacy this morning?" he asked.

Sarah nodded. "I did earlier. He was bleary-eyed and not the best for wear." She smiled affectionately. "He asked after you and I told him you were still asleep. He seemed envious."

"I'd like to talk to him later. I want to see what he thinks should be done about my lessons."

"Then, if I see him, I'll suggest that he make himself available."

Christopher nodded. The manner in which she'd phrased her reply was yet another indication of his new standing. Supposedly, Jeffrey Lacy was still a teacher and he a pupil, but now Lacy was making himself available to Christopher.

Shortly afterward, the servant reappeared to collect the empty plates. Christopher leaned back in his chair. The meal had been modest but he felt well fed. After clearing the table, the peasant girl lingered. Christopher, distracted by his own thoughts, failed to note her continued presence until Sarah caught his eye and leaned her head toward the peasant.

Then Christopher glanced at the girl. She stood directly beside his chair.

"Will there be anything else, sir?" she said, in the exact same tone Christopher had heard peasants use toward his father as long as he could remember.

"Ah, no, nothing at all. Nothing for me, I mean."

"I think I'd like a cup of coffee," Sarah said, interrupting his stammerings.

"And you, Adrienne?" Christopher said, reclaiming his composure quickly. "Would you like something else?"

"No, thank you, Christopher."

"Then one cup of coffee," Christopher told the peasant.

"Yes, sir," she said, bowing gracefully.

Once they were alone again, Christopher turned to his mother and said, "After breakfast, I want to show Adrienne the house."

"Have the peasants finished?"

"Yesterday. We won't try to move anything now, but I thought she should see where she'll be living."

The servant brought a steaming mug of coffee and set it in front of Sarah. Once again, Christopher dismissed the girl.

Sarah took a sip. "Will you be leaving tonight?"

"This afternoon. I'd like to get to Tumas before tomorrow evening."

"Your father's already gone?" Sarah said, turning to Adrienne.

"He left last night, yes."

"He could have stayed here if he wished."

"My father has many responsibilities. He doesn't like to stay away from home longer than necessary." Christopher sensed a hint of something else in her voice. Was it bitterness? Or derision?

"He said he wanted to make the castle ready for our stay," he said.

"I know," said Adrienne. "I heard him."

Later, as Sarah was draining the last of her coffee, Christopher turned to her once again. "Mother," he said, "there's something I've been meaning to ask you."

"Yes, what's that?" She and Adrienne had been discussing the old house into which the newlyweds would be moving upon their return from County Tumas. This was the same house—following a full year of cleaning, reconstruction, and renovation—where Ned had first tested his model car. For that reason—out of, perhaps, sentiment—Christopher had ordered the peasants not to touch the cluttered, dust-choked basement.

"I was wondering," Christopher said, "if there was some particular book, one I very much wanted to read and couldn't find in the library in the den, where should I go to look for it?"

"What book do you mean?"

"Nothing, actually. I was just wondering."

Sarah pondered momentarily. "Well, if I were you, I suppose I'd just ask someone else. We're not the only family in County Kaine who own books. There's Mr. Darcy."

"All of his books are about one thing." Christopher grinned. There was a time in his life—when he was fourteen and fifteen—when Mr. Darcy's library had seemed like the most fascinating place in all creation. "I was thinking more of an old book. Something from Stoner's time."

Sarah spread her hands slowly. "Then I guess you'd just have to ask the pedlars. One of them might be able to get it for you from Capital."

"I suppose they could," he said, watching her face intently, "but I was thinking of the monastery too. Don't they own some books? It's a stable institution. The monks have been in the same place for two hundred years. Couldn't I go there and look?"

"Not that I know of." She spoke flatly and her expression betrayed nothing. "I've never noticed any books at St. Sebastian's to speak of. Theological writings, of course, and *The Bible*. *The Book of Stones*."

"Isn't there a library?"

She shook her head and, for the first time, a hint of puzzlement crossed her features. "Perhaps you should ask Sir Malcolm. If there is, he'd surely know."

"I'll do that, Mother."

"Are you sure there's not something—some special book—that

you really want?" She eyed him expectantly.

Christopher shrugged with what he hoped seemed casualness. "I was just wondering."

With the noonday sun beating harshly upon his back, Christopher Janson guided his bride Adrienne across the strip of brown grass that separated the Janson family home from the smaller house where the two of them would soon reside. Christopher barely recognized the neatly painted, single floor, wood frame house as the same ramshackle, centuries vacant wreck in which he had played as a child.

He let Adrienne precede him through the front door. In the past year he had deliberately avoided entering the house even once. He had wanted to make this moment as special for him as it undoubtedly was for her.

Inside, the first thing Christopher noticed was the presence of a strong, unpleasant odor, a combination of dust and dirt, soap and oil, and he regretted that he had not come earlier in the day, in spite of his long-standing vow, and at least opened some windows to air out the rooms. He did not want Adrienne's initial reaction to the house to be clouded by a stink.

She moved deeper into the room. He went after her.

Except for the odor, everything lay exactly as he had intended and ordered. Within the small living room, a couch and two chairs were neatly and evenly arranged. Adrienne stepped toward the back. The rear bedroom was clean and scrubbed. There was a large bed, the blankets smoothly spread, and a wooden chair and writing desk. The odor, fortunately, was less powerful here. Adrienne visited the kitchen next. She glanced at the wood stove and opened and closed the ice chest. A small dining room, barely large enough for a table and two chairs, lay to the right of the kitchen. Adrienne peeked in there and then moved off to visit the last remaining room, a second bedroom, presently unfurnished. Christopher planned to use the room as an office later on, but that could wait until their return from Tumas. It wasn't until then, until after they'd completed the tour and returned to the living room, that either of them spoke. "Well, what do you think?" Christopher said.

"I think—" She paused for dramatic effect and then suddenly smiled. "I think it's perfect."

He couldn't help smelling that dreadful odor. "Are you sure?"

"It's everything I could have asked for." She dropped down on the couch and stretched her bare legs.

"It is small." He took the chair directly across from her, thinking of Blake's huge and spendidly furnished castle.

"I like small houses."

"And we'll still eat our meals at the big house."

"I thought I saw a stove in the kitchen."

"Well, yes, but a peasant could hardly fit—"

"What peasant? I can cook."

He gazed at her in surprise. He could not remember Sarah ever cooking a meal, and although he knew that most women did, even many with house peasants, he had certainly never expected such a thing from Adrienne. "Would you want to do that?"

She shrugged. "Sure. Why not? I don't mind."

Something in her tone disturbed him. He looked at her face but her expression was as rigid and controlled as any her father wore. "Is something wrong that you're not telling me about, Adrienne?"

She sighed, shaking her head. "No, it's not that—not you."

"Then what?"

"It's just . . . well, everything seems so settled. That's all. Settled and finished."

"I wanted to have the house completed before you arrived."

"I don't mean that. I mean everything, my whole life. Am I making sense? I know it's different for you, but ever since the first time we met I've thought of nothing else except how we'd get married and come here—or someplace—to live together. Now it's happened and I can't help wondering. What do we do now?"

"Well, we live," he said weakly.

"How?"

"Well, I've got the motorcar factory. And my exams. There's a lot—"

"For you, yes. But what about me? I have nothing to do with the factory."

"My mother can show you things. She always keeps busy."

"I'm not talking about being busy. I'm talking about something specific, a direction. Do you understand?"

He nodded.

"Then what should I do?"

"Share your life with mine. Be my wife. We're supposed to be one person formed from two. Stoner said that."

"I know." She smiled tentatively. "Please forgive me, Christopher. I have no right to speak this way, not now. Look, it's just . . . well, sometimes my life seems like a book when you know the end in advance because somebody's spoiled the story by telling it to you. Do you understand? Am I making sense?"

"Of course you are," he said, automatically. "I know what you mean."

Unable to relax, Adrienne Janson lay beneath her young husband—a ridge of vertical light slicing through the part in the curtains and striking the bed—and thought, well, at least it's better than last night; at least I'm not so tense and afraid this second time.

It was odd how Stoner, who had written frequently of marriage, had never once said a word about sex. Adrienne knew something about it. Besides Dav Lindstrom, there had been several men in Capital the past year. Christopher didn't know. That was why she didn't dare relax. If he found out, he would be hurt and disappointed, for Christopher, like any county man, wanted a wife who was unsullied and untouched, and she knew she was no longer that. Well, he wouldn't find out. She'd see to that. If it meant pretending, meant lying here without moving, without responding, without passion, then that was a sacrifice—her pleasure for his contentment—she willingly made. His body upon hers was warm. She could feel the hot sun on his shoulders. He smelled of sweat. She held him gently, her lips brushing his mouth. Her eyes were sealed. The bed rocked softly.

It was a fine house. She wished she could enjoy it more but realized that, when they came back from the castle in County Tumas, from her father and the life she had truly loathed, then it would seem even better. She liked Christopher, liked his family, should have been happy. The year in Capital had changed her. She couldn't talk to Christopher about it. The great city had seemed almost like another country. With her dark skin and notorious ancestry, she had attracted immediate attention. Maybe that was all it was. Just vanity. She hoped so. But she also knew that she could have remained in Capital with Aunt Hilary forever, and that when the time had come to depart, she had hated Christopher for making her go. Was that fair? Had her father had that in mind when he'd first sent her away? Perhaps later, after Sir Malcolm's death, she and Christopher could move to Capital. On the trip here, she had often thought of that. Christopher could obtain an appointment in one of the ministries. Aunt Hilary knew the Governor himself. It didn't matter. She understood that now. Christopher was a county man, like his father, like her father. In Capital he would feel as out of place as she did here right now in this bed.

Suddenly, he rolled away and she realized that he must have finished. It was difficult to determine what she ought to do next. As his fingers touched her breast, she turned slightly, opened her eyes, and tried to meet his gaze. The light in the room seemed harsh. Her eyes squinted.

"It'll be better for you later," he said.

"I don't understand. What do you mean?"

"The way you feel. There is a lot more to it than this."

Of course she knew that. "It was just fine." She nestled close to him. Christopher was a person with whom she felt comfortable. He was gentle, in his rather tentative fashion, and certainly kind. But what came next? That still bothered her. Today was fine, sure, but tomorrow and the day after, what then?

Feeling like a creature trapped physically in a dream, Ned Janson surveyed the dusty, messy interior of the old Bixby place and tried to make himself believe that he wasn't really observing paradise. Sacrilege, yes, but under the circumstances, nearly impossible to avoid. He pretended to keep busy pushing the broom, building mountainous piles out of the scattered debris and then, moments later, in sheer neglect, knocking them over again. He kept grinning, filled with delight, his eyes never seeing what was truly in front of them. Ned was blind to the mess, oblivious to the reality of the clutter. Like a visionary, Ned saw only the future, what soon would be.

Christopher had warned him to be discreet, to stay clear of this place and not arouse suspicion by too much interest or activity, and Ned intended to be cautious—he knew full well the danger involved if their true intentions were revealed too soon—but it couldn't be today. Christopher had departed with Adrienne in the coach for County Tumas a few hours ago and in the excitement and bustle Ned had quietly snuck away here. Night was already falling; the shadow of the broomstick stretched across the floor. The quality of the light mattered little. Ned observed with stubbornly keen precision. This was a dream, after all—a trance, a daze. He recalled something Lacy had once said about the act of creation, how the ideal image must always precede the finished work. Perhaps that was what was occurring now. He could see the finished factory, freshly painted, clean and scrubbed, fully functioning, as solid as the concrete floor. The cars themselves gleamed brightly. Ned counted four, one in each corner. There were 1995 Chevrolets, an ideal form. Ned knew the model from history books. The year was significant. The final proscription had gone into effect in 1996.

So why do it now? Why do it again? Ned knew Lacy would want to know. What was the purpose of a motorcar, the necessity for building one? Was it efficiency, just speed? And what was the necessity for that?

Ned knew he wasn't equipped to answer such questions. Christopher, perhaps, but not him. He didn't care about efficiency. Speed meant nothing to him. He liked his horse. He wasn't motivated by any overwhelming desire to travel from Point A to Point B in less time than ever before.

To Ned, this was strictly a personal matter.

Ned had discovered the one thing in life he could do better than anyone else. That one thing happened to be designing and building motorcars.

So, all questions aside, Lacy or not, Stoner or not, he had to do just that.

With Christopher, it was completely different. Ned admired his older brother. Whatever Christopher tried, he invariably succeeded. Each day in Lacy's schoolroom, Ned watched his brother spin delicate patterns around the finer points of geography, history, mathematics, literature, astrology. Christopher whizzed, while Ned lumbered. The entire world lay open to him. Christopher would journey to Capital, pass his examinations, enter the bureaucracy, rise to control a county or minstry.

Ned wished him well. He wasn't jealous. All Ned sought was his own role, his own chance to prove to everyone (including himself) that he could do one thing (build motorcars) better than anyone else (including Christopher).

So he had never hesitated.

Christopher had first suggested the idea of the factory. He was also the one who had initiated the purchase of the building and the one who had decided to borrow money from Sheridan Blake. The factory would carry Christopher's name. The credit for their achievement, if any, would largely go to him.

Ned didn't care. He needed to prove himself to himself, and no one else mattered as much.

Because of this, because of his private needs, Ned never doubted that what they were doing was, if not right and proper, then at least necessary.

If, after he had finished building the first motorcar and actually saw it running, word leaked out of their heresy and his father and others came to the factory and ordered them to desist or else burned the building to the ground, Ned didn't think he would be disappointed.

No. Once I have accomplished what I need to accomplish, he thought, then I can rest and be content.

Yet, deep down, he wondered. What if no one ordered them to stop? What if no one put a match to the building?

Then, if that was the case, they would surely go on and on, building more and more motorcars.

Then what?

Then it would no longer be a personal or private matter. Then it would just be wrong.

And that was why, for today at least, Ned much preferred dreaming to working.

Charlotte Janson lay in her bed on the top floor of the Janson family house and stared intently at the set of framed family pictures that stood on the dresser across the room. From left to right, there were individual portraits of Mother, Ned, Father, Christopher, and herself. Each painting, done in oil by a peasant from the enclave, measured ten inches by seven. She recalled with clarity the experience of her own sitting—she was fourteen at the time—and the painter, a frail man with dirty fingers. She never liked looking at her own picture. There was something disturbing about that almost familiar face, a conflict, the presence in the painting of both herself and some stranger. Father himself did not like the paintings, although Mother had insisted that they be done. None had ever been displayed. Charlotte had retrieved them several months ago from a hidden nook in the basement. Whenever anyone came into the room, she hid them under the bed. She didn't want anyone to know that she had them.

The portraits were excellent. She recognized everyone in the family despite the transformations effected by time and the artist. Father was considerably thinner, for instance, and Mother a bit more heavily lined. Ned had probably changed the most, but then Ned was the youngest when the portraits were done.

She studied Christopher. He sat in half-profile, his chin thrust toward the light, his eyes in shadow. Christopher seemed hardly to have changed at all. Here he was at sixteen, with a shock of wild hair, a slightly crooked smile, an expression that seemed to say, *I know who I am and don't care if you know too*. That was Christopher, all right. Christopher then and Christopher now. He was the least mysterious person she had ever known. She could have hated him, of course. She didn't. Anger, yes, and disappointment, but not hate. Hate was too subtle an emotion to be applied to someone as open and unvarnished as Christopher.

He had told her to stay away from Brother Julian. Julian lived at the monastery and the oath he had taken as a young boy required him to give absolute obedience to the directions of his superiors. Charlotte lived at home. She had taken no oath, and yet, as far as she could determine, she was as much, if not more, of a prisoner than any monk. No, not a prisoner. A prisoner was a person and she was not even that. She was property—a Janson family asset to be used as the head of the house saw fit.

She was already old enough. Christopher realized that full well. If anything, Father's illness had served to stave off the day of decision for another year, but now that Christopher was married and prepared to assume his inherited duties, she knew the search would soon begin. Where would he look? In the neighboring counties? In Capital itself? She knew that she would not be sold cheaply. Her prospective husband might be fat, fifty, stupid, and vulgar, but he wouldn't be poor. Christopher would search carefully, spreading his net on distant waters. One girl she knew had been sent many hundreds of miles to the East, into the land of the mountains and savages. She would likely never see her home or family again. A girl two years younger than Charlotte herself. She suddenly felt very afraid. The one certain prospect in her life until now was its lack of uncertainty. Once Christopher succeeded in finding the right man, her fortune, such as it was, would be sealed.

She often wondered if there wasn't some other kind of place, a world where the air was free and people did what they wanted, not what they were told. Jeffrey Lacy said that such a world had once existed and come crashing down because people, when given a choice, did what was good only for them and not what was good for everyone. She didn't see how that mattered. She wasn't interested in committing heresy or flying an airplane or owning a factory or building a steel mill. She just wanted to marry the man she loved.

Brother Julian.

Squeezing her eyes tightly shut, she tried to envision the kind of country she desired. What would it be like? Green hills? Cool forests? White cottages?

She opened her eyes. Why, that was just like here—it was County Kaine.

So it wasn't the physical place that mattered. It was the spiritual vision.

If you thought you were free, then you were free. Could that possibly be true?

A voice spoke in her head. It was a female voice, deep and cool, but it wasn't her own. *You must decide, Charlotte.*

As always, she turned, looking around the room, seeking the source of the voice. Of course, there was nothing. The voice was inside her—it spoke from within.

"But what can I do?" she cried aloud.

Marry him. The voice had never spoken so directly before.

"Julian?" she said with hope.

You love him.

"Yes," she said firmly.

Then you must choose. Which has the strongest call upon your soul? Is it earth or heaven? Your brother or your love?

"I love God," she said, "and Christ."

Then you must serve Him.

"God?"

Through Julian.

"Then it's right for us to marry?"

It's your duty.

Charlotte could barely restrain the exhilaration she felt. None of her voices—none of the many that came to her—had ever spoken so explicitly before.

"May I go to him?" she asked, standing tensely beside the bed.

Yes—do.

"Now?"

Yes, tell him.

She raced outside. It was a warm, clear, beautiful day, but she had no energy to squander upon such externals. She and Julian had a secret place where they sometimes met and she only hoped, through some freak of fate, that she might find him waiting there now.

In her excitement and haste she failed to notice Christopher and Adrienne coming up the path from the old house below. Only at the last moment did she manage to dart aside and fall to her stomach in the high grass.

Fortunately, Christopher and Adrienne were engrossed in a world of their own.

As they passed, Charlotte barely heard their voices.

She was hearing voices of her own once again—loud, insistent internal voices.

They urged her to race on.

Once Christopher and Adrienne had passed, she did.

Tonight when Mother in her sleep began to moan, then speak with the voice of the gods, Bill Walker lay motionless for only a brief period of time before, unable to endure the pain of what he suddenly understood, he sprang to his feet and dashed outside and rushed past the circle of men who guared the enclave against the ravages of wandering demons.

He ran defenseless into the night, driven by fear and horror. He stumbled often, tripped, fell, as the woods grew deeper and thicker. Finally, exhausted, cold with terror, he collapsed against the bulk of a broad tree, the leathery bark moist with the dew of approaching morning. Then he waited, unable to move another stop. Would this night ever reach its natural end?

His lips moved. Without thinking, Bill raised prayers to Kina, Goddess of the Forest, and Burna, Dark Lord of the Night, seeking their protection. He was more than just afraid. Demons lurked nearby. He felt their presence with senses sharper than sight. Tears streaked his face. He fought not to cry out. "I do not deserve your love," he admitted softly. "I am a foul and unworthy thing."

At last, through a gap in the foliage above, he saw the first faint light of dawn as it spread through the eastern sky.

Tentatively, he moved, swiveling his head and glancing at the silent form of the forest surrounding him. Then he stood. It was over. With the coming of day, the nightmare had faded. Chilled to the core, he hugged himself and watched as the gray light in the sky shifted gradually toward a golden hue.

Now what?

He hesitated, unable to decide where to turn. Should he go home? Did he dare? If he did, considering what the elders had said in the past, would surely be punished again, but when that had happened before, when he had been beaten, he had endured the pain stoically, willing to admit—if not aloud—that the elders were right and he was wrong.

But not this time. It was different. It wasn't that he had not listened to his mother but that he had—listened too well—and for the first time his mother's actual words had penetrated the barrier of his own fear and he had understood exactly what she was saying:

"Death . . . destruction . . . doom . . . a building upon the meadow . . . two brothers in blood in blood . . . fire . . . the father who is not a father . . . the machine that spits blood . . . black blood . . . death . . . all must die."

Clear? Yes. Why had he never bothered to listen before?

The brothers were Christopher and Ned. The building was the old Bixby Carriage Works. The machine that spit—a motorcar.

It all fit—like the pieces of a puzzle. Bill was aware of what the Janson brothers were planning because Ned had approached him the day before and asked him to help at the factory.

Bill had agreed to accept the work. Anything was better than sweating in the fields from dawn to dark.

Now he wondered. His mother had spoken of death, ruin, and destruction. He believed her.

What should he do?

Bill turned toward home. Despite the clarity of his thoughts, his mind raced like an engine out of control. Should he approach Christopher and Ned and explain what the future held in store? Didn't they deserve to know?

Bill frowned.

He knew how Christopher would regard his mother's prophecies: as lunacy, ravings, peasant superstition. Bill himself had often pretended to feel that way—until last night.

No, he concluded. He would say nothing—he could not. He would work in the factory as promised but no more. In time—in the gods' own time, which might be a minute, a day, a year, or a decade—something more would surely be revealed.

Bill chewed his lip and finally shrugged. Until then, there was nothing he could do.

As the battered old coach in which he rode swayed down the narrow road that threaded between the tall cliffs that divided County Kaine from County Tumas, Sheridan Blake leaned out the window and shook his fist and shouted at the peasant driver to make further haste. Blake was well aware that the man was driving the horses as hard as he dared, that the poor beasts already tottered at the brink of exhaustion, but he felt that an additional reminder—especially a shouted one—couldn't do any harm. Why not? he thought, dropping back into the seat with a heavy sigh. It was he, Blake, who was in a hurry, after all; it wasn't the driver. His hands clenched in his lap, trembling with unrelieved tension; his toes tapped a frantic dance. Why leave anything to whim or chance? Why run the risk of complacency? The driver might grow bored. The horses, freed from the stimulus of the whip, might choose to slacken the pace. No. Wasn't it always wiser to create one's own future rather than letting tomorrow arrive at its own speed in its own shape? He grinned. Even Jeffrey Lacy couldn't dispute that bit of pure Stonerist philosophizing.

With deliberate calm, Blake turned and gazed out the window. He studied the pattern of the stars, the slant of the moon's faint light, and decided that dawn ought to be breaking soon. The narrow strip of sky that showed past the flat peak of the cliff had assumed a grayish tint. He shook his head. Day and night meant nothing to him while he was traveling. Whatever the tint of the sky—blue or pink or black—he never slept. Even during the course of the journey between Tumas and Capital, he failed to nod for even a brief moment, and often upon arrival it took as long as a week to recover fully from the ordeal of the trip.

It wasn't entirely a matter of choice. He remained wide awake while traveling because he had long ago discovered that it was simply impossible to sleep. His constant wakefulness owed nothing to the rocking motion of the coach or the fierce wind that slashed through the windows or the thick dust that filled his nose and throat; such common discomforts could be easily ignored. The real reason, Blake believed, was the simple excitement that accompanied the act of motion itself, the exhilaration of steady hurtling progress. Sleep was a condition to be assumed while stationary. As long as he was moving, he couldn't rest. When he did sleep, when he left the waking world, he needed to return at the exact same location from which he had first departed. In a coach, that was impossible. And so, despite the genuine fatigue he felt, he knew he would not rest a wink till the gates of his castle in Tumas finally closed behind him.

His poor stomach rumbled too. Eating while traveling presented none of the obstacles of sleeping, but this time he just hadn't been able to afford to linger. He was in a hurry—a great hurry—and the splendid wedding feast he had helped consume had long since faded to a sweet tantalizing memory. Twice he had ordered the coach to halt at roadside stations established by the county bureaucracy for the convenience of the occasional traveler such as himself, but in both instances Blake had merely paced at the edge of the road and urged the peasants to hurry as they exchanged horses, his arms flapping with wild impatience like the wings of a great bird.

The hunger was bearable. He managed to ignore the pain for long moments at a time. The recollection of what he had discovered and observed in County Kaine dominated his mind, chasing aside all else, his fatigue, his hunger. He thought about the library of proscribed books and, for what must have been the hundredth time, wondered exactly how many volumes such a library might contain. A thousand? Ten thousand? Even more? Of course it wasn't the exact number that mattered; it was the contents—what the books were about. He had first learned of the existence of the library at St. Sebastian's several years before, but it was only now that he had actually set eyes upon it, even with the intervention of a wall of concrete between himself and the books, that the matter had reached the level of true obsession. He remembered the night before, how he had stood alone in the dark— this was before young Christopher had interrupted his reverie—and he could have sworn he could actually smell those books—if not see them—the layer of accumulated dust that clung to their spines, the rich and musty odor of vintage wisdom. Blake made a vow—then and now. Someday, in time, in due time, that library, those books, would belong to him. He refused to doubt his ability. This was a promise, a guarantee; it wasn't just idle fantasy. The vow lay firmly rooted in the established fact of the onrushing future, a time Blake fully intended to create personally. And when that happened, when he did obtain the library, his first act of possession would be to order holes pounded in all four walls of the building, so that a clean wind could enter those musty precincts and sweep away the air of complacency that had kept the books hidden for centuries and doomed men to waste their lives laboring to achieve basic material goals that, with the help of their ancestors' knowledge, might well have been accomplished in a few days' time.

Blake's conception of the library's contents was not, he believed, overly optimistic. He had already acquired one such library, a small collection of nineteen proscribed volumes kept by an obscure band of impoverished monks headquartered in an abandoned farmhouse not far from his own castle in County Tumas. Even then, even once he learned for certain what the monks possessed, it had taken five years of effort before he finally convinced the head of the order, a monk named Brother Simon—who had died at his own hand shortly afterward—to surrender the books in return for sufficient food and drink to prevent his flock from starving, and yet, among those very few books, Blake had discovered one that contained a detailed article concerning the refinement of steel, which had allowed him, after years of false starts, to complete final construction of his mill.

So, if among a mere nineteen books he had found one such jewel, how many might be discovered among the scores of volumes hidden at St. Sebastian's? It was a tantalizing question, one he could no longer drive from his thoughts.

Nor did Blake wish to. Overcome by sudden rapture, he slid low in his seat and shut his eyes. A vision formed in his mind. It was a photograph he had observed spread across the pages of another of those proscribed books: the skyline of a city called New York. Blake smiled. This was the past, true, but the beauty of the past lay in the fact that it might well be recreated. That was what he intended. The past would become the future and this terrible present would expire. If

Blake had his way, a time would come when a hundred new New Yorks would rise from the ashes of today, and a new dawn would truly gleam for all mankind.

And then, before he even guessed what was happening, Sheridan Blake suddenly fell asleep where he sat.

PART 4:

The Funeral

For a human society to exist as a functioning organic unit, the same care and attention must be expended in its creation as one would use in erecting a tall building. In fact, a truly proper society can best be envisioned as resembling a stone tower, where bricks are piled one upon another until the uppermost reaches of the tower disappear inside the clouds above.

And yet, one must further acknowledge the ultimately precarious nature of any such project; the tower may, at any moment, choose to topple. A single misplaced stone may bring destruction. To survive and prosper, as any competent engineer will testify, the tower must first possess a solid and firm foundation. The same, of course, is true of society.

Of what should this foundation consist? For the tower, I suggest steel and brick, stone and granite. For society, I offer two interrelated institutions: the first is marriage and the second family.

As a philosophic thinker, I am often criticized for my advocacy of a prompt return to the old monogamous tradition. Even wise thinkers capable

of comprehending much of my work rebel at this
point, asserting that monogamy was merely the
product of a decadent industrial state. Isn't it
better, I am asked, that we retain our present
flexible system rather than reverting to the
unsuccessful rigidity of the past?

To me, this question is best answered in the
asking: the fallacy lies in the use of the word
"flexible". No proper society can long endure while
permitting the same. There must always be only
one accepted way of acting, for flexibility equals
complexity, and simplicity is harmony.

Who among us, given a full life, can truly learn
to love one other person? Few, I suspect—or none.
Given this fact, then who dares ask for a second
such person, a third, or even more? The concept of
numerous loves is not merely foolish, it is
presumptuous and absurd.

The only legitimate purpose of marriage—I, of
course, have never taken a wife—is the procreation
of children, for without them no family can exist,
and without a family the solid structure of society
must eventually collapse. The whole must always
resemble the parts. A proper society exists in
harmony with and in duplication of the properly
functioning family unit.

A proper marriage is, by definition, a
monogamous one and such a marriage will, in
turn, produce a proper family, which through
example will influence others to build similar
family units. In this manner a strong and enduring
tower will eventually rise; it will not topple and
cannot fall. The foundation is firm.

Once forged, no marriage should ever be
ruptured, except by the death of one partner.
Divorce is the ultimate danger, for when a
marriage dissolves, then so does a family, and in
time an entire society will be infected with the
seeds of destruction. History shows this clearly. We
learn from the lessons of the past.

A man, a woman, their children: this is the
ultimate in human harmony.

Such a family can and will endure forever.

William Stoner, The Book
of Stones, circa 2045.

By the time that stone edifice known familiarly as the Great Dark Age at last came crumbling down, the Christian monastery system that had thrived throughout most of those years was also pretty much at its end.

Parallels are often drawn (by ignorant historians too quick to find a simple answer before asking a complex question) between the monasteries of the last dark age and those of an earlier one, medieval Europe. As any halfwit ought to be able to discern, this is utter nonsense. The monasteries of the medieval period were part and parcel of the prevailing institutional system of their time, while those of the Great Dark Age existed quite apart from the dominant order of Stonerism. Whether one approves personally or not, the fact is that this was a godless era, excepting as always the peasants, whose beliefs tended toward a sort of primitive Pantheism, a considerable distance from the conservative Christianity of the monasteries. Among the upper and middle classes, religious practices were followed more in word than deed. There were a few mystics. The monasteries preferred to ignore such maniacs. More importantly, the question of how the two systems functioned as repositories for the neglected knowledge of the past remains to be considered. Bluntly, the monasteries of the Great Dark Age were less concerned with preservation and more concerned with concealment. This was their big mistake. If the monks had been wise enough to burn every secret library in the land the moment the first industrial stirrings were heard, they might well have forestalled their own ruin indefinitely. They failed to do this and instead attempted to continue their past policy of concealment. When this failed, when the need of certain men to know the truth proved too great, then the monasteries were doomed to a sad and humble demise. And so, eventually, it came to be.

Daniel T. Janson, A History of Human Events Subsequent to Stoner's Time, 2378.

*   *   *

Christopher Janson peered unsteadily at the blank face of the door as it swung painfully open and then took a single stumbling stride forward and caught Sarah, his mother, by the arm as she emerged, head bowed, from the dark room beyond.

"What is it?" he said softly. The sun, streaming through a window at the end of the corridor, bathed the old carpet in warm colors. Ned and Charlotte waited against the far wall, gazing expectantly at their mother and brother.

"He's still alive," Sarah said. "Though just barely. He wants to speak to you."

"Me?" Christopher glanced back at Ned and Charlotte.

"Just you." She nodded toward the half-open door and added, in a gentler tone than before, "I think you'd better go in now."

"Does Vincent think—?"

"Ask him." She nudged Christopher softly. Exhaustion showed clearly on her face. "Don't miss him."

Christopher went through the door. After the bright light of the corridor, his vision was limited in here. He moved cautiously toward the shape of a bed. Heavy black curtains blocked the windows like shrouds for the dead.

A firm hand fell upon his shoulder.

Christopher turned.

"Oh, you," he said. It was Vincent, the medical man, a small, composed, darkly complected former peasant, whose knowledge of medicine extended far beyond the usual lore of roots and herbs.

"He'll be dead in less than an hour," Vincent said, his voice harsh. In the bed, something only dimly visible stirred.

"Not so loud," Christopher whispered.

"I felt you should know."

"Me, but not him."

"He knows," Vincent said, drawing away. "When it's this close, they always do."

Christopher could not dispute Vincent's knowledge of the ways of the dying. Hesitantly, he approached the bed.

"Christopher?" A throaty whisper, like a frog's croak.

"Yes, Father." Christopher looked down. He could see his father's skull, a thin shadow against the whiteness of the pillow.

"I'll bring a chair," said Vincent, from behind.

There was a scraping. Christopher dropped stiffly down. The chair was beneath him.

"Leave us alone," the shadow said.

"I shouldn't," said Vincent.

"Go."

"Are you certain?"

"Yes."

"I'll give you as long as you like." Barely discernible footsteps padded across the room. There was a slash of yellow light and then the door shut.

Christopher felt his father's cold hand seeking his. He pressed down softly.

"I know I'm dying," Malcolm said.

"No."

"Yes. Let's be honest. There's no reason to argue now."

"No."

"I know what you're doing at the Bixby place. I know about your motorcar works."

"Who told you?"

"I've known all along."

"Then I'll stop." Christopher felt tears in his eyes. He spoke from sheer desperation. His chest hurt, as if the air refused to leave his lungs. "I'll close the place today."

"Why?"

"Because it's wrong."

"Who thinks that? You—or me?"

"Stoner does."

"You're lying to me, Christopher."

"No, I'm not."

"You won't close it. You can't. I understand."

"It was Ned's idea. More his than mine. Even when we were small, he used to build models."

"It's past time for promises now." His voice was weaker, more distant. Christopher sensed that the physical pain which had riddled the old man's body these last weeks had gone. His words came without haste, as if this moment of clarity might endure forever. "If it wasn't you, then it would be another man's son. Stoner was wrong. Curiosity, ambition, invention. There's no conceivable way to rid the human soul of these plagues."

"Do they have to be that?"

"I honestly don't know. Men wiser than me, greater than me,

have tried to solve that question and failed."

"Did Stoner fail?" Christopher suddenly saw Malcolm's face clearly. It was as if a fog had dispersed. The expression was calm and yielding. He knows he's going to die, Christopher thought, and he's ready. If it was me, I'd fight till the end. (But he wasn't an old man, either. Age was as much a mystery to him as the religious fervor that drove some peasants.)

"In that regard, perhaps he did. Stoner's wisdom lay in the fact that he recognized that men were animals, not trees or vegetables. We're fallible beings, Christopher—it's our shared curse. What Stoner wanted to create—what he granted us—was a chance to catch our breaths. Two hundred years in which to step aside from the rush of material progress and think seriously about what it meant. Was it a long enough time? I can't answer that. Our distant descendants—in another two hundred years—they'll be the ones to say. The little ripples we start today will look like waves to them."

"I wish I'd told you about the cars," Christopher said.

"If you had, I'd have fought you."

"And made me stop?"

"I would have tried."

"And succeeded." Christopher was certain, if Sir Malcolm had ever ordered him to close down the motorcar works, he would not have disobeyed.

"If you say so, I can't argue."

"Don't you think it would have been better that way?"

"Not necessarily." Malcolm's grip on Christopher tightened. He seemed to be regaining his strength, shedding the years, re-discovering an almost youthful energy. "It's not only you that's involved, Christopher. There are others, as well, who have chosen similar paths."

"Like Sheridan Blake."

"Yes. If one must prevail, you or Blake, I'd selfishly prefer that it was you, Christopher. Blake is a frightening man, simul-taneously weak and strong. The world manipulates him. If he ever fulfills his designs, at least if I understand them correctly, then the world will once more have us by our throats, not vice versa. Beware of Blake, Christopher. He may be the most dangerous man alive."

"I believe I can deal with him," Christopher said, with a mixture of arrogance and pride.

"Because of Adrienne?"

Christopher shook his head, but it was likely that Malcolm had not seen the gesture. His eyes were nearly shut. The air, leaving his lungs, throat, and nostrils, rattled noisily. Christopher said, "I don't think Blake cares much for Adrienne anymore. When I've visited him lately, he hardly mentions her."

"Then that's something you should remember. It's Blake's strength. He cares nothing for anyone."

"I'll remember that."

"Now stay with me." Malcolm's grip was looser, and his voice had grown so weak that Christopher had to lean over the bed to hear distinctly. Malcolm said, "Stay with me until the end, Christopher. There's no need for anyone else to see."

"Should I get Vincent?"

"No. He's done all he can."

"Mother?"

"We've said our farewells."

"Then Ned and Charlotte. Don't you want to see them . . . one more time?"

"No. It's you who matters."

"Me?"

"You're the eldest. Stay."

"I won't forget you, Father," Christopher said, his voice rising suddenly and the tears threatening to fall at last.

Shortly afterward, Sir Malcolm Janson died.

Pausing in his oration, Brother Horace stared at the open grave in front of him and waited patiently for the clanking engine of Ned Janson's motorcar to subside. Then he went on. "If it is certain that we bring nothing with us into this world, it is equally certain that we are permitted to bear nothing out at the time of our inevitable departure. The true standard of a man's life must therefore consist of those things, both substantial and abstract, that he leaves behind for those who live after him. Using this measure, it must be said that Sir Malcolm Janson did indeed . . ."

Burning with rage, Christopher Janson turned and glared in the direction of his brother. The small crowd gathered at the gravesite buzzed in surprise at the unheralded apparition of the motorcar.

Leaning over, Christopher whispered in his mother's ear. "I'm going to talk to him."

"Not now," she said. "Brother Horace is—"

"I'll be right back." He jerked away.

As he moved through the crowd of mourners, Christopher felt their eyes turning to follow his progress. Well, this won't take long, he decided. Crossing the meadow, from where the top floor of the big house could easily be seen, Christopher approached the spot where Ned had parked the car.

Ned was leaning against the near front fender. When Christopher reached him, he stood upright. "Is something—"

"Damn you," Christopher said, struggling to keep his voice from rising. "How could you do something so stupid?"

"But I—"

"A car. A car at Father's funeral. Don't you have a brain in your head?"

"But he . . . he's dead. I was late. I—"

"You should have run."

"But he can't care."

"It's not him I'm worried about. It's them—our neighbors. What are they going to think? You might as well have stepped on his grave."

Ned shook his head. "I'm sorry. I didn't think."

"You can say that again." Christopher looked past his brother at the shining frame of the motorcar. It didn't at all resemble the photographs in the old books—the tires were made of wood—there was no roof or doors or windshield—but it worked; it ran. "Come on," he said, grabbing Ned's arm. "Let's get over there before we miss it all."

The brothers hurried back to the gravesite. Christopher deposited Ned at Sarah's side. Adrienne and Charlotte stood flanking them.

Brother Horace was saying, "Sir Malcolm Janson was that rare human being capable of following the precepts both of his own master, William Stoner, and mine, Jesus Christ. Sir Malcolm and I often discussed our separate loyalties and he confided in me that he found it difficult to accept in his heart the concept of God on Earth, and yet I do believe that no other man I have known has better typified the glories of a Christian life than Sir Malcolm. He was a good man, a kind man, a gentle man, an honest man, a wise man. I respected him as a human being and loved him as a friend. I'll miss him. In the next world, if heaven truly exists, then I can only hope I'll have the privilege of sharing his good company once again."

Head lowered, Brother Horace backed away from the grave. Two brawny peasants carrying shovels stepped forward. It was a warm, windless day. Christopher heard the hollow sound of dirt striking wood. When the sound came a second time, he led his mother away.

The majority of the crowd had already begun to disperse, heading toward the big house where their carriages and horses awaited to return them to nearby farms and houses. A few children went racing across the meadow to the motorcar. Christopher told Ned, "Chase those kids away from there and then drive back to the factory. I don't want that car taken out again until I tell you."

Ned started to argue, but Sarah reached out and touched his arm soothingly. "Do as Christopher says, Ned. I don't want any bickering—not today. Please go."

"If that's what you want, Mother," Ned said sullenly.

"I do."

"All right—fine." He looked at Christopher. "I'll see you later."

"At the factory."

Ned moved away. As he approached the car, waving his arms, the children scattered, laughing joyously.

"I'm sorry that happened," Christopher said. "I never thought he'd do something so stupid."

"Ned isn't very sensitive sometimes."

They had gone only a short distance from the grave. The peasants continued to work, tossing additional dirt into the rapidly filling hole. Besides the two of them, only Brother Horace remained in the vicinity. He now approached, bowing to Sarah. "I had hoped I might find Mr. Lacy here."

"He's at the house," Sarah said. "He meant no disrespect to Malcolm, but Mr. Lacy refuses to attend funerals as a matter of principle."

"Perhaps I can speak with him later," Brother Horace said. "Christopher, I'd also like a brief word with you, if you don't mind."

"No, not at all," said Christopher, wondering what the old monk could possibly want at this particular time.

"I'll go home and see to any remaining guests," Sarah said. "If you two want, you are welcome to join Adrienne and me for coffee later."

"That would indeed be a pleasure," Brother Horace said, "but I can only stay a few more moments, I'm afraid."

"Then you must come later. Christopher will be leaving for Capital next week. Come then—we'll be alone."

"Your examinations?" Brother Horace said. "So soon?"

"I thought it would be best under the circumstances not to wait."

Brother Horace nodded slowly. "Yes, I suppose I can understand that." He bowed to Sarah again. "Until later, my lady."

Once they were alone, Brother Horace indicated the green meadow stretching before them. "Shall we take a walk and find a place to sit?" he suggested.

"Yes, of course." The peasants had nearly finished with the grave. Using the backs of their shovels, they pounded the loose earth firmly into place. Sir Malcolm had chosen the site personally. It was a serene place and, except for the distant peak of the house, undisturbed by human tampering.

Out of earshot of the peasants, Brother Horace sat down in the grass and motioned Christopher down beside him. The ground was cold, the grass moist. "I hope you'll do well on your examinations," Brother Horace said.

"Mr. Lacy seems to think I should have no trouble."

"Mr. Lacy is a fine teacher."

"Yes."

"And an intelligent man. He and I agree on very little concerning this world or any other, but I would never disparage his mind."

"I have learned a great deal as his pupil."

"But that is not why I suggested this talk. The fact is, now that your father is dead, I believe I must confide in you. I have received a communication from Sheridan Blake only this morning."

"Blake? What does he want with you?"

"Here." Horace removed a wrinkled sheet of paper from inside his robes. "Read this and then I'll explain."

The letter was written in a broad, florid scrawl. It read:

Sir: It is my painful duty to inform you that, since you have failed to acknowledge my previous attempts at communication, I must now deliver a friendly ultimatum. Either, within a week of your receipt of this letter, you agree to my demands, or else I will be forced to commence direct action in the very near future. In order to avoid such an eventuality, I seek your immediate and helpful response.

The letter was signed, "S. Blake."

Christopher handed the paper back to Brother Horace. "Well, what does he want?"

"My library."

Christopher had to pretend ignorance. "What library?"

"The library of some four hundred proscribed books presently housed at the monastery. Your father was aware of its existence and somehow Blake learned of it as well. For the past few months, he has bombarded me with requests to gain entrance to the library. When the first such missive arrived, I spoke with your father. He recommended that I make no reply and I complied with his wishes. Each succeeding letter has been slightly more threatening than the one before. This one, frankly, has me worried. What does the man mean by 'commence direct action'?"

Christopher shook his head. "It may mean nothing. Blake is my father-in-law. I have had dealings with him in the past. He would not be adverse to a bluff."

"He has guns at his disposal. Sir Malcolm told me that."

"He wouldn't dare use them against you—against us."

"I can't say. I don't know the man. He has explained his reasoning to me—in previous letters. It appears he wants to build a dam in his county—to generate additional electicity."

"I know about the dam. He began construction some months ago."

"Yes, and apparently he is stymied. The technology to build such a dam just does not exist today. That is why he demands that I let him use the library."

Christopher restrained the anger he felt. The man had gone behind his back. Any understanding he and Blake might have reached in the past had surely been breached. What could be the full meaning of this? "Is he correct? Does the library contain the information he wants?"

"I have no way of knowing," Brother Horace said coldly. "It is as much forbidden for me to examine the books as Blake."

"Have you ever considered acceding to his demands?"

Brother Horace's features froze in an expression of shock. "You can't mean that. A man like Blake—set loose in my library."

Christopher smiled thinly. "You needn't set him loose. Find the book he seeks and let him have it. A dam is a harmless thing. It'll do good, not harm."

"But it's a question of principle, too," said Horace. "The books are proscribed. Stoner said—"

Wagging his head, Christopher came to his feet. "I'm aware of what Stoner said. You needn't remind me. I was asking a question, not making a judgment. I agree. We can't let Blake have that book or any other."

Brother Horace's relief was visible. His face wrinkled in a smile. "Then what do you recommend I should do?"

"The same as before. Don't answer the letter, don't even acknowledge it, do nothing. I'll speak to Blake myself."

"Speak to him? Personally?"

"On my way to Capital, I'll detour and stop in County Tumas. Adrienne intends to accompany me and she hasn't seen her father since shortly after our marriage. That will provide a good excuse to visit him."

"But what will you say?"

"I don't know. I'll lie if I have to, say that you've examined the library and found nothing of interest to him. What I say doesn't matter as long as it puts him off for a while. The point is to gain time to find out what he really intends."

"Do you think he'll believe you?" They were headed back toward the house now. The gravediggers had vanished. Christopher saw the frail wooden cross standing mutely under the cool sun.

"I'm his daughter's husband."

"Perhaps we should seek someone else's advice," Brother Horace said. "Perhaps this isn't a matter that should be decided by two men alone."

"Who do you mean?" Christopher said.

"Well, I was thinking of Mr. Lacy."

Christopher shook his head immediately. "No. This is none of Lacy's business."

"He may have an opinion."

"He always does. No," said Christopher, "with my father dead. I have a responsibility to make my own decisions. I hope to be a chief county bureaucrat within the year. I can't depend on Lacy all my life."

"No," Horace agreed solemnly, "but I hope that you're right." He still clutched the wrinkled letter in one hand.

"So do I," Christopher said. "So do I."

After Brother Horace had gone up to the house to reclaim his carriage, Christopher found himself turning and retracing his steps until he had returned to the site of his father's grave. Pausing there, he knelt down, head lowered, his eyes fixed upon that forlorn pile of neatly packed earth.

Father, he thought, it wasn't a bad life for you. Not an easy one, I know, and not really a happy one either, but a good one. You died at the exact right moment in time. It's all changing, Father. The whole damned world—or at least this one tiny corner of it that any of us really knows. It's going to be different from anything you ever knew. Everything and everyone is becoming more and more complex as each day passes. Your world was a simpler, easier place. A man could be good back then. It's much harder now, Father. I think it may be impossible for anyone to be you anymore.

Christopher couldn't help wondering how his father would have managed this. Had Sir Malcolm's previous actions—or lack of same—meant anything significant, or had he merely, realizing that death was imminent, been biding his time until Christopher could succeed him and make the crucial decisions? Why didn't you tell me? he wondered. Why didn't you ever give me some idea of what you expected of me? Sir Malcolm had been a quiet man—it was the source of his strength—one who shielded his inner thoughts most zealously, so that it had always been difficult, if not impossible, to guess where his mind might be leaning. Blake had bested Sir Malcolm once, in the matter of Christopher's own marriage. Was it possible that Sir Malcolm had feared the consequences of another open clash? Christopher didn't know. His father, buried in his grave, was no less a mystery now than during the years of his life.

Yes, it was a different world. And, yes, he deeply regretted that Sir Malcolm had never chosen to confide in him, especially during this long last year. Different world or not, he could have used some help, so that now, when the burden fell totally on his shoulders, he would have felt less adrift and isolated. What was it Brother Horace had said during the elegy? How Sir Malcolm Janson had proven that it was possible to live a good life with no more guidance than the examples of Stoner and Christ. Well, was that true? For Sir Malcolm, yes, perhaps, but for Christopher, in this changed world, no, never. It just wouldn't work that way anymore. What, after all, did Stoner have to say about threats of armed force? How would Christ have dealt with a loaded gun? To live today after their example—to live as Malcolm Janson had lived—could bring nothing more than frustration and failure. Christopher believed that the world had grown smaller. There was less room for simple goodness, none at all for compassion. This was a new world where the selfish and unscrupulous, men like Blake, were destined to rule. And me, too, Christopher thought coldly. I must learn to rule, too, for if I do not, if I fail, then no one else can prevent the hegemony of the Blakes.

Sir Malcolm had understood this much. It was the meaning of his last whispered warning to Christopher.

I will go to Blake's castle, Christopher decided, and I will lie to him about the books in the monastery library. I will gain additional time and then, when the inevitable moment of open conflict at last arrives, I will meet Blake eye to eye and I will defeat him.

That was the future. Here now, kneeling at this grave, it was impossible to forget the past.

If the true measure of a man lay in what he left behind, then Sir Malcolm had accomplished much in his life. If I turn out to be a quarter of the man he was, Christopher thought, then I will have achieved more than I ever possibly dreamed.

Christopher hoped Brother Horace was right. He hoped there was a heaven. Then he might meet his father once more.

Sarah Janson was not reading poetry, not aloud, not silently, not at all. She clutched a book in her hands, the page open to her eyes, but she saw nothing. There was something on her mind—a question—something she knew she needed to answer.

Did I love him?

That was the burning question. Did I love him? Just that. Four little words. Did I ever love my husband?

Sarah tried to think. This was hardly the first time she had asked herself this question, but it had been years since the most recent time, many years now. It was a question that, with the passage of time, had receded from its once paramount position in her life to the status of a minor niggling doubt, but now that he was dead and vanished from her life, the matter had become powerfully significant once again.

Did I ever love him?

Jeffrey Lacy sat nearby. He, too, had a book propped open in his lap, but she didn't know if he was reading or not. In the hours since dinner, Jeffrey had kept a private counsel, refusing to interrupt her self-imposed silence. She thought he must guess what she was thinking. Perhaps he wondered himself about the answer. Still, the question was hers alone to decide. No one could do it for her.

Did I love him?

She tried to recollect a specific occasion, some definite moment when Malcolm had meant something special to her. Yet, was that really fair? Was that what love entailed? She guessed that love entailed concern, consideration, and care—emotions she had always felt toward Malcolm—but despite this she couldn't seem to separate one particular moment from the myriad of others surrounding it and say, with honesty, "Yes, that was when I loved him." But was that even fair? When one person loved another, wasn't it a constant thing, like the flow of a waterfall? Did the moment she was seeking even exist? Should it? She had never wanted Malcolm to feel unhappy or frightened or disturbed or sad or hateful or petulant or bored or hungry. Did that mean anything? She wanted contentment for him. Was that love?

She tried to remember the time Christopher was born. There ought to be something special then. Of course Charlotte had followed and then finally Ned, but to her only Christopher was of extreme importance, for even birth becomes upon repetition a less than uncommon event.

She remembered Vincent—he was a far younger man then—

handsome, too—and his dry crackling laugh better than she remembered Malcolm. She did recall how, hearing her agonized moans, Malcolm had crossed the room—she could hear the steady thudding of his feet even now—and gripped her hand in his so firmly and snugly that she had somehow been convinced that from now on even the most unendurable pain was finite in duration and thus not to be feared. Yes, Malcolm was a strong, courageous, loyal, devout, and brave man, thoroughly in control of himself. She had always regarded him that way and perhaps—after a fashion—feared him. There was the gap in their ages—twenty-five years—a chasm which had somehow failed to lessen as their marriage endured and their lives inexorably became interwoven. Malcolm remained a distant, commanding figure, more like an older brother, an uncle—even a father—than a lover or husband, and during those final few years when the world had crept sullenly up and threatened to overwhelm his resolve and consume his pride, she had never lost a speck of the awe she felt toward him.

Was it possible to love a man whom one respected so much?

Brother Horace would have said, "Yes, of course." Brother Horace loved and respected his god.

But Malcolm wasn't a god—just a man.

As delicate as it was, Sarah made herself recall the nights they had spent together. She went to his room infrequently, rarely the past few years, but even now she could envision his domain clearly, a stark, cold, austere room, dominated by a wide bed, dark curtains, and several shelves of books. Until the day Malcolm died, she had never seen it in the light of day. The only illumination he had permitted when she visited him was a single flickering candle.

Did I love him then? she asked herself. In the dancing candlelight?

Wearily, she shook her head. The answer was no. Naturally not. If anything, they had lain farther apart then than ever. Together at night, they had remained separate. Their bodies meshed. Nothing more. The children were born. It wasn't love. She knew that part of it well enough. It wasn't even passion.

Then perhaps, she thought, if I ever loved him, I did so yesterday, the day he died. She concentrated on that occasion, on those final lonely minutes. She had not seen him die. Later, when

Christopher led her into the room, she had glimpsed only a frail shadow and, almost in revulsion, she had gone to the window and thrown aside the curtains.

No, that wasn't enough. Not that either. That was pity and grief and sorrow—not love.

Which, completing the circle, left her at the beginning again. What was love? How could she decide about Malcolm when the subject itself continued to elude her grasp. For a final moment, she concentrated. Love, she thought. What is it?

Then she smiled.

"I don't know," she said aloud.

I don't know, I don't care, and I don't need to know. If, after more than forty years of living, the mystery remains as insoluble as ever, then I surrender, I throw up my hands, I give up. I don't know what love is and I never will know. Nor do I need to. I can go on living—and loving—without ever knowing what I'm doing. I can—it's damned easy.

So yes, Sarah Janson decided. Hell, yes. I loved that man, loved my husband, loved him always and without cessation. I might not know what love is but I do know what I felt. I loved him always.

Jeffrey Lacy glanced up from his book. "Everything all right, Sarah?"

She nodded. "I think so. Yes."

"Good." He stood. "It's damned late, you know."

"I hadn't realized."

He came over and offered a hand. "Let's go to bed."

"Together?"

"However you want it."

"Together."

The dust in this room filled the air so thickly that Brother Horace could see individual particles floating like fish in the lantern light. He blew his nose into an old handkerchief. Stacks of books and loose paper covered the desk in front of him. Building dams, he thought, scratching his chin. Now how do I go about finding out about that?

Horace was tired. His head ached and his vision blurred. This was a place—the monastery library—where he dared venture only during these faint and uninhabited hours just prior to the advent of dawn. He fully understood the danger involved. In his lifetime, he had only confided in two men the secret of this library, and one of those—Sir Malcolm—was now dead. None of the monks or nuns knew. The building itself must be a mystery to them— dark and locked forever.

Leaning precariously forward, he grabbed hold of sheaf of yellowed papers and began methodically skimming the words printed there. As he turned the pages in his hand, he understood that no other man alive had ever set eyes upon these secrets. He remembered his own first time. He was young then—what?— barely forty—and his superior, Brother Ernest, had awakened him one night and led him stealthily to this very building and unfas- tened the lock and guided him inside. Horace recalled how he had stood frozen like a statue, awestricken by the mountains of books and papers surrounding him.

Brother Ernest, pointing with a finger, had spoken calmly. "I want you to take one book, one sheet of paper, and read it thoroughly."

After more than twenty years in the monastery, obedience was second nature to Horace.

He did exactly as directed.

Only then, when he finished the page—it concerned some obscure aspect of mathematics totally incomprehensible to him then and now—did he ask, "Why did you have me do that, sir?"

"Because what you read just now is proscribed."

"No. I can't . . . you can't . . ." The horror he had felt was as real as any other sin.

Brother Ernest smiled reassuringly. "Proscribed, Horace, but not by us. To keep this page concealed was the decision of man, not God, and we, as the servants of Christ, need obey only as far as our consciences dictate. Knowledge in itself is never evil. The uses to which it is put can be."

"I understand."

"Then read more if you wish."

Horace shook his head.

"Then come here and sit." Ernest indicated a desk—it was the same before which Horace now sat. There were two chairs. The monks sat side by side.

"When I am dead," Ernest began, without preamble, "the responsibility for this library will fall to your hands. I have told no one of its existence, excepting yourself, and you are to tell no others, excepting your own chosen successor." This was the first time Ernest had ever hinted to Horace that he had selected him as his replacement.

"Am I free to look at—to read these books?"

"You are, and with the knowledge you will acquire, the wonder of God will soon beat even more strongly in your heart. You must communicate this wonder and share it, but never the books themselves."

"I understand, sir."

"If I feared that you did not, I would not have chosen you to assume this task."

Yes, true, but what of Sheridan Blake? Brother Horace thought, snapping out of his self-imposed reverie. Horace firmly believed that he would rather die than let these books, entrusted into his care and keeping, fall into the hands of a man like Blake.

Would it come to that? A question of life or death? In spite of young Christopher's cockiness, Horace could not be sure.

He had met this man Blake only once, on Christopher's wedding day, and even then had spoken with him only briefly. Nonetheless, he felt he knew him well. There had been prophecies and omens—portents of a dark man who would come to wreak destruction upon the county. Peasant superstition? He wished he could be sure. The structure of contemporary society was like the shell of an egg. Once broken, it could never be repaired.

Was Blake the man who would do this? Blake and these books—this library?

It was even possible that Blake served, knowingly or otherwise, as the agent of yet another power, a darker power, one whose influence on earth had in recent years waned. The devil. Satan. Horace hesitated even to murmur that name in the privacy of his own thoughts.

Christopher felt he could control Blake. Sir Malcolm had felt similarly. But they could be wrong—both of them—and Stoner, too—if Horace's worst suspicions were correct.

Christopher and Malcolm were Stonerists. They refused to accept the concept of evil in the world; they said that it could not and did not exist.

Horace knew better. Horace knew evil.

He was seventeen years old when he had first entered the monastery. His father, whom he had deeply admired, served as chief bureaucrat within County Kaine. If Horace had taken the examinations in Capital and passed, that position would eventually have been his. Instead, because Horace had chosen Christ over Stoner, Malcolm Janson had succeeded in his place. That was part of the reason the two men had always been close. It was part of the reason why Horace, breaking the vow he had made to Brother Ernest, had confided to Malcolm the secret of the library. He did not regret that decision. He was my friend, he thought. Malcolm lived the life I could have led and he lived it well indeed.

Horace continued to pour through the papers on his desk, but even as he did, he realized the futility of this maneuver. Blake was not apt to accept a compromise. He wanted the library, Horace believed, and this matter of seeking information for building a dam was only an excuse, a subterfuge.

Yet Horace kept searching. What else could he do?

A sudden heavy thumping sounded against the door. Brother Horace looked up from the papers in his hand, startled by the noise.

The knocking came again, more softly this second time.

As night fell at last, Sheridan Blake moved into the garden and turned his head to watch, past the top branches of the saplings that ringed the edge of the yard, the spinning wheels of his two new windmills as they churned majestically in the faint evening breeze.

The young fool, thought Blake, scowling to himself. Was he really naive enough to think that he might appease me with such an obvious lie? Blake sneered at the tale Christopher Janson had told tonight: the entire library at St. Sebastian's composed of nothing but old novels. Sexual themes, the boy had explained, managing somehow to speak simultaneously with a straight face and a knowing leer. Nothing you might be interested in obtaining, dear father-in-law. Blake snorted. Sexual themes indeed. As if a man like Brother Horace and an institution like the church he served would be willing to expend the most meager quantity of energy to preserve and protect mere art. It wasn't that which they feared and adored—not art—it was facts, for facts alone were the stuff from which earthly power could be built.

Above his head, in the thin branches of the tallest of the saplings, two electric beacons burst to life, flooding the garden in sudden harsh light. He grinned, turning an abrupt but graceful pirouette, letting the cool light strike him on all sides. Yes, it was coming together now. The library, the windmills, the glory of electricity. There was nothing Christopher or Brother Horace or anyone else could do to halt the momentum of history.

With that library in my hands, thought Blake, I will harness forces more powerful than the wind. With those facts in my possession, I will control the knowledge of the keenest minds of a thousand human generations. I will rule the world. (Or at least, he thought somewhat more humbly, this meager portion of it.)

He was glad Christopher had come. He was even more pleased to learn that Tumas was merely a stopover on his journey to Capital. With Christopher—and especially Adrienne—miles away, he could move quickly, freely, and, if forced, harshly.

The library was a necessity. He had never expected to reach this point this soon, but he had. Without the books, he could progress no farther. The steel mill, the guns he had constructed, his windmills, even the miniature locomotive—these stood as the farthest outposts of his own knowledge.

And he knew they were mere toys. He needed more: dams, factories, electric light and heat, refined oil. A thousand or more different ways of helping people—his people. Blake wanted to fill bellies, warm bodies, set men free. When he died, more tears would be shed at his funeral than Malcolm Janson had ever dared dream might be shed at his. And for that, to seal the love that flowed between himself and his peasants, Blake needed the library.

He stood alone. Brother Horace, he knew, would never voluntarily surrender. And the powers in Capital, especially his brother-in-law Minister Talstead, would surely oppose him. Without Talstead's past assistance, Blake would not have come as far as he had, and yet in the future he knew he would have to battle on alone. Talstead had grown wiser with the passage of years and by now undoubtedly realized that the controlled—Blake—was now the controller. Talstead had always despised him. Soon he would fear him as well.

Blake thought about his army. He wondered if young Christopher, swaying in his coach as it traversed the last few miles to the castle, had ever guessed at what lay concealed just beyond the range of his vision. A real army. Not a large one, of course. Nothing like the millions of armed and seasoned troops who had once scourged the earth from sea to sea. A mere eighty-six men, peasants from his own lands. Fifty rifles. Half as many pistols. A single small cannon. But an army—soldiers—men ready to be plunged into the thick of battle at an instant's command.

Of course, that would never happen. Blake knew he would never willingly kill another, even at second hand. The army was a bluff. But a wise one. Even a man as stubborn as Brother Horace would drop to his knees at the sight of such a specter of possible violence. Men feared what they could not understand. And no man alive understood war.

He would get his library. It might be over and done before Christopher even left Capital for home.

He wished he could somehow observe when the boy heard the news. Or, even better, Talstead. Blake made no secret of his eagerness to gloat. He carried the wounds of a hundred old scores. Certain men had again and again humiliated him. But in the end he had won. Always before and this time, too. And victory was the only thing that mattered.

Yet Christopher Janson was different. The boy disturbed Blake. There was more to him than the usual arrogance of the second generation. Beneath the hard shell that he turned to the world, something deeper burned within. What? Blake doubted that even Christopher himself yet knew. And that was good. It would take five years, perhaps ten, for him to penetrate the barrier of his own self.

And by then I will own him, Blake thought. When I jerk the strings, Christopher Janson will dance.

He cupped his hands to his mouth. "Dav!" he shouted. "Dav Lindstrom! I know you are there!"

A grinning figure emerged from the shadows of the saplings. Lindstrom was a young man of Christopher's age but as dark as the other was light, a giant of a man with arms as thick as tree limbs.

Dav Lindstrom executed a stiff bow in front of his master. "You sent for me, sir."

"I did. Why were you skulking back there in the shadows?"

Lindstrom jerked his head toward the castle behind. "I knew you had company. It would be impolite to disturb your guests."

"I was alone."

"So I discovered. Sir."

With Dav Lindstrom, there was always a hint of mockery in his tone. Blake knew that Lindstrom did not like him, but that was not important. For a peasant, Lindstrom was extremely bright, dutifully efficient, and highly respected by his fellows. Without regard for personal likes or dislikes, Blake had not hesitated to appoint him his lieutenant.

"The two of them will be leaving the castle tomorrow at dawn," Blake said.

"Yes, I know."

Blake's eyes narrowed. "How, might I ask?"

Lindstrom shrugged. His smile spread. "On my way here, I noticed the coach being prepared."

"That was observant of you."

"Does it matter, sir?"

"Not especially. It's just that . . . well, frankly, I happen to know that you and my daughter—Lady Adrienne—sometimes played together as children—small children. I would rather that you didn't see her during her present stay."

"That doesn't seem likely, sir."

"Why not?"

"You said she was leaving at dawn."

"Oh, yes, of course." Blake felt flustered, and that feeling angered him. Who was Lindstrom, after all? Just another ignorant, illiterate peasant, fit for nothing more than the most menial forms of labor. What did he, Blake, who had risen from such a state of abject poverty have to fear from such a man?

Blake had long suspected that something more than mere child's play had once existed between Lindstrom and Adrienne, but that was in the past. He would not let it influence his actions now.

"As soon as the coach has left the grounds," Blake went on, his composure returned, his voice calm, "I want the troops mustered for drill and maneuvers. Do you understand? That will be shortly after dawn."

"I understand."

"Christopher's departure for Capital is a good omen for us. I have every intention of moving in his absence."

"Then that will be soon." Lindstrom showed no particular emotion, not even interest.

"In no more than a month."

"May I inform the troops?"

Blake shook his head. "What they don't know can't worry them."

Lindstrom did react this time, but it happened so quickly and was over so soon that Blake nearly missed seeing it. Lindstrom's eyes flashed with genuine anger. "As you wish, sir," he said, after a pause, his voice registering nothing. "Will there be anything else for the present?"

"I think not." Blake looked at the sky, suddenly impatient. The striking of the hour must be drawing near, and that was always a moment he hated to miss. "Go back to your men."

Lindstrom saluted, a gesture Blake had taught the men, then turned, retracing his steps through the barrier of the saplings.

Alone once again, Blake also turned, sprinting hastily across the garden toward a circular open spot in the middle of a flowerbed—tulips, largely, his favorite variety—where a waist-high stone pillar stood set in the soft ground.

Two months before, Blake had installed an electric timing device inside the hollow core of the pillar. He had obtained the information necessary for the creation of the device from an old book—unproscribed—detailing the art of clockmaking.

The stone pillar had once housed a sun dial. Blake had merely modernized the machinery of time telling.

Resting his hands on opposite sides of the pillar, Blake leaned over and gazed at the clockface chiseled in the top of the stone. One minute before eight o'clock. He watched impassively as the minute hand continued to move. Its progress was gradual, barely discernable, as it closed in upon the numeral "12."

Then it arrived.

Eight o'clock on the dot.

Blake leaned back.

The clockface glowed. A yellow light, like the twinkling of a star, on and off, on and off, a steady rhythm.

Then the music commenced—the chimes.

Blake shut his eyes, ignoring the flashing light, concentrating upon the tune. A lullaby. He'd known it all his life. Had his own mother once hummed it to him, cradle rocking in the night, peasant's hovel, dirt for a floor? Blake murmured in time to the music. *La-la-la-la-la-la*. It was lovely. His fingers gripped the rough stone pillar. *La-la-la-la-la-la*. He smiled.

Too soon, the minute was over. The music subsided and, when he opened his eyes, the clock had stopped flashing.

One minute past eight.

Turning with a heavy sigh, Blake went back to the castle to say good night to his guests.

The moment the door clicked shut behind the messenger, Minister of Corrections Arthur Talstead slammed his fist hard against the impassive wooden surface of his desk, sending a stream of papers scattering to the carpeted floor.

Blake, he thought bitterly. *Blake, Blake, Blake. The bastard.* Why did it seem, every time he was sure he had that man firmly under his thumb, the next time he looked Blake had managed to squirm free and assume in the interim an even more menacing posture than before?

And now, if this messenger could be believed, it was guns. A small army equipped with weapons fully capable of hurling steel pellets through soft human flesh. That bastard Blake. And a cannon, too. (So the messenger claimed.) This was madness. Sheer lunacy. But true. Talstead felt it in his bones. With Blake, the worst always was true.

His rage cooling gradually, Minister Talstead forced himself to stand and walk calmly toward the window where he could peer out and observe the glorious spectacle of the winking lights of the city.

This was his life's work—his legacy: electric lights burning by the hundreds in a city which for two centuries had known only candles and gas.

And Blake's legacy? What would that be? Guns, armies, war, and destruction.

He had known the man twenty years. What was he in those first years? A freak. A peasant who had somehow risen to a position of considerable power. Talstead himself was engaged in a power struggle in those years, a battle for the ear of the Governor. His enemy: a man named Jeffrey Lacy. Their major point of contention: whether a generator should be installed to bring electric power to the city.

Eventually, Talstead had won. Lacy was a forgotten man, long since vanished into the countryside. But in order to win that victory, Talstead had required allies, one of whom had been Blake. In return for his assistance, Blake had demanded two concessions. First, he had asked to be appointed to head the bureaucracy in his home county. Without even checking to see who presently held that position, Talstead had agreed. The second concession, however, had caught even Talstead by surprise.

"I'd like to marry your younger sister," Blake had said.

Talstead laughed. "You? A peasant?"

"With your permission, sir, and that of your father, of course."

It wasn't a joke. Or perhaps it was—perhaps that was why it seemed so hideous. Talstead's younger sister was a girl so gorgeous that he sometimes wished he might love her himself.

"I can't agree."

"Then I won't help you."

"You'll remain neutral?"

"I can promise nothing."

Talstead pondered. As bizarre as it sounded, Blake's offer was not entirely unappealing. It would offer a chance to achieve two victories in a simultaneous stroke: not only additional assistance in the battle against Lacy but also, by making Blake a relative, an opportunity to guarantee the loyalty of a man Talstead already considered dangerous.

"I'll speak to my father," he said at last.

And somehow—the details, fortunately, had faded from his memory—he had convinced the old man to let his daughter marry the son of a shepherd.

Still, in the end, Talstead had achieved only half a victory. Lacy had soon left Capital, driven into exile by the strength of the forces ranged against him, but within a few years, Blake had managed rather easily to slip from beneath Talstead's restraining thumb and emerge as dangerous as ever. The man was sly. His marriage, it turned out, meant nothing to him. Blake refused to be manipulated through the vulnerability of his own emotions.

Despite this—or perhaps because of it—Talstead had long granted Blake a relatively free hand in the governance of his home county. Blake was a great flatterer, who professed to admire his brother-in-law's philosophy. "Let County Tumas serve as an example of your program of cautious progress—a rural counterpart to your work here in Capital."

He saw the man once a year—seldom more often. He let him have his way. Electric power. Windmills. Coal mining.

But then he had heard of the steel mill.

In all of Capital, only one small such mill existed. How had Blake, the peasant, accomplished what he had? (And without a word, a hint. The whole thing smacked of treachery.)

Talstead undertook an immediate personal journey to County Tumas.

Blake met him at the stone castle he occupied as a home. "How did you do it?" Talstead demanded. "You never consulted me. You never asked for assistance or advice. How did you build that thing?"

"I used this," Blake said calmly, tapping his forehead with a fingertip. "Don't you believe me?"

Talstead had not. Even then, he guessed the truth. Blake had managed to gain access to one of the various libraries of proscribed books. Later, home again in Capital, his agents had confirmed his guess. Fortunately, it was only a small library, the one in County Tumas itself. A much larger one—as large as any Talstead knew about—existed in County Kaine but, luckily, the chief bureaucrat there, a man named Janson, was a devout Stonerist of impeccable lineage who would never tolerate the advances of a man like Blake.

Later, Talstead had heard of the marriage between Christopher Janson and Adrienne Blake.

That was when he had first begun to worry.

And now this was worse—much worse. Guns, an army, a cannon.

What did Blake want?

It was a terrible thing to behold: the puppet turned upon the puppeteer.

Blake could no longer be tolerated. He and everything for which he stood must be destroyed.

But how?

Talstead recalled that Christopher Janson, Blake's son-in-law, was presently in Capital, recently arrived to begin the process of taking his Stonerist examinations.

Perhaps the boy could help.

Talstead shook his head wearily. He could think of nothing else.

Turning from the window, he went to the door, opened it, and shouted for his daughter. "Glorianna, come here. I want you."

She was twenty-six years old, as tall as a man, with blonde hair that fell to her shoulders. She wore a long sheer gown. Glorianna was seldom home once darkness fell.

"Yes, Father," she said.

"Do you know a girl named Adrienne Blake?"

"She's Adrienne Janson now."

"Then you know her."

"She's staying with Aunt Hilary, she and her husband. You ought to know. She's your niece, too."

"What about the husband?"

"A county man. I don't think I've exchanged a word with him."

"I want to meet him."

"Him? Whatever for?"

"I need his help in a minor matter."

She shrugged. "Then come with me tonight. There's a party. I imagine he'll be there—both of them will be there."

Minister Talstead turned his head and gazed at the papers arranged on his desk. There was a further scattered accumulation on the floor where he had knocked them.

He sighed heavily. "All right. Give me fifteen minutes. I'll join you."

Glorianna smiled. She had taken to painting her lips recently, a new fashion, and the scarlet sheen gave her mouth a slightly ravenous look. "You at a party, Father? Well, what will happen next? Is the world itself going to end?"

"Just wait for me," he said, turning curtly and closing the door.

PART 5:

The City

The term "Civilization" is one which I deliberately avoid using with the utmost totality, although there are some who have claimed that the core of my philosophy consists of little else. While acknowledging the partial accuracy of this, I further proclaim that much of my hesitation at using the term lies rooted in the word itself. Civilization, properly speaking, is a creature born and matured in the cities of man. My philosophy upholds the exact opposite thesis: nothing on earth is more detrimental to civilization than a city.

I strongly advocate the glories of nonurban existence.

In the most successfully proper of past societies—in T'ang China, for example, or medieval Europe—rural life, the virtues of the country, predominated. Urban existence was, at best, regarded as no more than a necessary nuisance. In recent centuries, where the opposite has been true, where urban population has actually outnumbered rural, then civilization has quickly deteriorated and eventually collapsed. Thus, history itself tends to uphold the viability of my judgment.

*I cannot proclaim the inherent superiority of
country living. I find no special grace in the
farmer. I simply believe that the stability of rural
life, its intimate relationship with the natural
processes of climate, weather, and seasons, is more
conducive to the establishment of proper order and
regulation than the artificially imposed chaos of the
steel and glass cities of yesterday. Time operates at
a different pace in the country; clocks seem to run
slower. People seldom regard themselves as "too
busy" to display the casual but essential aspects of
a truly civilized society.*

*Because of this, in any proper society, urban
centers must be severely limited in number. I
recommend that a single city be used as a center of
government, commerce, and finance. Only one—
nothing more.*

*In order to endure under these limitations,
people must relearn the art of self-sufficiency.
Trade will be limited and necessities will be
produced as near to their probable point of
consumption as possible.*

*If I believed in the rule of law rather than
tradition, I would recommend the enactment of the
following piece of legislation: for more than ten
thousand persons to congregate in any one place is
a crime against society punishable by death.*

*The fact is, whether law or not, this statement
is true.*

William Stoner, The Book
of Stones, *circa* 2045.

*If there's one complimentary statement that can
be made about the Great Dark Age, it's this: there
were no wars then.*

*Incredible? You don't believe me? Well, look it
up. I speak the truth. No wars—not a one—not
even a good fierce battle.*

*If you don't believe it, think of how your long
dead ancestors would feel. If there's one thing that
has always seemed to develop naturally out of any
grouping of human beings, it's that these same
people will sooner or later end up trying to kill
each other in some more or less organized fashion.
Look at history. Look at Russia, France, Japan,*

*Vietnam, Korea, Manchuria, Paraguay, etc. Civil
wars and revolutionary wars, wars of national
liberation and wars to defeat fascism, World War
I, World War II, World War III.*

*And then the great collapse. And then no wars
at all.*

How come?

*Well, I think I can answer that. When nobody
has anything anybody else wants, then there's no
real motivation to go rushing in to grab it off.*

*During the Great Dark Age, all groups—if not
individuals—remained more or less equal: they
were all poor.*

*And, too, Stoner had roundly condemned the
act of warfare, though I'm not sure how much that
really mattered. Stoner condemned a lot of other
things, and nobody paid much attention to him
unless they wanted to.*

*If they followed his precepts this one time, it
was also because they possessed a good reason:
nobody had the slightest excuse to start a war.*

*Of course, like everything from the shape of a
rump to the price of good wine, this soon changed.*

> Daniel T. Janson, A
> History of Human Events
> Subsequent to Stoner's
> Time, 2378.

"He's my father-in-law," Christopher Janson told the young
woman in the long sheer gown who stood beside him on the
balcony. Her blonde hair spilled down her shoulders like a rich
golden crown.

"Then we have something in common," she said, turning and
shutting the glass doors that divided the murmur of the party from
this high sanctuary. Christopher had stepped outside for only a
moment, for fresh air, when she'd joined him. "I'm Glorianna
Talstead. Mr. Blake is my—" she laughed suddenly, a tinkling
sound of wry merriment "—my uncle, I guess. At least he was
once married to my father's younger sister. She died."

"Yes, I know." Christopher had several times observed Glorianna Talstead from afar since his arrival in Capital, but she had

never approached him—or paid him the slightest attention—until now. Adrienne said that Glorianna was regarded as the most beautiful woman in the city, and Christopher did not dispute that. "Blake lives in the county adjoining mine—in County Tumas."

"And what county is yours?" She drew closer to him, her head a bare inch below his. A peculiarly sweet odor clung to her. Perfume, he assumed.

"County Kaine."

"I never can remember them all." She turned briefly away, fixing her eyes on the myriad lights that glittered below. This apartment—it belonged to some minister or another, Christopher forgot which specifically—stood on the top floor of a ten-story building. "Can you believe it?" She turned to face him again, hands on her hips. "I'm twenty-six years old and I've never left Capital in my life."

"You ought to. The country—some of it—it can be beautiful."

"And you've never been here before."

"No, never."

"My father has been looking forward to meeting you."

"I—Adrienne—we were both hoping to meet him."

"Who's Adrienne?"

"My wife."

"Oh, her. The dark girl. Yes, she visited here some time ago. I think I may have met her then."

"Adrienne said your father rarely attends parties."

"Never. But he's here tonight."

"We're staying with his sister . . . your aunt."

"Father despises her."

"Oh." Christopher shook his head, wondering how much of his confusion was the result of the wine he had drunk and how much was the fault of this strange and beautiful girl. Alongside her, he felt very much like a peasant. He could feel the soil and grit clinging to his body. His clothes seemed like rags.

"But don't worry," Glorianna went on. "He didn't come here to see Aunt Hilary. He came to meet you."

"Me?" said Christopher, in genuine surprise.

Just then, as perfect in its timing as the alarm of a clock, the glass doors slid open and a tall, finely dressed, gray-haired man stepped through. Christopher did not need to be told that this was

Arthur Talstead, Minister of Corrections, perhaps the most powerful man in the entire government.

Christopher extended a hand tentatively as Talstead approached. "I'm Christopher Janson, sir. I'm deeply—"

Talstead cut him off curtly. "I'm Arthur Talstead." He shook hands forcibly. "I've been waiting to meet you."

"So your daughter . . . so Glorianna said."

"Your wife is Sheridan Blake's daughter, I believe."

"Yes, sir."

Talstead leaned against the balcony railing. "What do you know about Blake building an army?"

"An army?" Christopher glanced from Talstead to his daughter and then back again. Glorianna was smiling, but Christopher didn't think this was intended as a joke, "I don't know anything, sir. How could he . . ."

"Never mind how. I need to know why. Do you have a theory? Is there anything Blake wants that it might take an army to acquire?"

Christopher felt suddenly very cold, chilled. He started to reply when Glorianna interrupted him.

"Father, it's crowded out here. I'm going back inside."

"Yes, fine."

"Christopher," she said, swiveling toward him and reaching for his hand. "I do hope I'll have a chance to talk more with you later."

"Yes. Yes, I hope so, too."

Both Christopher and Talstead turned and watched silently as Glorianna made a swift and graceful exit.

Talstead shook his head. "I'm afraid we bored her. The affairs of the world do not interest Glorianna greatly. I'm afraid she'd much prefer to discuss sex or fashion or her own charms. Your father was very lucky. I love my daughter very much, but when I die, without a son, that will be the end of everything." He moved stiffly, as if trying to shake off a dream. "But you started to tell me something about Blake."

"Yes, sir. I can think of only one thing he might want. In my county, there's a monastery where—" He broke off suddenly, wondering if he might be violating Brother Horace's confidence by revealing the existence of the library to Talstead.

"A collection of proscribed books," Talstead said impatiently. "I'd thought of that."

"Then you know?"

"There's little I don't. How do you think Blake found out? I was a fool to trust him. There was a time, I'm afraid, when I refused to regard him with full seriousness." He stopped and scratched his pointed chin. "So you think Blake has an eye on those books?"

"I'm sure of it, sir. You see, he's already sent several letters to Brother Horace, demanding access. He said he wanted to build a dam and needed the books for technical assistance."

Talstead looked worried. "That may be true enough, but I doubt that it's all."

"So I thought, too, sir. So on my way here, I stopped at Blake's castle and spoke to him."

"What did you say?"

"I told him the library contained only novels." Christopher risked a tentative smile, but Talstead refused to return it. "I said there were no technical works of any kind."

"He'll never believe that."

"I only hoped to delay him—to put him off."

Talstead said nothing for a long moment, turning and gazing out at the sparkling lights of the city. When he turned back to Christopher, a set smile had formed on his face which served to conceal whatever true emotions may have lain buried within. "You did the best you could," he said. "Come on. Let's go in. It's cold out here."

Christopher stepped toward the glass doors, but suddenly Talstead reached out with a hand and stopped him. "Sir?" said Christopher, turning back.

Talstead kept his hand on Christopher's shoulder. "There is one other thing. Call it a suggestion, a word of advice, whatever, but it's something I wish you'd remember. Once you've left Capital and returned to your own county, if you ever have any trouble with Blake, anything you can't handle, then don't hesitate to contact me at once. I'll render whatever assistance is possible. You have my word."

Christopher understood that Talstead was offering to form an alliance, but something made him keep his answer vague. "I'll remember that, sir."

"And do it?" Talstead prodded.

"If it's ever necessary, yes, sir."

This seemed to satisfy Talstead. He marched briskly past Christopher and held the glass doors open. The sounds of the party—high-pitched voices laughing and chattering—reached them clearly. "Are you coming?"

Christopher shook his head. A minute ago, he had been ready to return but now he wanted time to think. "In a few moments, sir. I'd still like . . . I'm not used to so much smoke."

"The cigar habit hasn't reached the counties yet, has it?"

"No, sir." Christopher was tempted to mention the exception of Jeffrey Lacy, but if Talstead remembered Lacy—and Christopher was sure that he did—he also would remember not getting along with him. Lacy's presence in County Kaine could remain a secret if Talstead was not already aware.

"Then I'll hope to see you again sometime during your stay." Christopher nodded. "Yes, sir. I'd like that very much."

By the time Christopher returned to the party, neither Minister Talstead nor his daughter was present. He pushed his way gingerly through the crowded room until he reached Adrienne's side. She was seated with her Aunt Hilary, a skinny horse-faced woman who seemed constantly perched between exhilaration and despair.

"Guess what you just missed," Aunt Hilary said excitedly. "My brother, Arthur Talstead, has just graced us with his presence. And he was looking for you, too. He said he wanted to meet you."

"He found me," Christopher said. "I was out on the balcony."

"Oh." Aunt Hilary could not have sounded more disappointed if she had just been informed of the death of a close friend, but her grief was as brief in duration as her previous elation. "And what did he say to you?"

"He wanted to tell me how much he admired my father."

"Your—your father?" said Aunt Hilary, her eyes widening in surprise.

Christopher couldn't help himself. If there was one fact he had learned since his arrival in Capital it was that county people—any county people—were regarded as lower, more barbaric forms of life. Aunt Hilary was a particular advocate of this point of view, and Christopher had suffered her patronization on several occasions. "Minister Talstead said that he had known and admired my father for years."

"They—they knew each other?"

"Like two peas in the same pod." Christopher held out a hand for Adrienne. He knew he had to get out of here before his restraint broke and he started laughing. Adrienne seemed to understand. She came briskly to her feet.

"I'm afraid we're going to have to leave now, Aunt Hilary," she said. "Christopher's examinations begin tomorrow and he's going to need all the rest possible."

Aunt Hilary seemed stunned. "Be sure you return my carriage."

"I certainly wouldn't want to leave you stranded here all night."

"Wouldn't you?" There was a flash of anger, the depth of which shocked Christopher, in the woman's narrow eyes. "Your husband's new friend, my brother, wouldn't mind."

"I'm sorry, Aunt Hilary."

"Don't be, dear." Aunt Hilary had managed to recapture her vanished composure in a moment. "And don't be foolish and wait up for me, either. As far as this old woman is concerned, the night is as young as a puppy dog."

As the two of them moved toward the exit that would carry them to the staircase and then below, Christopher leaned over and said softly to his wife, "What was all that about?"

"She hates him," Adrienne said. "No, that's wrong. He hates her. I suppose you could say they represent the two different ways of life in this city. Uncle Arthur is all business and Aunt Hilary is all fun."

Christopher nodded. This conflict of styles was something he had noticed before. "Then he really did come here just to see me?"

She smiled. "He and Glorianna. Don't think I didn't see her out on the balcony with you."

"She's not like her father."

Adrienne shook her head. "I don't think there's anyone in the world quite like Glorianna."

"You don't like her, do you?"

They were on the staircase now. A cold wind blew up from

the open door below, tossing her hair back toward her face. She paused, pushing errant strands away from her eyes. "Like? Glorianna? I don't think I ever really thought of her in those terms. Glorianna isn't just a person. She's—I don't know—she's like an elemental force."

"I understand what you mean," he said, but was that true? Did he? There were times when Adrienne surprised him with her insight and maturity. Even after more than a year of intimate marriage, he felt as if he knew little about her.

The driver waited below with the carriage. While Adrienne climbed inside, Christopher gave the white-haired servant his instructions.

It was a brief ride to Aunt Hilary's small home. Despite the hugeness of the city, everyone seemed to live close together. Christopher had probably not traveled more than a mile's radius since his arrival. The white lights of the Governor's palatial mansion could be glimpsed where it squatted high atop a nearby hill overlooking the city.

"What was it Uncle Arthur wanted with you?" Adrienne asked, as the carriage swayed beneath them.

Christopher saw no reason not to tell the truth. "He wanted to talk about your father."

"I thought so."

"Why?"

"I don't know. I . . ." She paused, appearing to struggle with her own feelings in an attempt to read their true import. "It's just that during my whole life no matter how far away I am, it always seems that he's always with me, always nearby."

Christopher tried to make a joke. "Even when we're in bed?"

She turned and glared at him with an expression which, even in the sheltered interior of the coach, made him feel like shivering. "Even then," she said softly. "Sometimes."

Reaching out, he grasped her cold hand in his.

"Time's up," cried the official examiner, a thin wisp of a man with a permanent frown on his lips. Swooping down upon Christopher like a bird of prey, he captured the dozen sheets of paper that lay scattered across the examination desk.

Christopher stared in surprise. "But it can't be—"

"I'm afraid it is," said the examiner, with a sudden show of sympathetic sorrow. "There's never enough time—never. Your results will be forwarded through the local bureaucracy of—" He glanced at the papers in his hand. "—County Kaine." For some reason he insisted upon pronouncing the final *e*.

"But I wasn't finished. I—" He reached out weakly, as if trying to reclaim his work.

"You weren't, but your time was." The examiner was already moving away, clutching the papers close to his chest like booty to be treasured.

Christopher sat, stunned. The examination center was located in the central chamber of what had once been a church. Until today as many as a dozen other men and boys had shared the hall with him, but this morning, arriving for what he knew would be the final phase of his examinations, he had found himself absolutely alone. The vastness of the chamber had only emphasized his sense of isolation.

Slowly, he stood. Sunlight trickled through the stained windows, divided into a prismatic display of rainbow colors, and the vaulted ceiling seemed a hundred miles away. The examiner had vanished into some hidden recess.

Turning, Christopher headed for the distant doorway. His footsteps echoed like gunshots inside the huge cavern. He tried to shake off his fear of failure. The examinations were graded in terms of average performance. Could anyone else have accomplished more than he had in the meager time allotted for the task? Christopher wished he could think not. He had been asked to compose an essay from his own life describing the effect of Stoner's teachings upon his own subjective world. Unfortunately, he had barely been able to reach his own twelfth year.

Outside, Adrienne waited for him upon the high concrete steps that led to the muddy road below.

Seeing her brightened his mood considerably. He even managed a smile as she slid her hands into his. "What are you doing here?"

She returned his smile. "I thought, since this was your last day, you might want some company. When I was here the year before last I met several men who were taking examinations, and I remember how all of them said it was miserable on the last day.

how you think you must have failed."

"You mean I didn't?" he said lightly.

She squeezed his arm. "You know you're smart, Christopher."

He nodded. "So people keep telling me." But his mood had improved dramatically. He was glad she had come.

"Let's go for a walk." She steered him down to the edge of the road, a strip of hard dirt occupied by a few other pedestrians. This was an area of government buildings, many as tall as six and seven stories. By turning his head slightly and looking in the right direction, Christopher could once more observe the Governor's mansion.

"Uncle Arthur had most of these built," Adrienne explained, as they walked. "Ten years ago, nothing was here."

"Your father and Uncle Arthur have a lot in common."

"Do you really think so?"

He shrugged. "They both like to build things."

"I'd never thought of it that way before."

"Where are we going?"

"I don't care. Where do you want to go? Home? To Aunt Hilary's?"

"Not especially."

"Then let's just walk."

He nodded, experiencing a growing sense of contentment. It's all over and done, he thought, and in a few more days I'll be home again—in my real home—in the big white house in County Kaine—where I belong. He breathed the light misty air, with its deep scent of autumn, and clutched his wife's hand. A particularly ornate coach drawn by four of the biggest horses he had seen in his life rocked down the street, spraying mud. He had always wondered why the streets remained so wet when the sidewalks were dry and not a drop of rain had fallen in months. Aunt Hilary suggested that it was because the horses urinated, but he hadn't believed that, even though she apparently did.

"I imagine you're glad to have it finished," Adrienne said, after several blocks of mutual silence.

"In one way, yes, in another, no. This is going to alter my life—both our lives. It'll never be like the last year again. When we get back, we'll move into the big house. I won't be free anymore."

"You were already handling most of your father's work."

"But he was responsible. I could always talk to him. I can't do that now."

"Mr. Lacy will help."

"I wonder. Will he? I half expect, when we get back, Lacy will have moved on."

"But why?"

"Because his work is done."

"You?"

"And Ned, of course. Charlotte, too, in a way. I don't think there's anything else he needs to teach us."

"Then he should be proud of the way things have turned out."

He shifted his eyes, trying to study her expression, wanting to know if she meant what she said or was only trying to make him feel good, but as usual it was impossible to decide. She often amazed him, the easy way she had of shifting with his own changing moods, so that whatever she said or did always seemed to be the right thing. Who was Adrienne? he sometimes wondered. There were times when she worried him—almost frightened him.

"Sometimes I envy the other ones," he said, trying deliberately to recapture the tranquil mood he was in danger of losing.

"What other ones?"

"Well, my brother, for instance, Ned. Look at my father. He could never have been happy. He had to carry the weight of a whole county on his shoulders, and now I'm going to have to do the same. But not Ned. All he wants out of life is to build motorcars. One, then another, then another, and he's happy. Ned doesn't have worries or ambitions or responsibilities. Stoner wrote that there were no such things as good and evil acts, only good and evil men. He believed that a gentle man could do anything he wanted as long as he concentrated upon the act itself and ignored the results. A cesspool digger could live a life as proper and harmonious as a bureaucrat as long as he kept his sights fixed upon his own labors. Once he began to think of the results—of the money he would be paid or what he could purchase with that money—then he failed the precept."

"Do cesspool diggers make much money?" she asked.

He shook his head. "Actually, I was thinking of myself."

"Well, I don't like it. I think it's unfair. Who in the world is ever going to ignore something as important as results?"

"We should all try. It isn't supposed to be easy."

"Well, I don't think it should be impossible either."

"That's why I'm here to take the examinations and not you."

"It's also why you'll pass and I wouldn't."

He grinned. They had entered an entirely different part of the city now. A residential area unlike any he had observed before. Rows of flat-topped frame houses stood behind white picket fences. The road was narrow and dry enough to walk on. Two children, boys, shot out of one of the yards, dashing across the street and vaulting the opposite fence. Christopher could smell the odor of cooking food. It must be close to the dinner hour now.

Suddenly, Christopher sensed it was time to head back toward Aunt Hilary's house. He looked at the sky, which had darkened. It couldn't be the rain coming at last, could it?

But they went another block. Then another. Adrienne seemed to have no interest in turning back.

Once more the mood of the surrounding landscape altered drastically. The houses were much older, many with broken boards, unpainted walls, cracked windows. In some of the yards—there were few fences here—the grass grew as high as his knees. A crowd of children stood in the street, watching in silence as he and Adrienne passed. From inside one house, a woman's voice screamed. It might have been from anger or terror or neither one. Then a man answered gruffly.

Christopher leaned close to Adrienne. "I think we'd better go the other way."

"What other way?"

"Back toward Aunt Hilary's."

"Don't you like it here?"

"It's not that. I just think it's going to rain." He was lying but, oddly, he wasn't sure why.

"I think this is fascinating." She waved at the houses. A small girl, no more than five or six, ran past them, stopped, shouted a particularly vile obscenity in a thin reedy voice, then turned and ran on. Adrienne appeared not to have heard. "I never knew there were any peasants living in Capital until now—except for the servants, I mean."

Now that she had mentioned it, Christopher realized that she was correct. Perhaps that was the source of his anxiety. These people were peasants. Black hair. Flat noses. Bronzed skin. Why had he failed to notice before?

At the next corner, a group of a half-dozen men stood idly in a circle. They were young men, tall and broadly built, and Christopher had no difficulty recognizing them as peasants. Perhaps that explained his previous failure. Until now, he had seen nothing but children in these streets.

As he and Adrienne walked on, Christopher felt the dark resentful eyes of the men following him. There was a sudden shout. Whether directed at him or not, Christopher did not know. He quickened his pace, listening for pursuing footsteps. When none came, he relaxed. The sky was a dark threatening shade of gray.

"I never knew this existed," Adrienne said. "Why, there must be hundreds of people living here. I wonder how they exist. They can't raise their own food. There isn't room."

"Maybe they work."

"But where? Who for?"

"You should ask your aunt."

Adrienne laughed hollowly. "I'll bet she doesn't even know this exists, and she's lived here all her life. If I asked anyone, I'd ask Uncle Arthur. The cabs must skirt this area. It can't be much farther."

Overhead, thunder cracked. Christopher felt the first thick drops of rain on top of his head. Within a few more blocks, they had left the peasant district. The houses were new and clean again, the yards neat and trim. The rain began to fall heavily.

"There's a cab," said Adrienne, pointing toward an approaching carriage drawn by a white horse.

"Hey!" Christopher shouted, stepping into the street. "Hey, over here!"

The moment he and Adrienne entered Aunt Hilary's house, with the rain beating against the roof like a shower of pebbles, Christopher sensed something dramatic in the air. The atmosphere was tense, crackling with electricity. Aunt Hilary rushed to greet them. "Arthur is here," she cried. "He's been waiting almost a full hour." She pointed accusingly at Christopher. "He says he wants to talk to you."

He felt a knot of anxiety in his stomach. "Did he say what about?"

"Tell me? Arthur?" She laughed bitterly. "You must not know him very well."

Minister of Corrections Arthur Talstead waited in the small, delicately furnished living room. When Christopher entered, he stood up from a chair and extended a hand.

Christopher gripped it tentatively. "I am most pleased and honored to make—"

"As am I," Talstead said curtly. He glanced past Christopher's shoulder to where Hilary and Adrienne stood in the doorway. "I think this would be easier if we were alone."

"Yes, of course." Christopher turned. "If it's about my examinations—" he could think of nothing else that might have brought Talstead here where he had undoubtedly not set foot in decades "my wife can—"

"I know nothing of your examinations. Please dismiss them."

"Adrienne," said Christopher softly. "Aunt Hilary."

The women left the room without protest but, before making her final exit, Aunt Hilary swiveled her head on its birdlike neck and fixed her brother with a baleful glare. And now you come to drive me out of the rooms of my own home, she seemed to be saying.

When they were alone, Talstead laughed softly. "That old woman could drive any man to an early and welcome grave." Christopher doubted that Aunt Hilary was more than a few years older than Talstead himself. "No wonder she's never been able to snare a husband." He threw himself down abruptly in the chair he had vacated. "I'm afraid, Christopher, that I have some rather unpleasant news to share with you."

Christopher's first thought was that he had failed his examinations, but Talstead himself had denied that possibility. "But, sir, what could it possibly be?"

"Blake," Talstead said bluntly. "I hate to have to be the one to tell you but it's happened at last. The man has made his move."

"But how?"

"The reports that have so far reached me are not complete. The most I can tell you is this: some time early yesterday morning Sheridan Blake and an army of approximately a hundred armed peasants attacked and took control of the monastery at St. Sebastian's in your home county."

"Attacked? With guns?" Christopher couldn't believe what he was hearing. This was like a nightmare—no, it was worse than that. This was too incredible to be anyone's dream.

"And a single small cannon. There were casualties, I'm afraid. Several of your countymen were reportedly killed while resisting Blake's attack."

Christopher sat down in a chair, his head reeling. "And Brother Horace?"

"I have no specific data—only the basic facts. Blake's objective undoubtedly was the library. We must assume that he is now in possession of it."

Christopher nodded, no longer able to trust his voice. Men dead—murdered—and for what? For a few books. He should have let Blake have the library when he asked for it. Anything would be better than this.

"So what do you intend to do?"

Talstead's voice reached him as if from a great distance. Christopher lifted his head in surprise. "Do? What is there I can do?"

"You'll be returning to County Kaine, I assume."

"Well . . . yes. Of course. It is my home—our home."

"Then there are certain things I want you to do." Talstead's voice was brisk, firm, and businesslike. He could have been discussing the price of corn on the open market.

"What can I do now?" Christopher said bitterly.

"A great deal, Christopher. For one thing, I want you to talk to Blake. Find out exactly why he did this—this dreadful thing. Find out his strengths, his potentialities, his ambitions. Above all, find out his weaknesses. We're damned lucky you are who you are. Blake may not trust you, but he can hardly ignore you. I want you to act as my eyes and ears, Christopher. Find out what's happening in County Kaine—and tell me."

"You want me to spy." Christopher forced himself to stand. His knees felt weak, as if he had not eaten in several days.

"Not just for me. For yourself as well. You have more at stake in this than I do."

Christopher nodded. "My family was there. My mother, my brother, my sister."

"I'm sure Blake wouldn't have harmed them." Talstead was brisk again. He clapped his hands in an obvious attempt to shake Christopher from his lethargy. "On my way here I ordered a coach. I told the servants to pack your belongings." He pointed to the door. "There's no reason you can't be on your way inside an hour."

"My wife . . . she doesn't know."

"Then tell her on the way." Talstead came out of his chair like a snake springing to attack. He slipped an arm around Christopher's shoulders and turned him toward the door. "She's a bright woman and I'm sure she'll understand. Still, he is her father. I wouldn't confide in her more than necessary."

"She hates him," Christopher said.

But Talstead was no longer listening. He steered Christopher through the door and propelled him down the hallway. At the end of it Christopher could see his trunk and suitcases waiting. There was no sign of Adrienne at first and then, suddenly, she appeared from a side passage, a stricken look on her face. He wondered if, somehow, she already knew.

As the rapid crackle of gunfire penetrated the morning mist, Sheridan Blake stood high upon the crown of a hill and peered below, where a broad pillar of black smoke rose into the air. Turning, he slammed an angry fist against the steel hood of the car behind him. Why wasn't it over yet? What the hell was happening? It seemed as if hours had passed since he had heard the reverberation of that first shot. Blake turned back. The smoke seemed thicker than ever. What the hell were they burning? It couldn't be the monastery itself, the library. Damn that idiot Lindstrom! What was he doing down there?

A small dark man dressed in a burlap smock stood beside Blake. A former house servant, the man was employed by Blake to drive the motorcar presented to him by the Janson brothers in appreciation of the assistance he had rendered in helping start their factory. The man was gazing down at the smoke with narrow hooded eyes. "I think I know what it is that's burning, sir."

"Well, what is it?" cried Blake impatiently. "Do you think I'm in the mood for guessing games?"

"It's that car, sir. The one that broke through the men. Lindstrom got it with the cannon, I think."

Blake felt a tightness in the pit of his stomach. He knew that motorcar—had recognized its driver. "Is anyone—?" He started to say *dead* but revised his words. "Is anyone moving down there?"

"I can't see that well. Not that—"

"We should have brought a telescope, a spyglass. This is impossible. Can you see anything except the wrecked car?"

"Just the soldiers."

"Well, what about them?"

The man turned, throwing his shoulders helplessly. "They're fighting, sir. Surely, you can hear the bullets."

Blake could. Of course he could. Hear the bullets and smell the smoke. This wasn't how he'd wanted it. A show of strength. Bluff and blackmail. But not killing, not death. It was that damned Lindstrom. Him and Brother Horace. What was the old fool trying to prove? "Idiot!" Blake shouted. "Stupid old bastard! Surrender, damn you! Give me the books! Give me—"

The rest of his words were buried beneath the sudden blast of the cannon.

The driver leaped excitedly. "Got it, sir! Got the chapel cleanly!"

"It's burning," said Blake, peering past the hilltop.

"That's not it, sir," the driver corrected. "That's still the car you see. The chapel's got a big chunk knocked out of it, though. Those monks won't soon—"

"Drive me down," said Blake, with sudden decisiveness. "I can't stand here and watch anymore. I've got to stop this slaughter. Maybe they'll listen to me."

"Well, you are the commander, sir."

The two of them went to the car. Blake slid into the rear seat and waited impatiently while the driver took the wheel. The car was the newest to emerge from the Janson factory. It came equipped with an automatic starter, clutch, three forward gears, and round wooden tires.

When the driver pressed the switch, the engine coughed instantly to life.

"Just drive down the hill till I tell you to stop."

"Toward the monastery?"

"Yes, of course. Head for the cannon."

"That might be dangerous. I think those men have lost their heads. We don't want to end up like the other car."

"Those are my men, for God's sake. They're fighting for me."

The driver seemed reluctant. "I hope this brake holds."

The car tottered briefly at the brink of the hill, then dropped downward. Descent was gradual as the driver cautiously rode the handbrake. Blake felt like snapping at the man, urging him to hurry but restrained himself. An accident at this point would do no one any good. He observed the battle scene, uncertain of his own emotions. He was proud—he admitted that much. The army he had trained had performed to all expectations. It was only a shame that Sir Malcolm had died so soon. Revenge might have tasted sweeter with its proper recipient at hand.

Not that he'd wanted it this way. It wounded him to know that men were dying in that hell below. It wasn't his fault. The blood, if any, lay on the hands of Horace, Lacy, Christopher Janson. They should have surrendered. There was no reason to fight back.

The smoke filled his nostrils now. He tried to breathe through his mouth, ignoring the stink. A lone man suddenly darted out of the dark cloud ahead and raced past the car. Blake saw his face. It was a massive red sore.

Then, touching level ground, they were inside the cloud. Blake tapped the driver on the shoulder and urged him to hurry. Through near darkness, he could see the ruined relic of the chapel. The cannon must have hit it more than once. More than twice.

As the car reached the outer circle of soldiers, Blake's men turned and raised a shout. Blake heard the cannon bellow. The reverberation was enough to make him deaf. A portion of the chapel collapsed inward.

Blake stood in the rear seat, waving his arms. "Cease firing!" he cried. "Stop! Hold that cannon!"

The driver, perhaps misinterpreting Blake's words, hit the brake. The car skidded to a halt. Losing his balance, Blake pitched headfirst between the seats. Realizing the indignity of his posture, he struggled to regain his feet. Suddenly, he understood what had changed. There was silence all around. The shooting had stopped.

He felt a hand on his shoulder and turned his head. Dav Lindstrom stood beside the car. "I told them to stop," he explained. "The monks are ready to give up."

"Well, make sure it stays that way." Blake climbed awkwardly out of the car and stumbled when his feet touched ground. His right knee ached, presumably injured when he fell. "What makes you think so?" he asked Lindstrom.

The man pointed toward the chapel. With the shooting stopped, the smoke had cleared and the full extent of the destruction inflicted on the building could be seen. Blake shook his head pityingly, then turned an anxious gaze on the smaller building where the library was housed. That, according to his orders, had been left undamaged.

Blake started to move forward.

Lindstrom reached out and stopped him. "Where do you think you're going, sir?"

"To talk to them—to Brother Horace. I have to receive their surrender, don't I?"

For some reason, Lindstrom was grinning. "I suppose that's your privilege, Mr. Blake."

He went ahead. The men—his men—stepped deferentially back and let him pass. He could see the smoking wreck of the car. Two bodies lay sprawled on the ground a dozen yards from it. Blake pulled his eyes swiftly away from the sight. Oddly, even the measure of pride and triumph he had felt on the hill had vanished now. He sighed. It could only get better from here on out. Couldn't it?

The two men met on equal footing just beyond the shattered remains of the chapel gate.

Blake extended a hand tentatively and Brother Horace grasped it firmly.

"I—I've come to accept your surrender," Blake said.

Horace nodded curtly. "That you have." A trickle of blood ran from his forehead. Horace noticed Blake staring at the wound and smiled thinly. "A splinter of brick struck me. Nothing serious."

"I'm very glad of that," Blake said, with more feeling than he might have wished. "It was a mistake. You have to believe me. I never intended for anyone to shoot. I left specific orders that—"

"When you give a man a gun, it's hard to convince him not to use it."

"I never wanted anyone to die."

"Nor did I." Horace shrugged philosophically. "But these young men—yours as well as mine—they appeared to believe there was something worth dying for."

"A few old books." Blake laughed bitterly. There was a shrillness in his tone.

"They knew nothing of the books. That was our matter, Sheridan, not theirs."

"Then why?"

"Things that neither of us perhaps can understand."

Blake felt a flash of anger. Damn this old man. How dare he display such arrogance? This was victory—Blake's victory. Horace should be weeping. When he spoke, Blake tried to adopt a mollifying tone. "I don't want you to worry about the damage. I intend to put my men to work at once repairing this. Inside of a few weeks, you'll never know what happened here. You have my word, Horace. Tell your monks to continue to perform their normal duties. I want nothing interrupted. Tomorrow is Sunday. Do you understand?"

"The regular services will be conducted," said Horace.

"Then all I need is the key." Blake held out a hand. "Give me that and the repairs can begin. I'll want to inspect the library, select the volumes that fit my needs, and have them transported to Tumas."

"Ah, yes, the library." Horace spoke in a distant voice. A smile toyed with his lips.

Blake wanted to be generous. "You must understand that I'm doing this only because I believe I'm right. Are you aware that two hundred years ago nearly everyone in the world lived to seventy years? Not just the Malcolm Jansons. Everyone. Peasants. Workmen. We can have that world again, Horace, without its faults. The secret lies in those books. We haven't the right to keep them concealed any longer."

The smile on Horace's lips spread. "It isn't the number of years a man lives that is consequential," he said, quoting one of Stoner's most famous precepts, "it is the use to which he puts those years allotted him."

"Stoner never had to beg for his next meal," Blake said, bitterness rising up from within. What did Horace know of agony of hunger, the pain of dull work, petty superstition, debilitating disease? When a man's cards were dealt from a deck containing nothing but aces, kings, and queens, it was impossible for him to comprehend the despair of another man holding a losing hand.

"Then perhaps I ought to tell you about the library." The smile had vanished from Horace's face. His eyes were narrow, his gaze direct. "I will not give you the key."

"Then I—I . . ." Blake struggled not to shout. "I'll burn this place to the ground," he said tightly. "I won't have risked everything for . . . for nothing."

"The choice was yours to make. The door, as a matter of fact, is not locked. Go look for yourself. You have no need for a key."

Blake started to step away, then stopped himself. All at once he understood exactly what Horace was trying to explain. "The books aren't there," he said flatly.

Horace nodded. "They aren't."

Blake reached out and grasped the old man by his robes. "You destroyed them."

"I would never do that."

"Then you hid them."

"Yes."

"Where?"

"I won't tell you that."

"You will or—or—" Blake loosened his grip on Horace and dropped his arms tensely to his sides. "Tell me."

"I won't." Horace shook his head firmly.

It was a gray Saturday morning and Ned Janson lay on his back on the ground underneath his newest motorcar, clutching a loose wire in one hand. In spite of the fact that the squat bulk of the chassis blocked the sun's light, Ned experienced no difficulty working by touch alone. As he raised the wire to attach it where it belonged, he became slowly conscious of a commotion outside his limited field of immediate awareness. Pausing, he held the loose wire suspended in the air and listened intently. A strange crackling noise reached him. Then he heard a voice. Puzzled, he hastily connected the wire and slid out into the light.

"Ned! Ned Janson! Are you there?"

He recognized the voice. It was Bill Walker. Slapping the dust off his shirt and trousers, he stood up. "I'm over here, Bill. What do you want?"

Bill Walker came into view around the corner of the factory building. His face registered strain, as if he had run a long distance. He stopped in front of Ned, his breath coming in heaving gasps. "It's the monastery," he managed. "It's . . ."

Bill broke off, unable to continue. Ned let him have a moment to regain his breath, then asked, "What about the monastery?"

"Don't you hear it?" Bill cupped an ear. The crackling noise continued. "It's coming from there."

"What's coming from there?" Ned still hadn't managed to identify the noise.

"Gunfire."

"At the monastery?"

"Yes, it must be—it's Sheridan Blake. Peasants from Tumas. An army with guns, and they're attacking the monastery. It's just as my mother said it would be. She said—"

Ned leaped into the car. He couldn't for the life of him make sense of what Bill was saying, but whatever it meant, it had to be worth investigating. He used the automatic starter to ignite the engine. "You'd better come with me," he said, pointing to the empty space beside him on the seat.

Just then a massive explosion rocked the earth. Far ahead Ned saw a puff of black smoke rise in the air.

"They have a cannon, too," Bill Walker said bleakly.

"Get in," said Ned. Without waiting for a reply, he released the brake. Bill Walker climbed into the car as it rolled forward. Ned depressed the throttle. The car moved quickly, leaping across the green pasture which already showed the deep ruts of past motorcar trips.

"We're doomed," Bill Walker said calmly, his voice barely audible above the roar of the engine. "My mother foretold all of this. She said we were doomed."

"Did she say anything else? Did she say what this means?"

"She said it was machines that coughed fire and spat blood."

"In other words, guns." Ned nodded his head. He recalled Christopher once having mentioned that Sheridan Blake was making his own guns. Christopher wasn't here now—he was in Capital, taking his examinations—and Ned assumed that it was now his responsibility to take charge. Lacy was home in the white house. For a moment Ned considered going there first to seek guidance, but the despair on Bill Walker's face convinced him there wasn't time to spare. If he wanted to solve this puzzle, he would have to drive straight to the monastery.

The fastest route to reach there was directly overland. Ned turned that way, ignoring the regular road. He only hoped, going this way, the car wouldn't get bogged down in some deep mudhole. He kept the throttle close to full out. At top speed, the car was more than capable of hitting forty miles per hour.

They went uphill. Ned shifted gears carefully. He glanced at Bill Walker, but seeing his lips moving as if in prayer, he looked quickly away again. Whatever was happening at the monastery he would find out soon enough once he arrived.

The crackling noise—the gunfire—grew more distinct. The car passed grazing sheep and lolling cattle but no men. It was as if a giant hand had fallen upon the land and stripped it bare of human life. Ned felt lonely and isolated. Bill Walker continued to murmur, his actual words not quite decipherable.

Ned saw a man moving toward the car. Recognizing the dark robes the figure wore, Ned hit the brake. The car bucked to a stop. The man shouted a greeting. It was Brother Horace from the monastery at St. Sebastian's.

"Brother Horace, what are you doing out here?" Ned asked.

"Never mind." Horace hesitated an instant, then climbed into the back seat of the car. "You've got to take me home."

"It's where we're going, too." Ned released the brake and jerked the throttle. "Bill says that's gunfire you hear in the air."

"I know."

"He says someone—Sheridan Blake—is attacking your monastery."

"I know that too."

Ned could have asked a hundred questions. He resisted the impulse to begin and concentrated on the land ahead. Obviously, Horace knew more than Ned about whatever was going on. Undoubtedly, Christopher did too. His brother never confided in him.

"You must have a pretty good idea of what this is about," Ned said over his shoulder. He gripped the steering wheel tightly as the car moved across a particularly bumpy stretch of ground.

"It must be Blake come to seize the library." Horace held on to the seat as the car bounced and swayed. "Didn't Christopher tell you? We must get to the monastery as soon as possible."

"Nobody's going to get there faster than us." Ned focused his eyes on the ground ahead, searching for the smoothest stretches toward which to aim the wheels. The car plunged into a shallow stream, splashing water, and charged up the opposite bank, tires holding fast in the mud. Ned was proud of the machine he had built.

"I just can't believe he'd do this," Horace said, his voice choking. "We always assumed he'd give some warning. This is terrible. Men may be dying right this instant and for no good reason. It's hopeless. Pointless."

"We'll be there in just a moment," Ned said soothingly.

Horace didn't reply. Ned thought he might be sobbing. Bill Walker continued his passionate mumbling.

Ned swerved to avoid a blackberry thicket.

The last hill rose ahead. Ned drove the car toward the peak. Something whistled past his ear. He ducked automatically. "Get down!" he cried. "That was a bullet!"

A second shot zinged past. Ned slumped in the seat, holding his head low. On the hill opposite he could see another motorcar. Two men stood in front of it. He held the throttle as far down as it would go. He guessed they must be doing close to fifty miles per hour by now.

A short moment later the car reached the foot of the hill and burst through a thin circle of armed peasants. With his head bent down, Ned barely had a chance to look at them. The spire of the chapel rose ahead. To one side Ned caught sight of a huge dark shape. A cannon, he realized with astonishment. So Bill Walker had not been exaggerating, after all.

The front windshield shattered. Ned cried out as splinters of broken glass rained down on his head. He heard Bill Walker let out an agonized scream beside him. There was no time to see what was the matter. He released the throttle and gripped the brake. The car spun a hoop in the dust as the rear wheels froze.

Brother Horace was out of the car in a flash, racing toward the monastery.

Ned stood up. Bill Walker sat slumped in the seat, holding his face in his hands. Ned saw blood. "Horace—wait!" he called. "We've got to—"

A bullet pelted the car. Ned realized he could be killed if he stayed here. He reached over to assist Bill Walker and that was when it happened. As soon as he heard that awful noise like a great roaring in the earth, he knew that something had gone terribly wrong. He felt as if the ground beneath him had split into two pieces and left him standing in the middle. A cosmic whirlwind burst around him. He seemed to be flying, deaf and blind. Why couldn't he see anything? Hear anything? He was falling.

The fear of death swept over him like a high wave.

Was this what it was like to end your life?

He struck the ground.

The car, several yards away, was already burning.

Charlotte Janson, newly married, turned her head and smiled shyly at the lean profile of her husband. Charlotte Janson? she thought musingly. No, that wasn't right anymore. She was Charlotte Chambers now. Why, she hadn't even known Brother Julian's last name until he'd confided in her only moments before the ceremony.

"Are you all right?" he asked her, turning as he noticed her gaze fixed on him.

"Oh, I'm fine. Perfectly fine."

"I'm glad." He clicked his tongue, urging the horse that pulled the cart to slightly more haste. "I was worried, once it had actually happened, you might begin to have doubts."

"Not a one," she said, matching his smile. And that was true. If anything, she had to fight to hold back tears from filling her eyes with gratitude. She was glad—more than glad—joyous. She had never been so happy in her life as she was now—as Charlotte Chambers.

Even her voices had receded. Oh, she could still hear them— she supposed that, objectively, they were as loud as ever—but she no longer felt any urge to listen.

This man beside her on the hard wooden seat of the cart—this man whom she loved—was now her husband. And that seemed to make all the difference in the world.

"I wonder what that noise is about," Julian said, his face falling into a puzzled frown.

"What noise?" she said.

"Haven't you heard it? It's been going on for some time now. Listen. It sounds like firecrackers."

She shook her head, but now that he had mentioned it, yes, she could hear something. A steady crackling noise coming from somewhere behind them. "Maybe that's what it is. Maybe it's a celebration. For us."

"I don't think so." Julian's frown turned slowly into a smile. "Maybe it's Christopher—your brother. Maybe he's blowing his cork."

Charlotte laughed. "Oh, it couldn't be him. He's not due home for several days. We'll be miles and miles away from County Kaine before he even hears the news."

"I suppose that's best. For all concerned."

She nodded. Charlotte did not think she had ever loved Julian more deeply than she did at this very moment. Not that it hadn't been wonderful this morning, too. As long as her life went on, she would never forget this morning.

It hadn't been an idle whim. For more than a year she and Julian had formulated careful plans. And then it had come together. Father's death. Christopher's departure. There hadn't been any better time. Last night, together, they had visited Brother Horace and asked him to perform the ceremony. Charlotte had not wanted to go to him. When she thought of Brother Horace, she thought of her father and Christopher, but Julian insisted. "I've lived in the monastery since I was nine years old. If I'm leaving now, I have to tell Brother Horace. I won't feel truly married unless he's the one who says the words."

At first Brother Horace refused. Julian asked her to leave the room and spoke to the old man alone. She didn't know what he said, but when it was over, Brother Horace agreed to conduct the ceremony at dawn the next morning. He only tried once to talk her out of it.

"Charlotte, you're a child. Are you sure you really know what you're doing?"

"I'm sure, Brother Horace." She gazed at Julian as she spoke.

"You are aware that Sir Malcolm would not have approved of this."

"I love Julian."

"And Christopher? Your mother?"

"It doesn't matter. I don't mean to be selfish, but it just doesn't. I love Julian and we both love God. We have to be together so that we can serve Him properly."

Horace shook his head. "I know. Julian told me of your plans."

The site they had chosen for the ceremony was a tiny nook of land, a meadow, in the big forest that surrounded Crystal Lake. It was the place where for the past few years they had met privately when they wished to be alone. For Charlotte, it was a special part of the earth. At dawn the light of the sun actually seemed to strike there first, painting the nearby trees in bright swirling patterns of gold, brown, yellow, and red.

Horace brought a cart. When they reached the meadow, Julian turned to him and said, "We would like to begin at the first light of dawn."

Unfortunately, the sky proved to be clouded. That was the one disappointment in a day of supreme delights.

After the ceremony, Horace let them have his horse and cart. "Take it and flee, children," he said. "What's done is done and cannot be erased. Go and find your own calling. I wish you well."

"But how will you return to the monastery?" Julian asked practically.

"I'll walk. This is a fine morning, cool. Go now—both of you. I bless you as man and wife."

Charlotte thought that last was a particularly kind gesture on Horace's part, especially considering his initial reluctance to help. The cart and horse would ensure they were miles distant from County Tumas before Christopher returned. Their eventual destination was the small farm in County Saktom to the north where Julian's brother presently resided. On foot the journey would have taken more than a week, and they would have been forced to beg lodging as well as food.

With the cart, she now felt as free on the outside as within.

The crackling noise followed them through the forest.

"I love you," Charlotte said, reaching out and clasping her husband's hand.

"I love you, too," Julian said.

PART 6:

The Monastery

In a properly modulated society, the chronological age of an individual must serve as a primary means for determining intrinsic human worth. No wise man will ever neglect the terrible lesson to be learned from the cult of youth that ravaged civilization during the Terrible Years and from the manner in which the aged were forced into the idleness of so-called "retirement" at the very moment when they had entered the most rewarding and productive years of their lives.

With this example firmly in mind, I hereby declare that the man of fifty shall bow his head to the man of fifty-one and that the man of fifty-one shall in turn bow his head to the man of fifty-two. In all such instances, of course, the social standing of both men must be identical.

Nonetheless, I further denounce the myth of adulthood which also flourished in the Terrible Years. Who among us possesses sufficient wisdom to determine accurately exactly when any man attains true maturity? Does some magical boundary verifiably exist separating childhood from genuine adult status and, if so, what is this boundary? Is it sixteen years, eighteen, twenty-one, twenty-five, or thirty-two? All of these at one time or another have served as such a dividing point, and yet all are equally absurd. They are false numbers—deceptive lies that conceal the inner truth from view.

What is this truth?

Simply this: adulthood is not a matter of years; it is a question of wisdom alone.

I do therefore declare the establishment of a second series of examinations to be administered apart from those concerned with the bureaucracy. All men, regardless of class or station, will be required to complete these tests as soon as they turn sixteen and every year thereafter until a passing mark is achieved.

Those who achieve a passing score on the examinations will be considered full adults and accorded the privileges thereof.

These examinations will not be concerned with matters of established fact. Each will offer a specific problem, preferably in the form of a parable, to be understood and solved.

I am reminded here of the old tale of the strong man and the lean boy.

Pardon my digression:

Once long ago in a distant land a strong man of thirty-three years and a lean boy of nine summers undertook a journey together. Both desired to reach and enter the fabled city of the wise men in order to comprehend the teachings of these sages and become wise men themselves. The journey was an arduous one of many months duration but eventually the strong man and the lean boy reached the outer gate of the city they sought. A heavy door blocked their path. The strong man tried the latch, found it securely bolted, and pounded on the door with his fist.

A square panel in the center of the door slid back to reveal the visage of an ancient yellow-skinned man. "Who are you," cried the man, "and what do you wish of our city?"

"This boy and I," said the strong man, "have traveled many miles in order to enter your city and receive your teachings and become as wise as you."

"A most noble ambition." The old man pursed

his lips. "Unfortunately, if we were to allow all such pilgrims easy access to our city, soon there would be no room for those already here."

"Then you are a wise man?"

"I am."

"And you refuse to allow us to enter your city?"

"I do."

"Then you are as selfish as you are wise."

"Perhaps, but we must ask that you first pass a test."

The strong man considered this offer, stroking his chin slowly. "That seems fair."

"Thank you," said the wise man. "As you may have noticed this door, which happens to be the only entrance to the city, is securely bolted. What we ask is simply that you find a means—any means fair or foul—for gaining entrance to the city through this door. Once you have entered, you will be made welcome and all your desires will be served."

The strong man laughed heartily, for what the wise man had demanded was only what he had previously considered on his own. "Stand aside," he told the lean boy. "I will break the door with the strength of my body and soon we will be inside."

Without additional prelude, the strong man hurled his shoulder against the door.

Yet, in spite of the savageness of this assault, the door refused to budge.

"Again," said the strong man, and he tried once more.

He kicked the door.

He beat upon it furiously with his fists.

Again, he rammed his shoulder against the barrier.

For many hours, without cessation, the strong man pitted his strength against the unyielding door. In the end, thoroughly exhausted, he fell to the ground and lay without moving. His strength had deserted him now. He was beaten and knew it.

The lean boy, who had carefully observed the strong man's exertions from beginning to end, now stepped forward. Raising a fist, he tapped politely upon the door.

Almost instantly, the square panel slid back and

the withered face appeared. "What is it you want here in our city?"

The boy replied in a hushed tone. "Please, sir," he asked, "may I come through the gate?"

"Why, of course," said the man, grinning broadly. "All you need do is ask. Our city will always be open to one as wise as you."

And so the lean boy passed into the city of the wise men and became in due time famous throughout the world for his own wisdom.

> William Stoner, The Book of
> Stones, circa 2045.

In spite of the apparently firm grip of classical Stonerism upon the society of the Great Dark Age, any quick perusal of The Book of Stones in its unabridged format will instantly indicate that not every word Stoner wrote was later followed exactly to the letter. In fact, there were entire programs that Stoner considered absolutely essential to the practical pursuit of his philosophy that were utterly ignored when the time came to turn theory into practice.

How come, you ask, if these people thought Stoner was so smart, they refused to pay attention to some of the things he said?

Well, perhaps, I reply, it was because Stoner proved to be a whole lot smarter than most people wanted him to be.

So what are you talking about? ask you.

Well, for one thing, Stoner strongly advocated the establishment of a cult of wise men to stand at the summit of society and make decisions for all the relative imbeciles below. Needless to say, this cult never even came close to getting off the ground.

How come? you ask. ————

You shouldn't. The answer's so damned obvious that, if it was a snake, it'd bite. The county bureaucrats, once the reins of power fell into their hands, were not about to establish a competitive seat of power. No, sir. When you've got a room at the top of the house, you don't go building another one right over your own head.

Whose fault? Who to blame? The bureaucrats? Call them petty and selfish?

> *Well, maybe. But for me it makes better sense to blame the sainted Stoner himself for having neglected a basic aspect of human nature. If you intend to remake society society over into something practical and sensible, you'd better start with at least a smattering of awareness of plain old human selfishness.*
>
> Daniel T. Janson, A History of Human Events Subsequent to Stoner's Time, 2378.

Christopher Janson sat beside his napping wife on the plush padded seat of the coach Minister Talstead had provided and watched idly as the familiar meadows and forests of County Kaine swept past the window. Today was a lovely day, crisp if somewhat cool, as totally devoid of menace as a trilling robin in the low branches of a tree.

For that reason, when the coach at last rolled past the summit of the final hill and began a rapid descent toward the monastery at St. Sebastian's, Christopher felt a double sense of shock and horror at what he discovered ahead.

"Stop," he told the driver, his voice choking, as the coach reached the nearest building. "I think I'd better see if . . ."

Adrienne was staring out the window. It was difficult to know how long she had been awake or how much she had seen. She reached for his sleeve. "Shouldn't we go home?" Her voice was stricken, pleading. She must have seen everything. "There's nothing we can do here."

"Somebody has to do something." He threw open the door and jumped out of the coach, but as quickly as it had come, his anger evaporated, replaced by a welling numbness. He stood where he was, unable to make his feet move. If he hadn't known where he was, he would never have recognized the monastery. A few buildings remained undamaged—including, he noticed, the library—but most at least had large chunks torn from their frames, like meat stripped for a feast. A pile of stone rubble marked the site of the main chapel. Christopher took one hesitant step and noticed the charred skeleton of a motorcar. Whose? he wondered. Blake's, most likely. But how had it come to be burned? The wind whipped silently around him. He sensed it brushing his face, scattering his hair. Christopher felt as though he had moved instantaneously from one level of heaven to another of hell, from the world of the living to the domain of the dead. He gazed at his feet. Blood showed on the ground.

"Stay here," he told the driver, letting his words break the spell of despair. "I'm going to see if anyone's alive."

"I'll go, too." It was Adrienne. He had failed to notice when she joined him.

"No. I'll only be a moment." He went ahead. On the ground near a place where a stone gate had stood—no sign remained to mark its passing—a flash of reflected sunlight caught his eye. He bent down. It was a steel case—a cartridge shell. In spite of himself, he felt his anger returning. There were other spent shells scattered about. Now that he looked, he could see them. Each caught the sunlight, burning like stars fallen to earth.

He went around the building housing the library and suddenly came upon a number of monks and nuns. There were five or ten of them—it was difficult to count—moving between the various buildings like shadows in a dream. Reaching out, Christopher caught one of them—a young monk.

"Brother Horace? Is he—?"

The monk shook his head. "He's not here."

"Then where is he?"

"Perhaps the other man could explain." He jerked his head toward the opposite building. "You're Christopher Janson, aren't you, sir?"

"I am."

"Then he specifically said he wanted to see you when you arrived."

"Is it . . . Blake?"

The monk grinned, showing yellowed teeth, rotten in spite of his youth. The gesture seemed totally anomalous amid this destruction. Still, Christopher tried to understand. Five days had passed since the actual attack. Even grief and horror rarely lasted long.

"Then who?"

"I'm not at liberty to say the name. A friend, I believe."

Christopher nodded, as if confirming the monk's analysis, though he had no firm idea who this man might be. "What's everyone doing? Why has there been no attempt to repair the damage?"

"We are tending our wounded first, sir."

"Yes, of course." He felt an odd reluctance to leave the monk's company. And the questions kept coming to mind. "How many were killed?"

"Only nine."

"Nine men!" Christopher realized his hands were shaking.

"Eight. One was an elderly nun. She was praying in the chapel when the bomb—the cannon—hit."

"And the wounded?"

The monk seemed ready to blurt out a reply but caught himself in time and merely shrugged philosophically. "Who can count? All were injured in some fashion. My knee was cut by a flying rock."

"I see." With an effort of will, Christopher forced himself to turn away from the monk and approach the building where the mystery man waited. This, if his memory was correct, was where Horace had made his home. The lower floor of the building was badly damaged, with wooden support beams showing through the rubble, but the upper floor seemed largely untouched. Christopher ascended what was left of the staircase that led to Horace's rooms. Several steps were missing. He moved with caution.

When he reached the door, he knocked once. Almost immediately, it opened.

"Lacy," he said softly, not really surprised.

The bearded man nodded. He was smoking one of his fire sticks, and the gray cloud that wreathed his head gave him an oddly angelic appearance. "I saw your coach coming over the hill. I would have greeted you personally but at the present time I'm afraid that would be unwise."

"Why?"

"Blake is in the county."

"I know."

"Well, he doesn't know I'm here. And, for the time being, I intend to keep it that way." He shook his head swiftly, as if suddenly reminded of something he had forgotten. "But do come in. At least in here we can sit."

Christopher followed Lacy into the small, barely furnished room that had served Brother Horace as a home. There was a round wooden table and two chairs. Lacy poured wine from a bottle into two tall glasses. "I found this in the chapel," he explained. "I hope Brother Horace won't regard my partaking as sacrilege."

"How is Horace?" Christopher sipped the wine carefully. After what he had become accustomed to in Capital, this was a poor vintage indeed. He swallowed with difficulty. "He's not dead?"

Lacy shook his head slowly. "He's alive. In Capital, how much did you learn?"

"Only the basic facts. A messenger came. He must have ridden night and day. I left immediately."

"Did you talk to the messenger personally?"

"No. Minister Talstead told me."

"Talstead? You know him?"

"He's Adrienne's uncle."

"Yes." Lacy gulped the wine. "I remember."

There was a gentle knock on the door. It opened and Adrienne peered through the gap. The sleeves of her gown were rolled past her elbows. "I came after you," she told Christopher. "Vincent is in another building. I'm helping with the wounded."

Only then did Christopher notice the bright red stains on her hands. "I wish you'd waited."

"No, this is better for both of us. Hello, Mr. Lacy."

"Hello, Adrienne."

"When you're ready to go, find me," she told Christopher and went out.

"You married damned well," Lacy said, when they were alone again.

"I know. But you still haven't told me. Where's Horace? Where's Blake?"

"In the same place. Blake and his army are camped in a meadow about two miles from here. When you go home, make sure you avoid them. They've got Horace there, too. He's a prisoner."

For the first time today, Christopher experienced genuine astonishment. "Whatever for?"

"Because Blake thinks Horace knows where the books are."

"The books?"

Lacy grinned. "You needn't play coy with me. I know about the library. I've known about it for years."

"Horace told me. How did you learn?"

It was Lacy's turn to be coy. "I have my sources of information. That's not the point. The point is, in case you were worried, Blake failed to get what he came for."

It was back to astonishment again for Christopher. His head was beginning to feel dizzy. "But I saw the building—the library. It wasn't even touched in the attack."

"No, but the books weren't there, either."

"But how could . . ."

Lacy poked himself in the chest. "Me. I'm the guilty party. I moved them. When Blake opened the door the other day, he found nothing."

"Nothing? But that means—this whole thing—the attack—all the dead and wounded—it was for nothing."

"I know." Lacy stared at his big gnarled hands. "Nobody knows that better than I, I'm afraid." He looked up and met Christopher's eyes. "I was too damned cute for my own good. Horace knew. He was supposed to tell Blake when Blake arrived. The trouble was, he snuck up on us and Horace wasn't even here the day he hit."

"Oh, no," said Christopher, more revolted by the utter waste than anything else.

"I knew he was coming. Horace and I discussed it. He wasn't an easy man to convince, but I explained why I was positive Blake would attempt to move against the monastery during your absence. I had evidence—proof—and Horace agreed. It seems that I was correct in my surmise but wrong in the manner I handled it. I should have posted myself at the gate and made sure that Blake would never do—" he waved a hand weakly "—this."

"And Horace let you move the books, without knowing where."

"He knows."

"Where?"

"In the mine."

"The diamond mine? You can't hide anything there. It's just an empty hole in the ground."

Lacy shook his head. "There's more to that mine than you know, Christopher. More than anyone knows."

"What do you mean?"

"Never mind." Lacy shrugged. "I'll explain later."

"But if Horace knows, what's to keep him from telling Blake? I know he's a strong man, an honest man, but after this, who knows what Blake might do?"

"No one," Lacy admitted, "which is why I don't expect Horace to keep silent forever. The idea is for Blake to know—eventually."

"Why? Do you have a plan?"

Lacy turned vague. "You'll see in time."

"Why not now?"

"Because there's no need. Horace trusts me. I wish you'd do the same."

Christopher stared at his old teacher, wondering not for the first time who this man really was. Lacy was like a kaleidoscope, constantly revealing new dimensions. "I wish you trusted me enough to tell me more."

"It's not a question of trust. I—"

A gentle knocking came again at the door. Guessing who it was, Christopher looked at Lacy, who said, "Come in, Adrienne."

She stepped inside and glanced questioningly in Christopher's direction. Then she looked at Lacy. "You haven't told him yet."

"There were other things to discuss first." Lacy gazed at his wine glass as he spoke.

"Don't you think you should?"

He nodded. "Yes."

"I only just heard myself, but I think you should be the one to tell."

"I will," Lacy said.

Adrienne stepped back out. The blood now showed on the front of her gown, like scarlet polka dots.

"What was that all about?" Christopher asked quietly.

"About my being selfish. I'm sorry again, Christopher. There's something you have a right to know."

"What? Is . . . is . . ."

"It's Ned," Lacy said.

"He's dead."

Lacy looked up, shaking his head firmly. "Thank God, no.

But he was injured—wounded. He came here on the morning of the battle. He and Bill Walker together in a car. It must have been something to behold. They drove smack into the middle of everything."

"I saw the car," Christopher said softly. "Outside. It's a wreck."

"A direct cannon hit."

"And?"

"Bill Walker was blinded. The monks were caring for him, but he disappeared yesterday. I've been trying to locate him. I don't think . . . Bill's not right in his head anymore."

"Ned, too?"

"Ned's mental processes are fine. It was his legs. Vincent doubts that he'll ever walk again."

"I see," said Christopher. He sat motionlessly for a long, hushed moment.

"It was my fault," Lacy said.

Christopher shook his head. "Is he here?"

"No. At the house. Vincent felt it was safe to move him. I suppose you'll want . . ."

"Afterward, yes," Christopher said coldly.

"After what?"

"After I find out what you intend to do about Blake."

"Don't blame him—blame me. His motives were pure enough. I was the one who miscalculated."

"I'd rather blame him."

Lacy nodded, suddenly as emotionless as his former pupil. "Then I suppose that is your privilege."

Sarah, his mother, intercepted him in the dim upstairs hallway outside Ned's room. He hadn't seen her in weeks, not since the day of his departure for Capital, but there was barely a hint of recognition in his eyes. "Let me past," he said gruffly.

"No. The medical man's in there now. I know how you feel but I wish you'd wait."

"What medical man? Vincent is at the monastery."

"This man's name is Malone. Mr. Blake sent him."

Christopher lunged for the door. "Then get that bastard out of there."

Sarah caught his hand. Her strength, as always, was astonishing in a woman. "No. He's an excellent medical man. I know how you feel, but he has things that kill pain."

"Potions?"

"Drugs. Imported. They work."

"And Ned needs them?"

"His legs—they . . ." She broke off as Christopher stepped back.

"All right. Ned's the important one, not me. I won't interfere. I promise."

"Then I suppose it's all right if you go in." Without turning, she opened the door. Christopher followed her inside. Heavy curtains covered the lone window, and only a faint glimmer of sunshine managed to penetrate into the room. A short, stoop-shouldered man hovered near the bed.

At the sound of Christopher's approach, the man turned. He clutched a narrow glass vial in one hand. Bowing to Sarah, he said, "Mrs. Janson, I am honored." Then he looked at Christopher. "And you, sir?"

"This is my eldest son," Sarah said.

Christopher nodded toward the figure beneath the bedcovers. "I'm Ned's brother."

"I am honored to make your acquaintance, sir." The man extended his free hand. "I am Dr. Malone, at your service."

Christopher ignored the outstretched hand as easily as he ignored Malone's assumption of a title—doctor—which no longer bore any real meaning. He went to the bed and peered down.

Ned looked sick—very sick—a shadow of himself. When he saw Christopher, a glimmer of recognition crossed his features but nothing more.

Christopher stepped back. "What have you done to him?"

Malone shrugged. "There are drugs—to ease the pain." He held up the vial in his hand. "Before you entered, I had just completed an injection."

"Can he talk?"

"In a moment, yes."

"Then I'd prefer to be alone with him."

Malone looked at Sarah. When she nodded, he faced Christopher and said, "There can be no harm."

"I'll go, too," Sarah said.

Christopher turned back to the bed. "Adrienne is below. You might talk to her."

"I will."

Malone moved toward the door on feet that barely made a sound. "I will return within ten minutes."

"That will be fine," Christopher said.

"He may fall asleep suddenly. If he does, don't worry. It's an effect of the drug."

"I understand."

When the door shut and the others were gone, Christopher leaned over the bed and said in a loud voice, "Ned—it's me."

"Christopher," said a voice, faint and distant.

"I've come home."

"Good." Ned's swollen lips barely moved as he struggled to speak.

"You're going to get better."

His lips seemed to twitch. What was it? Was he trying to smile? "Sure, I am. I . . . the doctor keeps saying so too."

"Well, believe him."

"I do." His voice was stronger, his gaze more alert, but he paused between nearly every word to take a breath. From this, as well as the tenseness of his body, Christopher realized the agony Ned must be enduring. "The doctor . . . would . . . never lie . . . to me."

"Of course not."

"And Capital," said Ned. "You haven't told . . . me. How was it? Like . . . like the way we always thought."

"Even better," Christopher said, smiling. "I wish you could have come. It was magnificent, beautiful."

"I wish I . . . could . . . have come, too." Ned winced, his body suddenly twisting.

Christopher clutched his arm. "Does it hurt?"

"A little." Perspiration coated his forehead. "It won't be . . . long. They . . . the doctor . . . he wants to cut them off."

"Your legs?" Christopher felt sick. Lacy had not told him this.

"It's a . . . matter of . . . life and death. The skin . . . the flesh . . . it's burned away. If he cuts . . . I'll be . . . as good as new."

Christopher looked away. He felt a touch at his wrist. Glancing down, he saw Ned's fingers clutching the flesh. "Bill Walker," he said, pausing to breathe. "They won't . . . tell me . . . about him."

Christopher saw no reason to conceal the truth. "He was blinded."

Ned shut his eyes, and for a moment Christopher thought that, as Malone had predicted, he had fallen asleep. Then he opened them again. "I guess I'm . . . lucky."

"But I have some good news, too," Christopher said quickly. "Do you know why Blake attacked the monastery?"

Ned nodded against the whiteness of his pillow. "Books."

"Well, he didn't get them. Lacy hid every one of them before Blake even reached the county. Now we have him checked. We're going to beat him, Ned. We really are."

Ned nodded again. It was difficult to determine whether he had understood a word Christopher had said. Perhaps, like Christopher himself, he could only think of how the absence of the books meant that all this suffering was without meaning.

"You fought for what was right," Christopher said. "That's more important than any book. Don't think this was for nothing."

Ned smiled. "Look after the factory," he said.

The factory? Christopher hadn't even thought of the motorcar works since his return. "I will," he promised.

"It's important. They . . . it . . . it's all I've got now."

"No, it's not."

But Ned was sleeping. For a few moments, Christopher watched him—Ned's features oddly serene as he lay there—then he turned away.

Shortly afterward, Malone returned.

"Are you really going to cut off his legs?" Christopher asked.

"It is necessary. Without that—the poison—he will surely die. I intend to cut at the knee. I hope that will be sufficient."

Christopher suddenly understood that without this man his brother might already have died. "When?" he asked softly.

"I could start this minute. I should."

"Will you require any help?"

"Two strong men—peasants. I can't guarantee the potency of the drug. He may wake up."

"I'll get a man."

"No, at least two."

"I'll be the other one."

Christopher drank deeply, slamming the empty mug down on the table when he finished. Only then did he look up and meet his mother's gaze from across the room. "Malone says he's going to be all right," he told her.

"Thank God!" For a moment, he thought she might faint, but then, recovering her balance, she placed a hand on her forehead. "Thank God," she repeated in a softer tone.

"He never woke up the whole time. It was . . . clean. Malone knew what he was doing." Suddenly aware of the immensity of his fatigue, Christopher shut his eyes. A scene flashed through his mind that he wished he could forget. Ned. Malone. The knife. The sound of the saw cutting into bone. And the blood. He would never forget the sight of that blood.

"Can I see him now?"

Christopher shook his head. "Wait." The peasants had not finished cleaning Ned's room. It would be better if she waited until then.

"Will he be awake?"

"Not now. Malone said it might be three or four hours."

"Then I think I'll wait until then. I'd like . . . I think it would be better if Ned saw me when I visited him."

Christopher nodded. There were times his mother's wisdom amazed him. The shock of seeing her son lying there without legs would be lessened if Ned were awake to talk.

Sarah said, "Christopher?"

Her voice snapped him from his reverie. He met her gaze. "Yes, Mother?"

"I'd like to know what you intend to do about . . . about Blake."

"Do?" He reached automatically for more wine.

"Lacy left here the day of the attack and I haven't seen him since. Some of those men—those peasants of Mr. Blake—came here looking for him. Adrienne says you saw him at the monastery. If he's hiding there, I want to know why. I want to know what your plan is."

Christopher shook his head. "I wish I could tell you but the honest truth is that I don't know myself. Not everything."

"But Lacy has a plan?"

"Yes."

"Then tell me this much: will we be rid of Mr. Blake?"

"Lacy says we will, yes."

"And the peasants?"

That was a factor he had not discussed with Lacy. "I imagine, once Blake's gone, the others will leave, too."

"I worry about them more than Blake himself. Our own peasants talk. Blake's men are restless, they say. He's inflamed them with a blood lust."

"They're only peasants. They'll do as they're told."

"Blake is a peasant, Christopher."

He nodded slowly, staring down at his wine. The next progression was the most delicate, for if Blake was a peasant, then Adrienne must be one too, and if she was, knowing her character as well as he did, then how could he possibly make further generalizations? Perhaps that was what Sarah had intended him to realize. "Where's Charlotte?" he asked suddenly, lifting his head. "I haven't seen her since we got back."

"Charlotte's gone, Christopher." With those words, Sarah finally revealed the depth of her fatigue.

"What do you mean she's gone? It's not Blake, is it?"

"No. Charlotte left the morning of the attack. Brother Horace was kind enough to send word. Charlotte married Brother Julian and went away with him."

"Brother Julian!" Christopher slammed his mug against the tabletop, spilling a few drops of wine, but the force of his anger was weaker than he had expected. I'm too damned tired, he realized. "How could you let her do a stupid thing like that?"

"It wasn't in my power, Christopher. Or yours either, I'm afraid. I wish she'd talked to me."

"I can have it annulled. As soon as this mess with Blake is settled, that'll be next. I'm sure Horace will be agreeable."

"Brother Horace performed the ceremony. That's how he knew."

"Then Horace is a damned fool."

"No, I don't think so," she said sharply. "I think Horace merely recognized the inevitable. You ought to do the same, Christopher. They're married. They could be happy."

"Happy?" He laughed. "With a monk? With tattered sandals and moth-eaten burlap? I could have found Charlotte a husband second to none."

"I think she thought she'd already found that—without your help. Charlotte was—is—she's a very strange girl."

"Too strange for me. Is that what you mean?"

"I think you're tired." Sarah crossed the room and laid her hands, palms down, on top of his head. The gesture carried a familiar intimacy. When he was young—very young—Sarah had often touched him in this fashion; it had been her way of easing the strain that went with being six years old. "Why don't you go to bed? Sleep is something we all could need. Adrienne told me she'd wait for you."

"In a minute." He sat where he was, feeling her touch, letting the tension flow away. "I know I shouldn't have gotten angry. About Charlotte. It's just that, since we got back, there've been so damn many shocks to bear."

"Too many. Sometimes I get afraid."

"Of what? Of Blake?"

"No, not really. Blake is an aberration, a freak, and when he dies, everything he's done will die with him. It's not him I worry about. It's the way the whole world seems to be going. It's changing, Christopher, everything is, and that's something you ought to understand even better than I, because you're part of that change. It's frightening. Scary. Change is something we haven't experienced in a long, long time. Your father saw it coming. I believe it's here now. And you—you and Ned and Charlotte—will have to live with it."

She removed her hands from the top of his head and, bending quickly down, kissed him. Then, the soft fabric of her gown rustling gently, she left the room.

Adjusting his bulk in the chair he occupied, Jeffrey Lacy gazed at the handwritten page in the book spread open on the table and, moving the pen in his hand, dotted an *i* and crossed a *t*. Then he sat back and rubbed his eyes. Well, that seemed to do it. He reread the page a final time and, satisfied, dropped the pen. He was having trouble seeing clearly. That was just age, he decided. Age and a certain degree of deserved fatigue. Well, I am an old man, he thought. With advancing age, the eyes always went first—the eyes and the teeth. It didn't matter what he'd written. In his youth, Lacy had composed several other books—philosophical tomes— but the warm glow he remembered experiencing upon completing one of those was not echoed now. Those books had been written to be read; nobody would ever see a word of this one. It was a private work—a diary—his secret confessional. Begun nearly twenty years ago, the book was now finished: tonight's entry would be the last. He had chosen a title: *My Search for Stoner*. He liked that. Warm. Simple. Accurate. Evocative.

Pushing the book aside, Lacy extracted a clean sheet of paper from the desk drawer and picked up the pen again. *Dear Christopher*, he wrote. The message was deliberately terse, formal. In less than five minutes, he was done.

Then he stood. Crossing the room, he went to the door, opened it, and peered out at the night. Below, a large bonfire burned, tall flames climbing toward the sky. Lacy called to one of several dark shapes huddled near the fire. "Brother Timothy, may I see you for a moment?"

He waited until one of the shapes dislodged itself from the others, then went back inside. He poured a glass of wine and drank deeply. Footsteps sounded on the stairs outside.

Brother Timothy entered the room. He was a young man, stockily built, with black smoldering eyes. He stood hesitantly in the doorway. "Do you require my assistance, sir?"

"In two matters," said Lacy. He beckoned Timothy into the room. "I have a message I want you to deliver."

"Now, sir?"

Lacy shook his head. "Dawn will be soon enough. You can leave then. The message is for Christopher Janson. Be sure you deliver it personally into his hands. I don't want anyone else to see this." He folded the message neatly in half, concealing the written side, and handed it to Timothy.

"You said two things, sir."

"I want you to saddle me a horse."

"For morning?"

"For now."

"It's very late, sir. May I ask where you're going?"

"You may ask—" Lacy poured another glass of wine "—and

I guess it won't hurt to answer. I'm going over to Blake's camp. I'm going to convince him to let Brother Horace come home."

Brother Timothy appeared worried. "Couldn't you wait until morning, sir?"

Lacy drank. "Why? Don't you want Horace back?"

"We all fear for his safety, sir. It's just that—well, certain disturbing reports have been received."

"About Blake's men?"

Timothy nodded. "Yes, sir. It seems they're marauding, sir. Mr. Blake may not have brought sufficient supplies from County Tumas for such an extended stay. A farmhouse was raided tonight. Food stolen. A young girl was disturbed . . . molested."

"I was afraid of that," Lacy admitted. "It's my own fault. I wanted to wait until Christopher's return. I shouldn't have delayed this long."

"Delayed what, sir?"

"Putting an end to this." Lacy let the sentence hang without explanation. "You needn't worry. I'll take care of everything now."

"I only spoke so that you could take care. We monks have deeply appreciated your help these past few days. Without your guidance, we might not have—"

"Hey," said Lacy. "Don't talk as if you don't expect me to come back alive. I intend to be here snug in my bed long before you stir in the morning."

"I'm pleased to hear that, sir."

"Now go and get me that horse. I don't think it's fair to keep Mr. Blake waiting any longer."

"You can have my own mount, sir. It's the best horse in the corral."

"Fine, Brother Timothy, fine." Lacy ushered the young monk to the door and guided him out. And I'm a goddamned liar, he thought, turning back.

He drained the last of his wine. Well, now what? he thought, gazing wistfully around the room. More wine? He shook his head. It wasn't wine that he really craved. It was a smoke. He'd used up his last cigar the day before yesterday, and naturally none could be found on the monastery grounds. Well, perhaps Blake would turn out to have one to spare. If so, that would be damned near perfect. Lacy very much wanted to experience the thick acrid taste of good tobacco one more time before he died.

Restless, he picked the lantern off the table and went into the rear bedroom. He found what he was looking for on top of a small bedside table. He didn't need to glance at the titles to know what these books were. *The Holy Bible* and *The Book of Stones*. What else would Brother Horace keep beside his bed for late night reading? Lacy gripped one book in one hand and the other in another. Odd. With his eyes shut, he could not tell them apart. Both were similarly bound; both weighed approximately the same.

He replaced the books, turned, retrieved the lantern, and went out. He had no need to read from either book. If I haven't discovered the secrets of life by now, he thought, I'm never going to, and no book, not even one of those two, is apt to help me.

Carrying the diary, he went outside and waited beside the fire for Brother Timothy to bring the horse. A few monks and nuns— young ones mostly—knelt in a circle around flames. Lacy warmed his hands. He heard the patter of approaching hooves. A hand touched his shoulder. It was Timothy. "I've brought your horse, sir."

"Fine. I'll just be a moment." Lacy stared at the fire. He was playing a game, one he vividly recalled from his own youth. The purpose of the game was simple: among the flux of the flames, find the shapes—people, faces, objects, things. He remembered how once—he must have been about ten years old—he had glimpsed in the flames the wrinkled face of a very old man and boldly announced to all who would listen that that face was his own grown old. Well, it hadn't been. He could picture that face even now, and in no way did it resemble his own.

Carelessly, he threw the diary into the fire. The book landed squarely on top of a burning log and dropped into the bed of hot embers below. Lacy watched it burn. The cloth cover peeled back to reveal the scribbled pages underneath. *My Search for Stoner* he thought. Twenty years of work. Well, it was finished now. I've found him, thought Lacy.

Inside his tent on the dirt floor, Sheridan Blake sat curled in the folds of a blanket and softly cursed the good fortune of those men, his own loyal peasants, who outside the range of his vision—

if not his hearing—sat warm and laughing around the big fire. Bastards, he thought bitterly, shivering with cold. No wonder they laughed. Warm and secure. Well cared for. Free of worry. What can they know of a life such as mine burdened by a thousand conflicting anxieties? The men had been drinking, too. He could tell by the shrill tone of their laughter. Undoubtedly, Lindstrom had managed to acquire more wine from somewhere. Probably stolen it—looted it. Blake knew he ought to reprimand the man. Drunken troops—especially ones who were also hungry—presented a risk in any alien land. The trouble was, Blake didn't have the goddamned strength to move. He was weary, cold, beaten. It was Horace's fault. The old monk was lying, and Blake knew it, but what the hell could he do? Even now, as he sat huddled here, he could see Horace's grinning, lying face looming before him like a skull from hell. No, he was wrong. As he stared, the looming face altered shape. It wasn't Horace, after all—it was Lacy. Damn him, too. An old enemy after petty revenge. Well, he'd show them. Blake was determined. He'd discover the whereabouts of the missing books and leave this county with them in his possession, an act of total and final triumph. That would show Brother Horace; that would show Jeffrey Lacy.

Sure, it would—yes—but how?

That was what bothered him. Before he could take the books, he had to know where they were hidden. Horace knew, but Horace would not speak. Lacy knew, but Lacy could not be found. Why had Horace entrusted the library into Lacy's care in the first place? That disturbed Blake. He remembered screaming at Horace during their first interrogation session: *Lacy! Why Lacy? How can you trust a man who doesn't even believe in your own stupid god?*

"Because he showed me something," Horace had replied, with the same stoic acceptance he had displayed throughout the interview.

"Showed you what, you old fool?" Blake cried.

"Showed me truth," Horace answered softly.

Truth? Blake laughed aloud, wanting to spit. Truth? Now what in hell was that supposed to mean? The only truth Blake recognized was what he could experience with his own five good senses. He was damned cold right this minute—that was truth. And he was stymied, the bastards had him beaten, trapped like a mouse in a

flooded basement. That was truth, too. He had been camped here
six days. Little food remained, barely enough fodder for the
horses. Other than this tent and one other—where Horace slept—
there was no shelter from the cold nights. How much longer can
I endure? Blake wondered. One more day? Two at the most?
Maybe Lindstrom was right. Maybe they ought to torture Horace—
stick his fingers in the fire—force him to speak. Blake shook his
head wearily. Hell, Horace might welcome such a chance at mar-
tyrdom. No, it was useless, pointless. The trouble with Horace
was that he failed to recognize the limitations of truth. He insisted
upon believing in an abstraction as insubstantial as a god.

The tent flaps fell back suddenly and a man stepped through.
Momentarily startled, Blake sprang to his feet, but it was only
Dav Lindstrom.

He was grinning. "Something wrong, Mr. Blake? Did I scare
you?"

Blake controlled his fury. "I left strict word not to be disturbed."

"There's a visitor I thought you might like to see."

"Who? Christopher Janson?" Lindstrom's breath reeked of
wine. Blake took a step backward. "If it is, send him away."

"Janson's home—or so I understand—but this isn't him. It's
Lacy. Jeffrey Lacy."

"Good Christ! Why didn't you tell me sooner?" Blake rushed
past Lindstrom and peered through the tent flaps. The fire was a
huge thing, and various shapes moved around it. One might have
been Lacy. He turned to Lindstrom. "If you have him, bring him
here. Don't you understand this is what we've been waiting for?
Lacy knows where the books are hidden."

"So does the old monk. I haven't noticed him giving us much
help."

"Forget about that fool." Blake clenched and unclenched his
fists. "If I want your opinion, I'll request it. Bring Lacy here."

"Of course, sir." Lindstrom bowed with exaggerated stiffness
and backed out.

Blake refused to let Lindstrom's insolence modify his own
growing sense of excitement. He grinned. That goddamned
Lacy—caught at last. This might be it—finally. Blake paced up
and down within the constrictive boundaries of the tent. When the

flaps again opened, two men stepped through. The first was Lindstrom. Lacy followed.

His face was a blank, cool mask. "Well, Sheridan, I understand
you've been wanting to talk to me and so—" He broke off suddenly
and his expression became reflective. "Say, you wouldn't happen
to have a cigar, would you?"

Blake shook his head. "I don't smoke."

"And your men? Your troops?"

"A peasant can hardly afford such delicacies," Blake said, his
voice taut. He could feel the anger growing within him.

"True enough." Lacy dropped to the floor. "But a damn pity
nonetheless."

"I didn't have you brought here to discuss your personal
habits," Blake said tightly. "Where have you been? My men were
ordered to comb every square inch of the county."

"And I'm sure they did. Unfortunately for you, I managed to
figure out one safe place and have been holed up there. After what
you'd done to the monastery, I doubted you'd be too eager to
come poking around the ruins."

"Are you trying to say you came here voluntarily?"

"I did indeed. Ask your lieutenant here. It's my understanding
you're interested in locating certain missing books. I'm ready and
eager to show you where they are."

Blake glanced at Lindstrom, who shrugged his shoulders. "It's
true. He rode into camp on a horse as big as life."

"Then get out of here. Your presence is no longer required.
I'll interrogate this man personally."

"As you wish, sir." Lindstrom started to back out. With a hand
on the tent flaps, he paused. "Just remember: none of us can eat
books."

"Bastard," said Blake, when he and Lacy were alone.

"What's the problem?" Lacy said, with a show of concern.
"Don't the troops appreciate all you've done to set them free?"

"Spare me your mockery." Blake knelt on the floor beside
Lacy. No longer cold, he let the blanket fall in a heap beside him.
"You and Horace tricked me. I have no idea how you learned of
my intentions, but I'm stymied, and I admit that. Without the
books, my entire plan of attack is rendered useless. So where do
we go from here?"

"First I want to know about Brother Horace." Lacy appeared calm. His gaze was direct. "Have you harmed him?"

"Of course not. Do you think I'm a savage? Horace is perfectly fine."

"Then release him. He can take my horse and ride back to the monastery."

Blake's eyes narrowed. "Naturally, I'll expect something in return."

"And you'll get it." Lacy smiled thinly. "Let Horace go and I'll take you to the missing library."

Blake hesitated. "You're lying, of course."

"If I am, what do you have to lose? Let Horace go, and you've still got me. I know as much as he does."

"Horace is an old man. He might prove to be more susceptible to persuasion."

"Horace will never tell you a damned thing, and you know it." Lacy leaned back on his heels. "The decision is yours to make."

"And you promise to turn the library over to me?"

"I promise to show you where it is, yes."

"On your word of honor?"

"On my word of honor."

Blake considered briefly. Then he stood and went out. Lindstrom sat among the men around the fire. Blake told him to release Brother Horace. Lindstrom said nothing. He crossed to the other tent and reappeared momentarily, accompanied by the old monk.

"Give him the horse Lacy brought," Blake called across the clearing. "Send him back to the monastery."

Blake waited until Horace had ridden away, then returned to his own tent.

Lacy did not appear to have moved. "He's gone," Blake said.

"Fine."

"Don't you want to check?"

"No, I believe you." Lacy stood up. "Shall we go, then?"

Blake could not conceal his surprise. "To the library? Now?"

"That was our deal. You released Horace and now it's my turn."

Blake was suddenly skeptical. "Since you know where the books are hidden, why don't you just tell me? I'm sure I'll be able to locate the correct spot."

Lacy shook his head. "And I'm sure you won't. No, Blake. It's either my way or no way. I trusted you about Horace. Now trust me."

Blake had never trusted a man in his life. It was damned difficult to begin now. He was aware this might well be a trap, a way of luring him forth to meet his own death. Still, he was armed. He could feel the comforting weight of the gun in his waistband. "If anything happens to me, if you have friends waiting out there, I'll shoot you first, Lacy. I swear it. You'll be dead before anyone lays a hand on me."

"Fair enough." Lacy stepped toward the exit. Past a shoulder, he said, "It's still a pity you don't have a cigar."

Blake let him leave, then followed. Waiting for horses beside the fire with his own men listening, Blake said, "I still don't trust you. If you'd only waited, stayed hidden a few more days, I'd have had to leave the county. You would have won."

"Yes," Lacy agreed, "but for how long? You would have come back, Blake. I know that, and you know that. There are two kinds of people—those who give up and those who don't."

"And I don't give up?" Blake asked.

"I'm doing this," Lacy said, "because I don't have a single goddamned choice. But I do wish I had a cigar," he added, in a slightly softer tone.

Dav Lindstrom glared at the shadowy figures of the two riders as they slipped into the night, then turned and spat into the fire. Books, he thought bitterly. Goddamned books. That was all Blake worried about, and yet there wasn't a man in this camp—excepting Blake himself—who could read one word. Books? Lindstrom looked at the men seated with him around the fire. He counted heads. Twenty-five, thirty, thirty-five. That was all that remained. And where the hell were the others? Lindstrom could only guess. Out in the county. Stealing, looting, pillaging, doing what hungry armies had always done. And what did Blake care about it? The fool, excited by whatever lies that sly bastard Lacy had cooked up about the precious books, hadn't even noticed that more than half his army had vanished. What did Blake know about how the men felt? They were lonely, tired, bored, cold, hungry, but above all they were sickened to death by what Blake had forced them to do at the monastery. Lindstrom knew how they felt. Lindstrom knew there wasn't a man alive who'd stayed that way by feeding his belly with pieces of paper out of books.

He stood and moved slightly apart from the others. It was a considerate act. He knew the men preferred it that way. He was one of them—a peasant born and bred—but he was Blake's lieutenant, too. In the mill, where he served as foreman, things were different. The men respected him there, his knowledge of the smelting process, his sense of what was safe and right and proper in a dangerous job. This wasn't the mill. He was no soldier. And the men were scared. Not a one of them had ever before journeyed more than ten miles from the place of his birth. Lindstrom was scared, too. At the first sign of any weakness on his part, he knew the men would turn on him like wolves and tear the flesh from his bones.

Lindstrom would never forget the sound of that first damned shot. It was a mistake—no order had been given—but the men had reacted as if something had snapped inside them all at once. It was bloodlust—like a dog catching the scent of a terrified rabbit. Back home, Blake had vowed it would all be easy. Six days march. Surround the monastery. Attack at dawn. No practical resistance. A few monks, a few nuns. And then that first unexpected shot had blown up in their faces.

Or was it just that? Maybe, as the oracles insisted, events were predestined. Everyone denied shooting first. A nervous mistake. Finger clenched too tight on the trigger. No one really to blame. But then what? Then everyone else had started firing, too. Including Lindstrom. Firing wildly. Killing. Maiming. He, himself, had called for the cannon. Why? Lindstrom knew he had never wanted to harm anyone. The carnage—once he could recognize it—had sickened him. But he had done it—fired his gun—murdered innocent men and women. Even the monks—the most passive of human beings—had not been immune to the disease of bloodlust. Lindstrom remembered one of them racing toward him kitchen knife in hand, the blade already dripping with blood, and the blank look in the man's eyes the instant before Lindstrom had shot him down was worse than anything he expected to see this side of the gates of hell.

No. It wasn't worth thinking about. Wasn't worth remember

ing. Lindstrom sat on the ground beside Blake's tent and stretched
out his legs. He could still feel the lulling heat of the fire. His
eyes were heavy. He shut them. The monk's face. Red heat. Red
knife. Blood. Fire. Flame. Sleep. Yes, he would do that. He
would sleep until dawn. Perhaps by then Blake would return with
the books and they could leave this county—and its ugly waking
dreams—forever.

It was odd. Bill Walker was a blind man, and yet he swore
he could see with more clarity than ever.
As he walked:
A tree blocked his path.
(He stepped around it.)
A narrow creek bubbled in front of him.
(He sprang across it.)
A fallen branch lay upon the trail.
(He went over it.)
A snake crawled through the grass.
(He moved warily.)
The gods cried out.
(He cried back.)
Blind—yes—eyes burned—sightless sockets in a black man's
head. Yet he walked. For hours. Days. Nights. With confidence,
Bill Walker roamed the woods. Crazy, some might say. A blind
man gone mad. Bill knew better. Not crazy: sane. Not blind:
seeing. Like his own mother, whom he had despised. Her powers
were his now. The gods appeared before him and spoke. Bill
spoke too.
He fell to his knees.
Shedi, Goddess of the Woodlands, materialized before him,
floating with neither shape nor substance, formless, unbounded.
Bill slammed his head against the hard ground. *Shedi, I do
our bidding*, he cried without speaking.
Go, she said.
Where?
Everywhere.
Why?
To speak.
Prophesy?

Yes.
I can't.
You can. Try.
He tried: *The red black blue smoke consumes entrails—*
To them!
Yes!
From the seeing—
Yes!
—to the sightless.
Yes! (He laughed.)
Do you love God?
I do.
Then go.

Bill went. He ran. Like one of the great oceans, the forest swirled deep and black around him. And green. He smelled the color. On his knees, he crawled. On his heels, he ran.

From the sky, rain began to fall.

Bill stopped. Tossing his head, he let the sweet lonely raindrops splash upon his face. He removed his clothing, lay naked on his back, and opened his mouth hungrily. I have erred, he thought calmly. I am not one with the gods. I am the gods.

Standing, he ran again. It was odd. Keenly aware of his own blindness, thoroughly convinced that he no longer saw as most men did, Bill could not recall how this had come to be; he remembered only the fire.

Yet where was it? And when? And how?

Was it, perhaps, hell?

He considered the possibility. In hell, he knew, there was constant unrelenting fire. Had he been struck blind there? Bill shook his head at last. No. Hell—even the monks agreed—was the proper abode of the dead. And Bill was not dead. Blind, yes. Alive, yes. A dead man did not sip the falling rain.

Thin fingers brushed his arm. A soft, old man's voice spoke: "Child, where do you come from? Where are you going?"

A young woman whispered: "I think he's blind, Father."

"Do you know him?"

"Not unless . . ."

The old man gripped his arm. "Are you lost? Can we help you?"

"I don't think he's eaten in days," said the woman. "And his feet are like open sores."

"He's covered in mud."

"If we don't help him, he's apt to die."

Fingers tightened. "Child, won't you come home with us?"

Bill laughed.

"Come and we'll—"

Bill screamed.

They vanished—old man and daughter—as swiftly as they had come.

Bill ran on.

Ninety-nine days of destruction. On the forty-ninth midnight, the gods awaken. The eighteen days of material destruction. Bill possessed some familiarity with the Cult of Numerals practiced by certain elders. Time meant nothing to him. Blindness had freed him from the curse of the sun's agonized journey through the sky. Bill licked his own flesh. He nibbled the skin of one arm and bit deeply into a thigh, drawing blood. He was content, fine, not hungry. He thought of the thirteen cycles of death and life. He thought of nothing. Shedi materialized and spoke glowingly of his gift. He bowed.

Ahead, voices.

Crouching, Bill paused. Then, cautiously, he crept through the tall grass.

Tense voices. Many men. One woman. Emotions ran high. He could smell the fear—and lust!

An explosion tore at the earth. An explosion like the one that had blinded him that dreadful day. Motorcar . . . Ned Janson . . . monastery . . . explosion . . . cannon . . . his eyes . . . his eyes . . .

He bit his lip to keep from screaming as the terrible flood of remembrance swept over him.

Then the woman did scream.

Bill remembered now. Blake's men. Blake had blinded him.

Voices: "Grab her! Hold her! Don't let her get away!"

With fingers caked by blood and dirt, Bill touched the sightless orbs of his eyes. The bandage he had once worn had long since disappeared, and his eyes were wide open, naked to the wind. Bill touched the sores and then, gradually, inserted a finger from each hand deep inside the gaping sockets.

The pain rushed over him like a cleansing bath. He whimpered, blood in his mouth, but never screamed.

Then, his ordeal accomplished, Bill sprang. Swinging his arms like clubs, he charged among the men, driving them back. Bill laughed gleefully. A rock leaped into his hands. He hurled it forward. Blood flowed. Not his own. He knew the scent keenly. Bill was killing these men—these men who had blinded him—killing them one by one with the fury of his own forever dead eyes.

"Hurry," murmured Charlotte Chambers, speaking as much for her own benefit as that of her husband, Julian. "Please try to hurry."

"I'm doing the best I can," he said tightly. "The horse is tired. If I push him much farther, he'll collapse."

"I think it's too late already."

"Should we turn back?"

"No."

"But if it's already—"

"Don't you understand anything?" she cried.

Her contempt hurt him. "You were the one who said it was too late."

"Yes, but I saw it." She gripped his sleeve. "I saw Ned lying in the dirt. Don't you understand that? I just can't ignore it. I have to go to him now."

"But why, if—"

"He's my brother."

"But what if you're wrong?"

She laughed. "Wrong?"

"It's possible, isn't it?" He went on doggedly in the face of her ridicule. "You can't be sure, can you? What if nothing happened? What if we get back there and find everything just as it was, except that now Christopher's home? What are we going to do then? Tell me that."

She answered patiently. "My voices spoke to me. How can I ignore them?"

"Try plugging your ears."

"You told me you believed."

"I do, but . . ."

"Then hurry, damn it. That's all you have to do. Just hurry."

It was several days before. The voices had not reached her until the cart was only a few miles from the home of Julian's brother. Early morning. Broad daylight. Perhaps, because she had seldom slept at night, the voices had failed to speak to her before.

Go back, they said insistently.

"What?" Charlotte spoke aloud, twisting her head.

"I didn't say anything," said Julian.

"No, not you. Hush, Julian."

A fire at the monastery.

"Oh."

And death.

"Oh, no."

Murder.

"No!"

He stopped the horse and turned to stare at her. "Charlotte, what are you doing? Who are you talking to?"

Your brother bleeds.

"Not Christopher, not—"

Ned.

"Oh, God, how could—"

Go back.

"I can't. They'll—"

Go.

And then she had witnessed the vision. At first the scene had failed to coalesce, reminding her strangely of the line drawings in an old Bible she had once seen, depictions of the sufferings of the eternally damned. Then she had recognized the spire. The chapel. The monastery. The buildings were . . . terribly wounded. Walls shattered. Roofs torn. Many fires were burning. Then, in the center of this horror, she had seen the wreck of the motorcar. Ned's car. Then Ned himself. He lay sprawled in the midst of hell, his naked legs protruding from his body like charred blackened logs.

Charlotte leaned her head out over the cart and vomited.

Later, as soon as she could, she explained her vision to Julian. He turned the cart around and commenced the long return journey to County Kaine.

Even then, Charlotte had been aware that it was already too

late. Her vision had shown the past, not the future. The voices had spoken too late.

Julian pointed at the darkness in front of them. "I don't think we can be too far away now. See that dark shape past the top of the trees? I think that's the big hill in front of the monastery. If you want, we could be there in twenty minutes."

Charlotte shook her head. "I want to go to the house first."

"If Christopher's there—"

"Oh, damn Christopher!" In her anger, she heard herself shouting, sick of her husband's fear. "We're married, aren't we? What can Christopher do to alter that? I'm your wife, Julian."

"I know that, but if we have nothing to fear, then why didn't we just stay here?"

"Because I didn't want—" She stopped, lifting her nose to the air. "Smell that."

He sniffed tentatively. "Smell what?"

"I smell death."

"Oh, Charlotte, don't talk that way. You know it—"

"It's true. I can smell it. Death is everywhere. Death is—"

Harsh yellow light flared out of the darkness. Struck momentarily blind, Charlotte threw up her hands. The horse stopped. Squinting, Charlotte could see the dark oval skull of a peasant. The man was holding the horse by its neck. Other men came forward—peasants also. One held the torch which had blinded her.

Julian stood up awkwardly in the cart. "Who are you men? What do you want here?"

"Why, we live here, friend," said the one with the torch. Others continued to emerge from the forest. There were nine altogether—ten.

"I don't know you," Julian said.

"And we don't know you, either. All we want is to borrow your horse and cart."

"Get your hands away from there. I—I'm a monk. This is Christopher Janson's sister. She—"

One of the men, one of the last to arrive, a peasant so dark that his teeth shone in his face, reached calmly into his trousers and drew out a slim metallic object. A sharp explosion burst from his hand, and there was a brief flash of fire. Julian cried out clasped his chest, and toppled backward. Charlotte caught him. Blood spread across his shirt. She smelled death.

It was Julian's death.

She screamed.

"Grab her! Hold her! Don't let her get away!"

Charlotte wasn't moving. She clasped Julian in her arms and rocked him like a baby. Hands fell upon her, tearing her gown. She felt, knew, cared nothing. The voices were back, whispering in her mind.

PART 7

The Wise Man

Once during recent years, a man of considerable wisdom came to visit me. He was a young man, surely no more than thirty, who preferred to keep his name and home a private matter.

The young man asked many questions. Since the majority of these possessed considerable penetration, I soon relaxed in his presence, expounding my theories of life and society.

Eventually, as morning dawned, spent with fatigue, I asked to be released from the interview.

The young man held up a single finger. "Please, sir," he said. "One more question, and then I can depart contented."

Though weary, I could not refuse. "Proceed."

"Sir," he said, "how can you be sure that you are not mistaken?"

The question was one no one had asked me before. For a moment, startled, I could not speak. Yet his question was a serious one and deserved a dignified response. "Because of the pattern I have formed," I answered at last. "Because my philosophy, like a puzzle, is composed of separate

181

pieces which, when fitted together, form a sensible whole."

"But wouldn't these same pieces, if reversed, if turned on their backs, also form a whole?"

"I'm afraid I do not . . ."

He held up a finger. "The one factor I fear you neglect, learned sir, is the human one. During my meager worldly experience, I have developed but one hypothesis: that men, acting as a group, will invariably perform any given function in the exact opposite manner anticipated. Because of this hypothesis, I find it difficult not to conceive of your philosophy in its opposite form. That is, while everything you have told me today is true, it is also—simultaneously—false."

In my wounded pride, I attempted to refute the young man's statements.

He heard me out in dignified silence, then bowed and departed.

I have neither seen nor heard of the man since. Nor have I been able to prove him wrong.

> William Stoner, The Book
> Stones, circa 2045.

One of the more amazing aspects of Great Dar Age Stonerist society was the rapidity with which fell apart, the unexpected fragility of the binding threads.

To somebody living in the midst of such a society, it must have looked pretty stable. Hey, th is a perfect world and it's going to last forever.

Sure. Why not? Hadn't Stoner, in his infinite wisdom, covered all the angles? Doubt was vanished; improvisation tossed overboard.

So how come it all came tumbling down?

One way to understand is to envision Stoneri society as a big glass palace, perfect in form. Sta inside or outside the palace and no flaw can be detected. It's magnificent, grandiose, and whole.

But strike it with a hammer.

Any place you choose. One firm whap and— Crack!

The glass shatters. The palace falls. All you're left with is so many billion sharp splinters.

That's how it was with Stonerism.

For two hundred years, it shimmered in the
sun. Then came the hammer.
Whap.

> *Daniel T. Janson,* A
> History of Human Events
> Subsequent to Stoner's
> Time, 2378.

Jeffrey Lacy held up a hand, signaling to Sheridan Blake, who
rode a few yards behind, that they had reached their destination.
"Pull up," he called. "This is the place."

Dismounting beside Lacy, Blake showed his anger. "You
damned liar. What kind of fool do you take me for? This isn't
anything."

"I'm afraid it is, Sheridan." Lacy nodded at the sloping rocky
cliff that climbed to their right. "There's a cave over there. The
locals call it the diamond mine."

"Don't you think I'm aware of the place? My men searched
it a dozen times over."

"Well, they didn't search deeply enough. Come on. Let's get
this started."

Blake followed reluctantly. "If you're lying, if this is some
stupid trick . . ."

"Then it's as much a waste of my time as yours." The moonlight
showed the narrow slit of the cave mouth. Lacy squatted on his
heels, turned sideways, and managed to squirm through the gap.
Without waiting for Blake to follow, he stood up. The cave was
much broader inside, and the roof stood a full ten feet from the
floor. Lacy edged over to the right wall and placed one hand,
palm open, upon the surface. Then he moved forward, feeling his
way along the wall. Glancing back, he saw Blake apparently
trapped half in and half out of the cave. Lacy said, "Can you
make it?"

"I hope so." Blake gave a loud grunt and the rest of his body
popped through. "Damn you, Lacy. This had better be good."

"Trust me, Sheridan." He continued to move. .

"I should have brought a lantern."

"We won't need it if—" Lacy stopped. "Here, I think this is

it." There was a smooth place on the wall, a slight indentation perhaps six inches square.

"This is what?" Blake moved in close. "I can't see anything."

"You're not supposed to." Lacy balled his hand into a fist and struck the smooth place a solid blow. He counted to ten, drew back his hand, struck again. Another ten count. A third blow.

The wall slid back in a dazzling burst of white light.

Blake cried out in surprise and threw a hand in front of his eyes. "What in God's name—"

"It's not Him," Lacy said. "It's merely an elevator."

"My men never reported this."

"Nor should they have been expected to. When I first came here, it took me months to find the secret. And I had a fair idea of what I was looking for."

"What?"

"You'll see." Lacy marched straight ahead into the white-walled cage of the elevator. As always, the dull thud of metal underfoot was like an echo from the past. "Coming?" he asked Blake.

"The books are . . . there?"

Lacy pointed to the floor. "Down below."

Blake nodded. With an obvious effort of will, he strode forward.

Reaching out, Lacy touched the heat sensitive button that controlled the elevator. As soon as he did, the doors slid silently shut.

Then the elevator fell.

"It's a long way down," Lacy explained calmly, as the elevator descended. "Half-a-mile, I'd estimate."

Blake was holding his stomach. "I assume this damned thing knows when to stop."

"It has so far." Lacy stroked the nearest wall in a show of apparent tenderness. "This is a damned smart elevator."

The machine slowed gradually. It came to a final smooth stop and the doors opened.

"Well, here we are," said Lacy, stepping forward and spreading his arms. "What do you think?" He turned in time to observe a marvelous succession of shifting expressions crossing Blake's face. First there was shock, then dismay, then amazement, then wonder, then awe, then delight. The delight dawned when Blake spotted several neat piles of books and papers stacked in one corner of the room.

"The library," he said, pushing past Lacy and racing eagerly across the room. When he reached the nearest pile, Blake scooped up a book in each hand and gazed at the others with the eyes of a famished man confronted by an array of choice delicacies.

"Now see?" said Lacy, sauntering across to join Blake. "I told you they were here, didn't I?"

Blake seemed too excited to speak. With a shrug, Lacy turned away. There was only this one room—a huge cavern, the ceiling a full thirty feet distant. Lacy sat down in a padded swivel chair set in the concrete floor near the center of the room. He had visited this place on many occasions during the past. According to his research, at least three more levels existed below this one, but he had never been able to discover a means for reaching them, and additional exploration no longer seemed very important. Besides his own chair, several others stood scattered around the room along with three conference tables. A large number of gray metal filing cabinets—all securely locked, he had learned—leaned against the wall to his left, while the right wall, apparently blank, was actually a map of the world ready to be revealed at the touch of the proper button. The remaining wall, the one opposite the elevator, was a network of shifting, winking, flashing colored lights. These, Lacy knew, represented the visible face of the giant computer. Blake had not yet noticed its presence in the room.

Lacy crossed his legs and folded his arms and spoke conversationally: "Find anything interesting yet?"

Blake sat cross-legged on the floor, a book open in his lap. He looked up. "What did you say?"

"I asked if you'd found what you were looking for."

"No." Blake closed the book. "But I will. It's here—it's all here—everything I've wanted in my life. With these books, I can continue the work of turning County Tumas into a showplace for all mankind. Do you know what I think I'll do, Lacy? I'm going to build a building. A big one. Like the ones in Capital—but even bigger. I want to build a building so tall that on a cloudy day you won't be able to see the top. And I can do it, too. With these books, I can—" He stopped, his expression frozen. Lacy followed the line of his gaze. Blake had finally spotted the computer. He stood slowly. "What in hell is that?"

"A computer," Lacy said easily.

Blake shook his head. "You're lying. A computer is a gigantic electronic thinking machine. The last ones perished during the collapse."

"All except one." Lacy jerked his head. "That one. Sheridan Blake, meet DKM-4003."

"You don't mean to claim it's still functioning?"

"As well as ever, if not better. DKM-4003, like you and me, gets smarter as he gets older, and he was pretty wise to begin with. In the early twenty-first century, when he was built, DKM-4003 was regarded as the most sophisticated computer yet developed. He possessed immediate access to ninety-nine percent of the world's public and private stored data."

"But why is it here? Why is it buried underground?"

Lacy stood up and beckoned Blake to join him. "Let's ask him a question," he said. "Any question you want." He stopped in front of the network of flashing lights. "Go ahead—he's friendly."

Blake frowned suspiciously. "I didn't come here to play games with a machine."

"These aren't games." Lacy put an arm around Blake's shoulders and drew him closer to the flashing lights. "Ask him to describe the mode for a perfect society. Now that's not a game, is it?"

Blake shook his head. Curiosity and interest had displaced his past suspicion. "How do I go about asking that?"

"Just say the words. Preface your question—and be sure that it's a question—with the machine's name. Just say DKM-4003. That's the key."

"And how will it reply?"

"It will. Go ahead."

In a firm clear voice, glancing at Lacy as he spoke, Blake said, "DKM-4003, what is the mode for a perfect society?"

The voice replied almost the instant Blake finished. The flat dead tones seemed to emanate from all the walls of the room at once. "Order and diligence are the correct modes for the proper and perfect society."

Blake grinned nervously. "If that was it, the damned thing sounds like Stoner."

"It is," said Lacy calmly.

"What?" Blake stared.

"DKM-4003 and William Stoner are one and the same creature."

For a long moment, Blake's jaw hung slack. Then he showed anger. "Don't take me for a fool. Stoner was a man who died two centuries ago."

"That, unfortunately, is not true."

"Prove it."

"Prove it yourself." Lacy pointed to the wall of lights. "Ask him."

"This is absurd."

"Then I'll ask him for you." Lacy turned slightly and raised his voice. "DKM-4003, what is the exact identity of the entity commonly known as William Stoner?"

"The exact identity of William Stoner," said the voice of the computer, "is that of a construct of various related data."

Blake laughed. "See? The thing's making no sense."

"DKM-4003," Lacy went on stubbornly, "how did *The Book of Stones* come to be written?"

"The volume known as *The Book of Stones* was compiled and edited from DKM-4003 printouts numbered 0023574778 through 0023575098 inclusive."

"DKM-4003, who composed these printouts?"

"The computer DKM-4003 created the printouts from various related data sources, as well as through calculation of probable event factors."

"DKM-4003, would it then be correct to say that you—DKM-4003—and William Stoner are actually one and the same person?"

"As far as William Stoner can be said to exist as an independent entity, that is a correct statement."

There was no triumph on Lacy's face when he turned. "Satisfied, Mr. Blake?"

"I . . . I honestly don't know. As far as I'm concerned, the thing still doesn't make good sense."

"Then let me explain more fully. DKM-4003 was originally designed as a weapon of war, programmed to predict trends on the basis of past and present history and thus calculate the probable flow of future events."

"He was an oracle?"

"Very nearly. And a good one, too, apparently. He correctly predicted the coming collapse. Unfortunately, his warnings went unheeded and civilization, as we all know, fell into ruin. During the first years of the collapse, the existence of DKM-4003 was largely forgotten, but he lived on here underground accompanied by those men assigned to care for him. These men were not merely soldiers. Their number included various scientists, philosophers, and historians. They were good and honorable men, deeply disturbed by the pattern of events and their own failure to control what had happened. For that reason, they determined to make an effort to prevent a cataclysm like the collapse from ever occurring again. They set DKM-4003 the task of preparing a treatise explaining in careful detail how to create and maintain a truly stable society. That treatise has come down to us in the form of *The Book of Stones*."

"And how did you happen to stumble upon the truth of all this?" Blake asked.

"It was your fault. You and Talstead and the others who conspired to exile me from Capital. I visited the East. Bored with life, I decided to investigate the various relics that remain back there. I decided to write a book. A biography. The story of the historical William Stoner."

"Are there real libraries still intact in the East?" asked Blake.

"In a manner of speaking, yes. But only because no one is interested in such things. There are no monasteries. No church. Only a few men can read. It's a different world back there, a bizarre and terrible land full of suffering and savagery, where kings are crowned and murdered on the same day and where the word of Stoner has never penetrated. Still, it was there—in the ruins of an underground archive—where I first stumbled upon a description of DKM-4003. Later, I found maps and was able to deduce that the machine's actual location was here in County Kaine. I knew nothing then of its connection with Stoner. In fact, after years of futile searching, I had given up my original idea, for I could find nothing concerning Stoner written down anywhere. So I came back here. I was vaguely aware of the legend that Stoner had lived in County Kaine, but neither that nor the possible discovery of the computer played a major role in my decision to come here to teach. Still, once I was here, curiosity got the better of me. I found this cave. In time I learned the secret of the elevator. I descended and found DKM-4003. I learned to ask him questions. Naturally, I was interested to know what, if anything, he knew of Stoner. So I asked. The answer you now know as well as I."

Blake nodded thoughtfully. "Then you've known this for several years and said nothing."

"Besides you and I, only one other person, Brother Horace, is aware of the truth. DKM-4003 informed me of your impending attack. I, in turn, told Horace. To convince him that I wasn't mad, I brought him here."

"Then Horace could have told me all this."

"Yes, but Horace never would have. Oddly, I think he was almost pleased to find out the real truth about Stoner. Like many devout Christians, he's long had doubts about the divinity of our secular messiah."

"Then this machine must know damn near everything. It makes that library—" he waved a hand vaguely "—seem terribly inconsequential. I wonder, Lacy, if you're fully aware of the significance of this discovery. Do you really know what this means? With the help of this computer, we can begin to rebuild the world."

"I've considered that," Lacy said softly. "In fact, why don't you ask DKM-4003 about it. As a personal question if you want. Something about your own future."

"Mine?"

"If you're curious. I've supplied DKM-4003 with all the facts I know concerning the history of the past two hundred years. As I said, it warned me when to expect your attack upon the monastery. It ought to be able to tell you anything you want to know."

"Well," said Blake. He considered for a moment. "I'm not sure of the exact words to use."

Lacy smiled gently, aware that Blake was still somewhat leery of the computer. "All right, I'll do it for you. DKM-4003, where will Sheridan Blake's career lead if present trends continue?"

DKM-4003 replied instantly: "Sheridan Blake will establish dominion over two-thirds of the North American continent and, through his example, reestablish human technology at the level known prior to the collapse."

"See?" cried Blake in triumph. "It does know. And, with its help, I cannot fail."

Nodding solemnly, Lacy marched forward with sudden swift

determination. He moved past Blake and stood close to the face of the computer. In an even voice, he said, "DKM-4003, begin self-destruct procedures with operational zero established at three minutes from now."

Blake looked confused. "What did you just say? That wasn't a question. You told me it had to be a question."

"That was an order." Lacy turned. "I told him to commit suicide."

Blake showed his horror. "You couldn't—you wouldn't—you—"

Lacy cut him off. "Among the material I originally found in the east was that specific order. It was a classified matter, which means that only a select few were to know about it. In two minutes and some seconds, DKM-4003 is going to blow himself up."

"No!" cried Blake. Without warning, he rushed forward and pushed Lacy aside. "Don't do it! DKM-4003, listen to me! Ignore what that man told you! Do nothing—do nothing at all!"

The face of the computer blinked impassively.

Lacy placed a hand on Blake's shoulder. "Don't waste your breath, Sheridan. There's no way of countermanding that particular order."

Blake spun, springing at Lacy with hands outstretched, but Lacy stepped easily aside. Blake flew past him, landed on his belly on the concrete floor, and slid across the slick surface.

Lacy stood over him. "Spare yourself the effort, Sheridan. In another minute or two, we'll both be dead. Can't you find a happier way of filling your last few seconds?"

"Dead?" Blake looked up, stunned. "Dead? Us?"

"I suspect so. When DKM-4003 goes, he's apt to take most of this rock with him. You and I are damned close to the source, Sheridan. I don't see how we can expect to survive."

Blake's eyes bulged with sudden fear. He began moving his hands in front of him like a swimmer straining to reach a distant shore. Scrambling to his feet, he dashed for the elevator. The doors were already shut, presenting a solid white front. Blake pounded on the wall with his fists.

"Don't bother," said Lacy. "That's part of the standard procedure. The elevator is jammed halfway up the shaft. It's not going to come back."

"Why?" said Blake. His shoulders sagging, he looked like a beaten man. "Why have you done this to me?"

"Because of what DKM-4003 told me—about you—about your future. If you were to live and proceed with your plans, a second and much more terrible collapse would occur within a century."

"You can't stop progress."

"I know that. The world we inhabit today is neither perfect nor eternal. All I want is to give history a chance to unfold in its own naturally cautious manner. It's not that I'm eager to die. Or eager to kill you, either. It just happens to be necessary."

"And the books? The library? The computer?"

"I think it's best for all concerned if they die too."

"Who the hell do you think you are, Lacy? God?"

"No, not me. But not you, either."

Blake slid to the floor. He put his face in hands. "All I wanted—all I ever wanted—was to help my people."

"And you have," Lacy said quietly. "In your own way, you've helped a great many people."

Approximately thirty seconds later, the diamond mine exploded in a blast that could be heard and felt for ten miles around.

Christopher Janson dreamed a dream in which he stood waist deep in a pool of thick mud, and no matter which way he turned, trying to reach the shore, the mud seemed to grow deeper with every step he took.

Christopher wasn't alone. Sheridan Blake stood upon the bank, and every time Christopher tried to take a step, Blake called out tauntingly, saying it was the wrong way, calling him a fool, saying he would smother unless he found the right way to move. In one hand, Blake clutched the end of a long stick, which he would sometimes extend across the pool, right to the tips of Christopher's straining fingers—but never closer. Blake would laugh as Christopher tried to catch the stick. "You need a longer arm," he cried. "You need to grow some more."

Then, suddenly, right in the midst of this tableau, the whole earth gave a giant shake. On the bank, Blake yelped in surprise, dropped his stick and toppled forward. Just as Blake was about to strike headfirst in the muddy pool, Christopher opened his eyes.

Darkness loomed around him.

Still, he recognized the familiar precincts of his own bedroom. Cold fingers clutched his arms. He turned and saw Adrienne in bed beside him. "Did you hear that?" she asked, whispering.

"Hear what?"

"I don't know. Like a giant explosion. The whole house shook."

"An earthquake?"

"No. I've felt them before. This was more . . . more sudden."

Christopher pushed the bedcovers aside and stood up. "Something woke me, too. I was having a dream." He found his clothes on a chair and began to dress.

"Where are you going?" Her voice sounded nervous.

"To Father's den. I think I'll read."

"You could do that here."

"No, you sleep." Dressed, he approached the bed, leaned over, and kissed her lips. "I'll see you at breakfast."

He grabbed a lantern off the bed table, stepped into the corridor, closed the door, and ignited the wick with a match from his pocket. Then he headed toward the den, surrounded by a circle of light. Reaching the end of the hall, he turned left and pushed open the door.

Since Sir Malcolm's death, Christopher had rarely visited the den, even though Mother had made it clear that the room was his to use. Still, he felt like an intruder here—even now, at this particularly lonely time of day. Stepping past three chairs set in a row—one was the chair with the broken spring favored by Sir Malcolm—he crossed to the window, drew back the curtain, and peered out. False dawn could be observed as a streak of gray light in the eastern sky. Turning back, Christopher sat in one of the chairs—not Father's—and folded his hands in his lap.

He had lied to Adrienne, if unintentionally. Now that he was here, he didn't feel the slightest interest in reading. Two neat shelves of books loomed directly overhead, like hatchets ready to fall. Christopher had had enough trouble with books lately. He just couldn't bring himself to want to read one. Instead, he stared at his hands and let his thoughts wander. He remembered the dream he had had—the one with Blake and the muddy pool. Many peasants believed that dreams revealed the course of future events, but Lacy had always insisted that the opposite was true—dreams reflected the past. Christopher didn't have an opinion. Past or future, his latest dream had involved Sheridan Blake. Where was Blake now? Christopher wondered. Asleep? Christopher thought not. Blake was not the sort of man to waste a minute in fruitless slumber unless sheer fatigue forced him to rest and he no longer possessed sufficient strength to resist its entreaties.

Christopher also thought about Lacy. Even though Christopher had sent several messengers to the monastery, Lacy had not yet chosen to respond. He was alive—the messengers testified to that—and out of Blake's hands. But what was he doing? What was he thinking? What were his plans?

Christopher sighed and shifted his body in the chair. More than anything else, his thoughts kept returning to Capital. Did he miss the glamour of the city, the tall buildings soaring into the sky, the thousands of electric lights winking like stars fallen to earth? He thought of Minister Talstead. And Glorianna. Capital was a magnificent place indeed. Yet he knew it wasn't his kind of place. He was a county man. This was his home.

Restless and bored with thinking, he came to his feet and went back to the window. Dawn could be seen with more clarity this time: the sky was tinged a shade of pink. He gazed across the land, observing the campfires of the peasant enclave. Poor Bill Walker, he thought. Blinded in the same accident that had cost Ned his legs. No, not an accident. War. Blake was to blame for what had occurred, and he must be made to pay.

As Christopher continued to watch from the window, he noticed a flash of movement. Peering intently, he managed to discern the shape of a horse and rider. As the horse drew closer, Christopher realized that the rider wore the dark robes of a monk. Rubbing his chin, he stepped back from the window. A message at last from Lacy? At this early hour of the morning? Suppressing his excitement, Christopher went back to the chair and sat down stiffly. It might well turn out to be nothing. The monk might have come on another errand entirely. A death among the servants. Many possibilities existed. Christopher waited. Not patiently. His fingers twisted like snakes in his lap.

A few long moments later, a gentle knock sounded at the door. Startled in spite of himself, Christopher jumped. Then, in a deliberately calm voice, he said, "Come in, please."

It was an old woman—a house peasant. She seemed uncomfortable in the presence of her master. "We saw the light burning, sir, and thought... hoped it might be you." The face of a young monk appeared at her shoulder. "It's a message, sir," she added.

"From Lacy?" said Christopher, looking at the monk. Brother Timothy, if he recalled correctly.

"Yes, sir. I was instructed to make delivery at dawn."

"Then come in."

Bowing, the old woman departed. Brother Timothy moved into the room and handed Christopher a folded sheet of paper. As Christopher started to open the message, Timothy could restrain his excitement no longer. "Did you see it, too, sir?" he burst out. "Did you hear that terrible noise?"

"Noise?" said Christopher, glancing up quizzically. "What noise?"

"It must have been some sort of explosion, sir."

"When was this?"

"Just as I was leaving the monastery. The whole sky burst into flame. Do you know what it might have been, sir?"

Christopher shook his head. Was this explosion the same one that had entered his dream and awakened Adrienne? "Perhaps it was Blake shooting off his cannon."

"It was much more powerful than that, sir. I faced the cannon on the day of the attack."

"Perhaps I ought to read this first," Christopher said, losing interest in the mystery. He held the paper open in his lap and read slowly:

> *Dear Christopher,*
>
> *This is penned to inform you, somewhat in advance of the fact, of the recent deaths of myself and Mr. Sheridan Blake. Brother Horace can supply you with the essential details of an explanation, but suffice to say at this time that the books removed from the monastery library have also been destroyed. This is, I admit, a rather sad and impersonal end to our long and cordial relationship. Still, County Kaine is yours now to do with as you will. I would only recommend that the remnants of Blake's army be driven from the county at your earliest convenience. Recall the*

teachings of Stoner. Remember me to your mother with dignity and great respect.

The message was not signed.

His hands shaking, Christopher looked up at the monk. "Are you aware of what this says?"

"I wasn't asked to read it," Timothy said stiffly.

"Then I'll tell you: it says both Lacy and Blake are dead."

"But that's not possible." Timothy shook his head slowly. "Mr. Lacy was alive and well when he wrote that message not six hours ago."

"He's at the monastery now?"

"No, sir. He left."

"Where did he go?"

"To Mr. Blake's camp. He said he wanted to have Brother Horace set free."

"And did he?"

"Brother Horace returned to the monastery about two hours after Mr. Lacy left. He was alone."

"Did you talk to him?"

"He went directly to his own quarters. He seemed . . . very tired, I guess."

Christopher nodded, climbing to his feet. "Then perhaps I ought to talk to him. According to Lacy's note, Horace knows something about this."

"Perhaps he does, but, sir, I can't help wondering . . . What about that terrible explosion? Do you think it might have had something to do with it, too?"

"I wouldn't know." Christopher went to the window and looked out. Was it merely imagination, or was there indeed a cloud of dark smoke hanging in the sky? He turned. "I know something else we have to do now."

"Sir?" said Brother Timothy.

"Will you accompany me to Blake's camp?"

"Of course, sir, if you wish. But . . ." He hesitated.

"Yes?" said Christopher.

"I was just thinking. If Mr. Blake really is dead, there's no telling what his men may be like. And they do have guns. Going to their camp may prove dangerous."

"True." Christopher paced. "Then perhaps you and I had better not go alone. I know what we'll do: stop at the peasant enclave and recruit a few helpers. Janson's army, we'll call them."

"Then you intend to attack Blake's men?"

"Yes," Christopher said, surprised by his own certainty, "I do intend that."

"We'll need weapons. Swords, knives, clubs, anything."

"I suspect the peasants can help us in that respect. With any luck—any determination—we'll drive those bastards out of this county by nightfall."

"Then you do believe that Mr. Blake is dead?"

"If he isn't, we'll drive him out, too." But Christopher was convinced. Lacy would not have lied: Blake was as dead as any man could be.

I have seen the way, thought Charlotte Chambers, now widowed, as she reached out and hugged the broken creature beside her. I have seen the way as illuminated for me by Lord God Christ Himself and, having found that clear path, will never stray from its rightful course from this moment forward into dark eternity.

Charlotte leaned forward in her seat and let the whip brush gently against the sweating hindquarters of the horse. She wasn't in a hurry. With Julian dead, with her husband vanished from her life, it no longer mattered where she went or how quickly she arrived.

"We'll go east," she said, her voice firm. "Savages live in those lands, creatures who hold with no god but the point of their own swords. Lacy told me about them. We must go there, you and I, and preach the word of the Lord."

"Yes, Charlotte." He trembled on the seat beside her. Bill Walker. Blind. It had taken some time for her to recognize him, but now she fervently believed that she loved him. Bill Walker—yes—but transformed, touched by the hand of God. His eyes were red sores. He had saved her from those servants of Satan. God in His divine wisdom had brought them together.

Charlotte laughed suddenly and reached over to hug Bill again. Blind, she thought, and yet he had taught her—the truly blind—how to see. When the servants of Satan had fallen upon her, she had prayed: *Please, dear God in heaven, Whom I have adored, if I have offended Thee, I plead only for a sign to show that the sacred path of salvation is not closed to me.*

(She had expected nothing—already damned, she believed.)

And then it had happened. The instant the words left her lips. Bill Walker. The blind man. He had set upon her attackers. The avenging angel of the Lord. A great explosion rocked the earth. A bright fire tore at the sky. The men ran. Charlotte wept. On her knees, she expressed her gratitude to the Lord. She hugged Bill Walker and loved him.

She was naked now. Holding Bill, she drew him close to her breast. He had uttered barely a word since he had first appeared to her, and yet she felt she knew his most intimate thoughts clearly. "We will preach among the heathen," she explained. "When they hear the truth of my salvation, they will no longer question the power and glory of God."

A chill clung to the morning air. Bill shivered and made a gurgling sound in his throat. Charlotte leaned close and put her ear to his lips.

Bill said, "You are . . . Charlotte?"

Tears stung her eyes. "I . . . I am," she said.

He tilted his head and stared at her with sightless eyes. "I love you," he said.

The entire family sat down to share breakfast. From his place at the head of the table, Christopher Janson sipped his coffee and let the relaxed hum of conversation flow around him.

Mother sat to his left, still dressed in black. For whom? he wondered, not for the first time. Father, almost everyone assumed, or Charlotte, but Christopher thought that it might well be neither: Mother mourned the death of Jeffrey Lacy. Christopher vividly recalled the agony in her eyes when he'd first informed her of Lacy's death and how he had understood then for the first time the true nature of her feelings for the man she had brought to County Kaine to teach her three children the truth of the universe.

Adrienne sat at the far end of the table. Despite the death of her own father, she wore nothing resembling mourning. It intrigued Christopher to realize that Adrienne knew him far better than he would ever know her. She was pregnant now. The child—son, he hoped—was expected in six months.

Opposite Sarah sat Ned. He attacked his food with all the old eagerness, swallowing fierce bites. Ned was presently working on steam-driven wheelchair which, he insisted, would soon allow him to move about with the facility and freedom of any man.

"I asked if you were going with me today."

Christopher looked at Ned and blinked. "Going where?"

"To the factory. The new model is finished and I want you to see it."

"Oh," said Christopher, shaking his head to clear the last of his reverie. "I wish I could, but I have a meeting. This afternoon?"

"Are you meeting with that peasant Lindstrom again?" Ned made no effort to conceal his distaste.

"We have to settle some matters concerning the operation of the steel mill."

"Well, I wish he'd go home again."

"I invited him here."

"Is he still trying to get you to move there?"

Christopher glanced at Adrienne before shrugging. "He says it would be wisest. I think he's right. The peasants would work harder at the dam if they knew I was watching them."

"We'll never go," Adrienne said flatly.

"Of course not," Christopher added quickly.

"Then you ought to make that clear to Lindstrom," she said.

"Oh, I have." Christopher was casual. He sympathized with Adrienne's reluctance to return to her own home. "He's not trying to force me. He's just stating his opinion."

"Then you ought to state yours and be done with it."

Christopher nodded with what he hoped she interpreted as agreement. This was hardly the time for making a major decision, and yet he realized that Lindstrom's viewpoint had much to be said for it. If Christopher did intend to exercise authority over both County Kaine and County Tumas, he would eventually have to be willing to spend at least half of every year residing in each place. After the birth of the child. That would be soon enough to decide. He could inform Adrienne of his decision then.

"This man Lindstrom is nothing but a murderer anyway," Adrienne said, with sudden and unexpected passion. "I don't think you should allow him the authority you do."

"A full amnesty was granted to everyone who followed you

father. I have to treat Lindstrom the same as any other man. And he does have the respect of the peasants in Tumas." Christopher became aware of a figure at his elbow. Turning, he discovered a house peasant holding a envelope in his hands.

The peasant bowed. "For you, sir. From Capital."

Christopher opened the envelope. There was a letter inside. He read it, then glanced at the postscript, written in a different hand.

"What is it, Christopher?" Sarah asked, speaking for the others as well.

Christopher tucked the letter into a pocket and grinned. "It's from Minister Talstead. I passed my examinations."

Ned clapped his hands enthusiastically while the others smiled.

Christopher looked at Adrienne. "And he's invited us to spend a few days with him at his home beginning the first of the month."

"Uncle Arthur's home?" Adrienne seemed less than exhilarated by the prospect. "Whatever for?"

"To discuss my new official duties," said Christopher.

"Chief eounty bureaucrat?" Ned said.

Christopher nodded. "For County Kaine and County Tumas."

"Well, congratulations to a very great man," Ned said, extending a hand. "Two counties. That is a hell of an honor. Lacy, if he were here, would be damned proud."

Sarah winced at the mention of Lacy. "I want to congratulate you, too, Christopher. I'm very proud."

"Thank you, Mother."

"And is that all he says?" said Adrienne. "He didn't say anything about me or Aunt Hilary or anyone in the family?"

Christopher shook his head. He hadn't mentioned the postscript to the letter—in Glorianna's tiny hand. She had wanted to inform him of her delight at his impending visit. "You don't have to go if you don't want to," he said, moving away from the table at last.

Come Explore the Fantastic World of Berkley's Fantasy Titles

_____**MICHAEL AND THE MAGIC MAN**   04630-3—$1.95
Kathleen M. Sidney

_____**A SHADOW OF ALL NIGHT FALLING**   04260-X—$1.95
Glen Cook

_____**VISION OF TAROT**   04441-6—$1.95
Piers Anthony

_____**THE WORD FOR WORLD IS FOREST**   03910-2—$1.75
Ursula Le Guin

_____**WATCHTOWER**   04295-2—$1.95
Elizabeth A. Lynn

FRANK HERBERT
...is science fiction

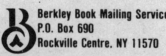